PRAISE FOR
TRUE

"A sweet, romantic, dynamic coming-of-age new adult that takes a much-needed detour from the usual emotionally draining, overly dramatic offerings . . . Crisp writing and a smooth story line makes it incredibly easy to become fully invested in this book."

—*Smexy Books*

"By turns sweet, steamy, gritty, and heartbreaking, *True* is an outstanding read."
—*On a Book Bender*

"One of those books that you just can't and won't put down . . . Extremely realistic and relatable . . . [A] dramatic and beautiful story."
—*Harlequin Junkie*

"Ms. McCarthy did a wonderful job with this story."
—*Under the Covers*

PRAISE FOR THE NOVELS OF ERIN MCCARTHY

"Quite a few chuckles, some face-fanning moments, and one heck of a love story."
—*A Romance Review*

"Readers won't be able to resist McCarthy's sweetly sexy and sentimental tale."
—*Booklist*

"[McCarthy] is fabulous with smoking-hot romances!"
—*The Romance Reade* ... *on*

"Just the right amount of humor interspersed ...

"One of the romance-writing ind ... . Ms. McCarthy spins a fascinating tale th... ...ranormal story with a blistering romance . . . Funn... ...and very entertaining."
—*...ance Reviews Today*

Titles by Erin McCarthy

A DATE WITH THE OTHER SIDE
HEIRESS FOR HIRE
SEEING IS BELIEVING

The Fast Track Series
FLAT-OUT SEXY
HARD AND FAST
HOT FINISH
THE CHASE
SLOW RIDE
JACKED UP
FULL THROTTLE

The Vegas Vampires Series
HIGH STAKES
BIT THE JACKPOT
BLED DRY
SUCKER BET

The Deadly Sins Series
MY IMMORTAL
FALLEN
THE TAKING

The True Believers Series
TRUE
SWEET
BELIEVE

Anthologies

THE NAKED TRUTH
(with Donna Kauffman, Beverly Brandt,and Alesia Holliday)

AN ENCHANTED SEASON
(with Maggie Shayne, Nalini Singh, and Jean Johnson)

THE POWER OF LOVE
(with Lori Foster, Toni Blake, Dianne Castell, Karen Kelley,
Rosemary Laurey, Janice Maynard, LuAnn McLane, Lucy Monroe,
Patricia Sargeant, Kay Stockham, and J. C. Wilder)

FIRST BLOOD
(with Susan Sizemore, Chris Marie Green, and Meljean Brook)

ERIN McCARTHY

TRUE

BERKLEY BOOKS, NEW YORK

THE BERKLEY PUBLISHING GROUP
Published by the Penguin Group
Penguin Group (USA) LLC
375 Hudson Street, New York, New York 10014

USA • Canada • UK • Ireland • Australia • New Zealand • India • South Africa • China

penguin.com

A Penguin Random House Company

This book is an original publication of The Berkley Publishing Group.

Library of Congress Cataloging-in-Publication Data

McCarthy, Erin, 1971–
True / Erin McCarthy.
pages cm.—(True believers ; 1)
ISBN 978-0-425-27446-0 (pbk.)
1. Roommates—Fiction. 2. Virginity—Fiction. I. Title.
PS3613.C34575T78 2014
813'.6—dc23
2013045412

PUBLISHING HISTORY
InterMix eBook edition / May 2013
Berkley trade paperback edition / April 2014

PRINTED IN THE UNITED STATES OF AMERICA

10 9 8 7 6 5 4 3 2 1

Cover design by Rita Frangie.
Photo © kiuikson/shutterstock images.
Interior text design by Kristin del Rosario.

CHAPTER ONE

GETTING DRUNK WAS NOT IN MY PLANS FOR FRIDAY NIGHT.

Neither was admitting to my roommates, Jessica and Kylie, that I was a virgin.

But they left me alone with Grant.

I knew what Jessica and Tyler, Kylie and Nathan were going to do in the guys' respective bedrooms. Well, it's not like I actually knew from personal experience what they were doing—but I hoped their sex fest wouldn't take that long. I had studying to do for an inorganic chemistry exam on Monday. Plus, I had to read six chapters of Hemingway about boozy, washed-up writers and their cheating wives, which was always a challenge for me, since I preferred the facts of math and science. Puzzling out literature and the social dynamics of characters struck me as a waste of time, especially given their activities.

Alcohol and sex. Ironic, really.

But Jessica was my ride. It was too far to walk back to the dorms, and it was the kind of off-campus neighborhood that had my dad raising his eyebrows and suggesting I go to college in some cow town like Bowling Green, where there were no dirty couches on sagging front porches and no residents smoking crack in full view of the street.

So walking back was not happening, because I didn't smoke crack and I was no risk-taker. At all. Yet sitting there alone with Grant while my roommates were off having a good time almost seemed riskier than strolling through the ghetto. Because it was sort of like perching over a public toilet seat without actually touching anything. It was difficult. Awkward.

Plus, it was very, very quiet. He didn't speak. And I didn't either, so there was a lot of sitting and a lot of awkwardness and a lot of trying to be entirely motionless so I wouldn't be moving more than him. Since he was barely breathing, this was a hard thing to do.

I actually felt sorry for Grant, which was just crazy because I wasn't exactly the Girl Everyone Wants to Be. But Grant was cute, with long hair that dropped into his eyes, high cheekbones, and thick, girlish eyelashes. He was too thin and wore his black T-shirts, always tight and wrinkled, with various rude expressions like *Bite Me* and *What the F Are You Looking At?* His dirty jeans hung off nonexistent hips that rivaled Mary Kate Olsen's, and not because he was looking to be fashionable. I don't think he ate enough, honestly. Nathan had told me Grant's father was a drunk, and his mother was a freak who stabbed her coworker at Taco Bell with a pen and was in some psych ward downtown. No one was shopping for vegetables at Kroger in Grant's house.

So I had kind of an awkward girl crush on Grant because it smelled of Possibility. Like it was not totally out of the realm of possibility that he could actually want to be with me, in some sort of male-female capacity.

"Smoke?" Grant asked, holding his pack of Marlboro Reds out to me, gaze shooting around to avoid the connection with mine, as we sat in the main room of Nathan's apartment.

"No, thanks." It was the eyes that made me understand that here was someone I didn't have to be afraid of, didn't have to feel threatened or intimidated by. Because even though his eyes never met mine, Grant had haunted eyes. Aching, vulnerable, gray eyes.

I wanted him to kiss me. Even as I took a huge swig out of the beer he had given me five minutes before, I was thinking that if only he would recognize what I saw, everything would be awesome. We were absolutely perfect for each other. Two totally sensitive, pale, quiet people. I'd never shove him around the way Tyler did, under the guise of bro wrestling. I'd never embarrass him or set his clothes on fire for fun like his alleged best friend, Nathan, did.

His hand shook a little as he flicked his Bic on to light the cigarette he'd stuffed in his mouth. There was an oak end table between us, each perched in a plaid easy chair, a movie playing on the TV screen in front of us. Some sort of bad Tom Cruise drama. I've never liked Tom Cruise. He always reminded me of someone's creepy cousin, who smiles too big before he touches your butt and whispers something gross in your ear with hot whiskey breath.

Grant was studying the TV, though, very seriously, his smoke floating out into nice, sexy ovals. He could make smoke rings.

I thought my only talent was converting oxygen to carbon dioxide, though to give myself credit, I did really well in school—I always have. I was in the Honors Scholar program, and I was on track for magna cum laude, which made my rooming with Jessica and Kylie even more ironic than reading Hemingway. They were social superstars, while if there were a subject called Casual Conversation and Flirting 101, I would have been flunking it.

I'd never had a boyfriend. No sweaty, handholding, note-passing middle school boyfriend. No guy in high school who had me wear his football jersey to pep rallies. No TA in college who suddenly recognized the value of a quality brain and spent coffee shop nights studying with me. None of the above.

I wasn't exactly sure why, because I didn't consider myself ugly with a capital *U*. Maybe slightly plain, definitely quiet, but not repulsive in any way. No body odor, bad breath, or strange growths in obvious places, no bald spots or facial tics. I did have a few guys who wanted to make out and attempt to shove their hands down my pants, but no one wanted to date me.

Which is why I knew I should make a move on Grant somehow. Because here was my chance to score a boyfriend. To have make-out sessions and share popcorn at the movies, to text each other on a minute-by-minute basis using sickly sweet nicknames. Just to see what it was like, a relationship, to try it on for size like a great pair of sexy heels.

Maybe it would even result in having my name tattooed on Grant's bicep. It was a short name, Rory, so it would fit on his skinny arm. Something permanent that said that someone else in this world thought enough of me to ink me into infinity.

In reality, Grant and I had remained completely silent for fifteen, twenty minutes. He'd even stopped asking me if I wanted another beer. He had the uncanny ability to sense when I'd drained one without even looking over at me, and he immediately offered another by just holding out the can. I didn't really want this many, but I couldn't bring myself to say no. His silent offer was the only thing connecting us at all, besides the fact that we were both human and happened to be sitting in the same room.

I was starting to feel a serious buzz from the three back-to-back beers I'd had, and I was wondering how much longer until my supposedly large brain managed to put forth a flirtatious comment for me to sling at Grant, with an artful hair flip. A lot of girls I knew talked more as they drank, but so far, my tongue still seemed to be stuck to the roof of my mouth, and my ears were ringing.

"Do you think . . . ?" Grant started to say, his whole body suddenly turning to me.

Startled, I choked a little, beer going up my nose. I didn't know he was going to look at me. Not prepared. No coy smile in place. I blinked at him, hoping that just maybe he'd say something that could lead to something, and I would have a turn at this strange mating game we all seemed to want to play.

"Do you think Tyler and Jessica are serious about each other or are they just hooking up? Or could I, you know . . ."

I sank back into burgundy plaid. My turn was not today. I was stupid to think it ever would be.

"No," I managed to say. "They're definitely serious." Even though I knew it wasn't true, that Jessica wasn't serious about anything right now. But I was feeling mean and a little sick, and drunk in a not-so-good way. It was rare for me to get angry, but I suddenly felt just that.

Because even Grant, who was like a terrified grasshopper clinging to the windshield of a speeding car, was too good for me.

I lifted my beer to my mouth and sucked hard, eyes focusing on Tom on the TV and his cheesy grin.

"She says she adores him," I added, to emphasize my point, driven to speak by an itchy humiliation that prickled over my skin. It wasn't a lie—she had said that. But Jessica adored her Hello Kitty slippers, and her iPhone, and Greek yogurt. It was her catchall word for anything that was pleasing her at that very moment. Tyler had been pleasing her half an hour ago. Whether he still was now was anyone's guess.

Grant looked down the hallway, toward the bedroom. He didn't say anything, but I could see it. That pathetic, hopeless wanting. The desire for what you want but can't have. The need for someone to like you.

I recognized it because I saw it in my own face every day.

So I drained my fourth beer completely, my teeth starting to numb, my breathing sounding loud and labored to my ears. I knew I should slow down, drink water, stand up, but it was easier to feel sorry for myself, hidden behind a beer can, deep in the recesses of the plaid chair, my new best friend.

When Grant leaned over and suddenly covered my mouth with his, I was so shocked I made a startled yelp and dropped the nearly empty can in my lap, dribbles of cold beer spilling onto my jeans. Grant had eaten up the distance between the two chairs and was leaning on the oak table with one hand, grabbing the back of my head with the other. Confused, I sat there unresponsive for a second, my beer brain chugging along slowly, processing. Grant was kissing me.

I kissed back. Because, well, this is what I wanted, right? Grant to kiss me.

But then I remembered Grant wasn't really interested in me. He was into Jessica. I knew that. And his mouth was hard, his tongue thrusting and swollen. I started to pull back, desperate for air. He tasted like stale cigarettes, and he smelled like he did laps in a swimming pool of Axe body spray.

"Pass that on to Jessica," he said, panting hard, tossing his hair out of his eyes.

I blinked. I may have been the awkward girl, but I didn't want to be second-best. A sexual stand-in for my hot roommate. Humiliation flooded over me, drenching my skin in heat from head to toe as I flushed with embarrassment and anger. When he started to move in again for another kiss, I put my hand on his chest to stop him.

"Tell her yourself," I spat out, standing up, the beer can tumbling to the dirty carpet. I wasn't sure where I was going, but it was away from him.

Only Grant grabbed me by the arm as I walked past and pulled me down onto his lap. Before I could react, he had his arms completely around me, his warm lips on my neck, the hard nudge of what I figured had to be his erection at the back of my thighs. Fear flooded my mouth. He didn't look this strong. He didn't look strong at all, yet his grip on me was tight, his sloppy, wet kisses trailing lower down my chest, under my T-shirt.

When I tried to stand, his hands held my arms so tightly it felt like my wristbones were being snapped, and I was too out of it from the beer to have great coordination. Trying to back up, I ended up sliding down his lap, between his legs and to the floor.

"Now that's what I'm talking about," he said, loosening his hold on me to take down his zipper. "Good girl."

When he pulled out his erection, a mere foot from my face, I couldn't believe what I was looking at, all smooth skin and dark hair, just out there, all casual. Right in front of my face. I realized he thought I was going to give him a blow job. That I was actually offering to give him oral sex, for no reason, with no conversation or lead-in, just a few shitty kisses when he referenced my roommate. That somehow, he was insane enough to think that I would willingly go down on him. Nauseated, I turned my head, so I didn't have to look at his junk.

The beer was going to come back up. I drank it too fast and it was sloshing around in my gut, ready to rush up my throat in a Bud Light tsunami, crashing out over my teeth onto his lap if I didn't get some fresh air, didn't get away from him.

"Let me go," I said, trying to get my feet on the floor so I could stand.

But he had my hair at the back of my head, and I realized the only way out was to go low, not try to stand. But if I fell to the floor completely, then he could fall *on* me, which meant that if I didn't get out of this in the next sixty seconds, I might wind up having sex on the hard, filthy carpet of this crappy rental apartment. I'd rather give oral sex than lose my virginity to this douche bag, who I had thought was nice, who I had thought would never victimize anyone because he'd been the victim.

Neither was a good choice.

But if I faked oral, I could bite him instead. Sink my teeth down into his most sensitive spot and get away. Call a cab. I was just panicked enough that I figured I could actually do it, get away or at least go down fighting.

So I tried to stand instead of falling down, and he yanked my hair so hard tears came to my eyes. I had long, dark red hair, which made it easy for him to entwine his fingers to control my head and my neck, holding me so I couldn't move.

"Stop! I'm serious." I braced my knee on the bottom of the chair, my hand on his chest to keep my head as far from him as possible. "I'm going to be sick," I added, because it was true, and I figured no guy wanted to be puked on.

But he ignored me and said, "Open your mouth."

So I punched his wrist, trying to break his hold, desperate, panicked, my vision blurred from tears and too many beers, my stomach churning violently. "No! Please, don't!"

"Let her go, Grant. *Now.*"

He did, and I fell to the ground, gasping, scrambling backward, my floral rain boots giving me traction to butt-scoot out of his reach. Tyler was standing in the hallway, not wearing a shirt, a beer in his hand. He had clearly been to the kitchen, clearly seen what had been happening, clearly planned to stop it.

Relief had my hands shaking and I zipped up my hoodie, wanting my T-shirt covered, wanting all of me covered, gone.

"Mind your own fucking business," Grant said.

"No. I won't. She said no." Tyler was tall, broad-shouldered, his chest and biceps covered in tattoos. He looked at me, and I shrank back a little. His eyes looked angry in the fluorescent glow of the stove light. "Did you say no, Rory?"

"Yes. I said no," I added, wanting to clarify.

Grant's foot came out, and he kicked my arm, hard. "You did not, you dick tease."

He kicked me. I couldn't believe that he just kicked me. I yelped, and before I could respond, Tyler was between me and Grant, pulling him to his feet.

"I heard her say no. Now get the hell out of here. Go home. What is wrong with you? You don't treat a chick like that."

They scuffled a little, Grant shoving Tyler's arms off him as he made his way to the door. "Man, I was doing her a favor. No one else wants her."

Tyler's response to that was to punch Grant in the face, knocking him into the wall. "Shut the fuck up, or I'll beat your ass into tomorrow."

Grant peeled himself off the wall, shot me a look of hatred, then left, the door slamming hard behind him. The tears were rolling down my face, whether I liked it or not. The realization that I was almost raped settled over me, and his hateful words lay on top of that, a final insult. He was right. No one wanted me. But that didn't mean I could be treated like shit. It didn't mean I wasn't a person, that I should toss over my dignity and accept whatever attention I got, no matter how selfish and crude it was.

"You okay?" Tyler asked, popping open his beer and holding it in front of me.

I shook my head. Because I didn't want the beer. And because I wasn't okay.

"I'm sorry. I didn't know he would do something like that. I feel really bad." He set his beer down on the end table. "Do you want me to give you a ride home? Jessica's asleep."

Great. All I wanted to do was retreat to our dorm and cry in my bed, but Jessica was taking a post-coital nap. It was bold for me, but I decided to accept his offer, even though I knew I was putting him out. "Yeah, if you don't mind."

"Sure, no problem. Just let me get my keys." He made a face. "And a shirt. It's cold out there for October."

He went back into the bedroom and when he came out, Jessica was actually with him. "Rory, are you okay?" She rushed over to me, blond hair flying behind her, dressed in men's pajama pants and a huge sweatshirt. "Tyler told me what happened."

Her arms wrapped around me and I let her hug me, grateful for the contact and her concern.

"What an asshole. If I see him, I'm going to cut his dick off and shove it down his throat. Let's see how he likes cock crammed in his mouth."

Her vehemence made me feel better. "I should have . . ." I started—but then stopped myself. I should have what? I shouldn't have done anything differently. I was just sitting in my chair and he

made a world of assumptions and I said no, and that was the truth
of it. I wasn't going to blame myself that he'd taken a fist to the face.

"No, screw that," Jessica said. "You didn't do anything wrong.
And I'm sorry I left you alone with that prick."

"I'll be right back," Tyler said, his phone buzzing in his hand.
He retreated into the bedroom as Kylie came out, her hair a hot
mess, makeup streaked.

"What's going on?"

"Grant tried to rape Rory," Jessica said in such a loud,
matter-of-fact voice I couldn't help but wince.

"What? Are you effing kidding me?" Kylie could have been
Jessica's twin. They were both tall, blond, tan, toned. They were
getting vague degrees in Gen Ed and would probably wind up
wedding planners and golf wives, while I was intending to go to
med school to be a coroner. I was more comfortable with dead
people than living ones. But for whatever reason, Kylie and Jessica
liked me. And I liked them. Their reaction cemented that feeling.
They both looked like if they had had a baseball bat and five minutes alone with Grant, he'd wish he'd never been born.

I didn't want to fight Grant. I just wanted to forget it had ever
happened. "I did kiss him," I said, because I felt guilty for that.
That was leading him on, a little.

"So? A kiss is not a promise of pussy," Kylie said.

She was right. "I know," I said, miserable, confused, stomach
upset. I sat down on the end table, looking at my boots. "But I
mean, it's not like I haven't thought about being with Grant. I have.
But he was so . . . and I don't want it, my first time, to be like
this . . . and I should have done . . . something."

So much for telling myself I wasn't going to do that. There I was,
worried, feeling like I'd had some part in what had happened.

"Your first time? Wait a minute, are you saying you're a virgin?" Jessica was staring at me blankly. "For real?"

Oops. I hadn't really meant to share that. It wasn't exactly a deep, dark secret, and it really couldn't have been that much of a shock to her, but it wasn't necessarily something I wanted to go around talking about. "Um. Yes. I just haven't . . ."

Had the opportunity.

"There hasn't been anyone . . ." I reached for the beer Tyler had abandoned and took a sip. I was drunk, but not nearly enough to not suddenly feel completely and totally middle school mortified.

"Oh." Kylie looked bewildered. "Well, that's cool. Lots of girls make that choice."

"It hasn't been a choice. Not exactly. I mean, if I could, I think I would." I did. I was twenty, and I had all the same physical feelings as other people. Just no one to explore them with. In a way that wasn't a quickie on the stained carpet.

"Well, why can't you?" Jessica asked.

"Because no one is offering. I guess technically Grant offered, but I don't want it like that." I was sorry I'd brought it up at all. It wasn't a discussion I wanted to have with Tyler and Nathan a few feet away.

"So you want, like, romance?"

Was that what we called it? "I guess."

Tyler came back into the room, pushing his cell phone into his front pocket. "You ready?"

"Yeah." I found my crossbody bag on the floor and put it over my head.

"Tyler, Rory wants romance," Jessica told him. "What do you think of that?"

My face burned with embarrassment. I didn't want to be the

subject of discussion. I didn't want Tyler to stare at me the way he was, dark eyes scrutinizing mine. He was the typical bad-boy type—which was why Jessica liked him—and I was the kind of girl he would never notice. And he hadn't ever noticed me, not really. I was the quiet friend of Jessica and Kylie whose presence he tolerated. But now his eyes were sweeping over me, assessing, and I couldn't read his expression.

"I think she should have whatever she wants." He reached out and took the beer can from my hand, his fingers brushing mine. "But nothing says romance like a six-pack. I need to pick up more beer."

I shivered from his touch and from the inscrutable look he was giving me.

"I'm staying here," Jessica stated. "It's too cold outside to go home. See you tomorrow, Rory."

Kylie was already curled up on the couch, in a praying position, half asleep as she gave a weak wave. "Bye, sweetie."

"Okay, bye," I said, shoving my hands in the front pockets of my jeans, wishing I had worn a thicker coat. I was cold, and I wanted a hot shower to wash away the beer and the fear and the feel of Grant's wet lips on me. But first I had to sit in the car alone with Tyler. A perfect ending to a crap night. Awkward small talk with my roommate's Friend with Benefits, who had punched his own friend on my behalf.

As I followed Tyler down the metal stairs, the smell of fried foods strong in the hallway, I thought that was the end of any talk about my virginity.

I didn't know it was just the beginning.

CHAPTER TWO

NATHAN'S APARTMENT WAS ON MCMICKEN STREET, OFF-STREET parking only. Tyler's car was a rusted-out sedan, at least twenty years old, with a maroon door that stood out in stark contrast against the car's white body.

"It's unlocked," he told me as he stepped into the street.

So I pried open the passenger side and climbed in, shivering, crossing my arms over my chest. I checked for a seat belt, but there didn't seem to be one, and so I just sat there, stiff, my rain boots shuffling through a pile of discarded fast-food bags and Coke cans. I didn't know what to say to Tyler. I wanted to thank him for rescuing me. Because that's what he had done. I wasn't sure I could have gotten away from Grant on my own.

I forced myself to glance at him, but he was just looking back over his shoulder as he pulled out of the spot. He had a strong jaw and a little bump in the center of his nose that I had never noticed before. With his sweatshirt swallowing him, and in profile, somehow he looked younger, less intimidating than when his tattoos were on full display, and his dark eyes were staring at me. It gave me the courage to say, "Thanks."

My voice came out like a hoarse whisper and I cleared my throat, embarrassed.

"No problem," he said. "You can't walk through this neighborhood by yourself at night. This fucking hill alone would kill you if the ghetto rats didn't."

Whether or not Straight Street got its name from the fact that it was virtually a ninety-degree incline or not, I didn't know. It was definitely unwalkable, even during the day. But I wasn't talking about his giving me a ride, though I was grateful for that. "Yeah, but thanks for . . . Grant." I didn't want to get more specific than that.

He turned now, and I was sorry he did when he gave me a look that I couldn't read. "Sure. If you find yourself in that situation again, punch him in the nuts. But you can do better than Grant, trust me."

"Yeah." I wasn't sure if it were true or not, but I did know that I would much rather be alone than have those wet, narrow lips anywhere on me, and that demanding grip on my arm, the back of my head.

"I mean, you've waited this long to have sex, you shouldn't waste your virginity on an Oxy junkie."

So he had heard me talking to Jessica and Kylie. I gripped my purse tighter in my lap, that churning sensation in my stomach starting again. The car was heaving and bucking as it struggled to make it up the steep hill, and the engine whined as Tyler gave it more gas. The street was empty, most of the houses darkened because it was after two, and I suddenly felt as trapped in the car as I had in the apartment. I didn't want to talk about this with Tyler. Or anyone.

"Oxy?" I asked, to buy time. Dodge and weave when the subject was uncomfortable. But I'd never been particularly good at dodging anything. I was the girl in grade school gym who didn't move fast enough and took a rubber ball in the nose.

"OxyContin. Grant likes to snort it. When he can't get his hands on any for a while, he gets a little edgy. I told Nathan he shouldn't let him come around anymore, but Nathan is loyal."

So Grant did drugs. I guess I wasn't surprised, not really. He had the requisite dysfunctional family, the nervous twitch. It made sense. I was disappointed, though, because it meant that I had inaccurately assessed Grant. I had seen him as a male version of myself, quiet from a lack of social skills, nervous. But it wasn't that at all, and I had projected what I wanted onto him.

The thought made me want to cry again.

"So you're not?" I said, then immediately regretted it. It sounded almost accusatory, when the truth was, the silence was stretching out, a long rubber band that snapped with my unintentionally harsh words.

"Not when you're doing drugs and kicking girls."

That made sense to me.

I didn't really know Tyler at all, other than he was Jessica's and Kylie's party buddy, and on occasion, he and Jessica hooked up. He almost never came to our dorm room, and I had only been around him a few times at parties and at the apartment. We didn't share any classes, and he'd never made much of an effort to talk to me.

But suddenly I liked him a whole lot better.

Unsure what to say, as usual, I tucked my hair behind my ear, but I was spared from having to answer by his phone ringing. He glanced at the screen and swore.

"Yeah?" he said, after tapping the screen, turning the steering wheel with his left elbow, heading toward campus.

I wondered if it were Jessica. But I realized that it couldn't be Jessica, because she wouldn't have called him. She was a texter and she always used an absurd shorthand with acronyms that no one but she understood, like LULB, which she insisted stood for *Love You Little Bitch*. Or my personal favorite, *W?* Jessica sometimes meant it as a general question, as in she didn't understand what was happening, which most people would assume, or sometimes as *What time?* though no one but her ever knew which one she intended.

"No. In the kitchen. No," he said into his phone, more emphatically. "I didn't take it. The cat probably ate it."

The woman talking to him was so loud that I could hear her, though the words were garbled.

"Well, stop leaving your shit lying around," he said, and with a sound of disgust pulled the phone from his ear and dropped it into a dirty change compartment next to the gear shift. "Moms are a complete pain in the ass."

If I hadn't been drunk, I probably wouldn't have said anything at all. I would have just agreed or most likely, just nodded. But my mouth seemed to move faster than my brain. "I don't remember my mom being a pain in the ass at all. She was always smiling."

Tyler glanced at me. "Remember? She run out on you or what?"

I wondered what the statistical odds were that someone would assume abandonment over death. "No. She died. Of cancer. When I was eight." The beer was working overtime. I never told anyone that unless they really pressed me, because the C word immediately brought both sympathy and fear to people's faces. They felt instantly bad for me, yet at the same time they were momentarily afraid that it would touch their life like it had mine, and they had to whisper the word. *Cancer.* Like if they spoke it too loudly it would be conjured up in their bodies like a destructive demon straight from hell. People had told me that straight out, that cancer was from the devil, a horrible affliction of otherworldly implications, unstoppable.

Others had told me that the government most likely had a vaccination for cancer but was keeping a lid on it, to drive the medical economy. This seemed unlikely to me for more than a dozen reasons, not the least of which was that it didn't make sense on a cellular level. It wasn't a virus but a mutation. Yet I understood people wanted an answer for the randomness of why it struck, why it killed.

I had stopped asking why a long time ago.

Tyler seemed to get that. His response wasn't an uncomfortable apology. He said, "Well, that's about as fucking unfair as it gets, isn't it? My mom is a selfish bitch and she'll probably live to be ninety, and yet yours died."

It was kind of nice not to get the same pat response of sympathy, the one where everyone was sorry, but at the same time so damn glad it wasn't them. I appreciated his matter-of-fact attitude. "You don't get along with your mom?"

"Nope." Tyler pulled into the driveway that led to my dorm. "She's not all bad, though. She did give birth to me." He turned and shot me a grin.

It was so unexpected that, for a second, I blinked, then I let out a startled laugh. The sound was foreign and awkward to my ears, but Tyler didn't seem to notice. His face changed when he smiled, and his eyes warmed. In the dark, they still looked like deep, black holes, but with his lips upturned and the corners of his eyes crinkling, he wasn't so intense, so remote.

That was when I realized why I'd always been slightly nervous around Tyler. He was what people always accused me of being—there but not present. Easygoing, but distant. Smiling, but intense. Maybe it was the alcohol, my ears still buzzing, my insides hot, my skin cold and clammy, but for the first time I didn't feel uncomfortable around him.

"So are you really a virgin?" he asked, sounding genuinely curious. "Or were you just saying that?"

No longer comfortable. It went away faster than you could say *Awkward Moment*.

Why he thought I would want to talk about that made no sense to me at all. I was drunk, but I wasn't *insane*. If I hadn't even told my roommates until that night, why the hell would I sit in Tyler's car and spill my guts? I wasn't the confessional type. I never had been.

So I just looked at him.

"I'm going to take that as a yes."

I wanted to tell him to mind his own goddamn business. To stop pressing a girl he didn't know for intimate details about her sexual experience. That it was rude. But I remembered that he had, in fact, saved the very virginity he was questioning, so I didn't want to be a bitch. I just shrugged. Really, what difference did it make? I was already a collegiate abnormality. Likes to study! Hates to talk! Won't go tanning! See this freak show exhibit in her natural dorm habitat . . .

But I actually surprised myself by opening my mouth and saying, "Yes, I am."

My admission silenced him for a second, but then he drummed his thumbs on the steering wheel as he put the car in Park in front of my dorm, a seventies-built tower of glass and steel. Light from the streetlight was flooding into his car, showing even more clearly how dirty and ancient it was with a slot for a cassette player crammed full of what looked like parking tickets.

"Do you have a purity ring or whatever?"

Now that I was in, and the beer had loosened my lips, I said the first thing that came into my head. "I prefer to call it my hymen."

Tyler let out a laugh. "No, I mean one of those rings you wear on your finger . . ." He looked at me, understanding dawning. "Oh, wait, you're being sarcastic, aren't you?"

I nodded.

Which made him laugh harder. "Rory, you are an interesting chick."

Interesting wasn't exactly a riveting compliment, but he hadn't called me a freak, which was how I felt sometimes. As if I had been assembled in a different way altogether than everyone around me, and while I liked the end result, everyone else was confused about how to interpret my very existence. They watched me, suspicious, as if I were a Transformer and they were waiting for metal arms to spring out from my chest cavity.

I didn't think that I'd ever seen him laugh before, or maybe I had just never noticed, my attention focused on Grant, who I had thought was more likely to fall in with my plan of exploring human mating and relationships. But then again, Jessica and Kylie tended to dominate all conversation in a group setting, so maybe their own perfectly affected laughter had drowned out Tyler's.

But for some stupid reason, I liked to think that he was laughing just for me.

Which was when I knew I was even more drunk than I realized and I needed to get away from him before I sat there blinking at him like a baby owl indefinitely. Before I put some sort of hero worship onto him that he might deserve, but didn't mean a damn thing. Before I substituted one pointless crush for another.

I shoved open the door, half falling out, clinging to the handle and the remnants of my dignity, like he could hear my stupid thoughts. "Thanks," I said over my shoulder, barely glancing back as I exited the car, clutching my bag.

There was no response, and when I struggled to slam the heavy door, which seemed to weigh a million pounds and required more coordination than my icy fingers had, I realized that he was just staring at me. There was a cigarette in his mouth, and he was lifting the car lighter up to it, his hand guiding it to its destination without thought. As he sucked on it to catch the paper and tobacco on fire, his eyes never left mine.

The smile was gone. There was nothing but a cool scrutiny.

I shivered.

Then I walked as fast as I could to my dorm, digging in my bag for my swipe card.

Once inside, I paused at the front desk to check in and I glanced out the front doors.

His car was still there, and I could see the shadow of his outline, the tiny red glow of his cigarette.

"HOW ARE YOU FEELING?" KYLIE ASKED, COMING INTO OUR room with more noise than could possibly be necessary.

I pried my eyes open and gave a mumbled, "Like shit," before crawling back under my blanket. I had woken up at five in the morning and had gone into the bathroom we shared with the room next door to throw up. It had shot out like a garden hose on high, and I had slid down onto the cool tiles, regretting my lack of dinner, regretting those stupid beers that I'd only had because I was nervous being around a guy who had turned out to be a douche bag.

None of it was logical. I didn't do stupid things, as a rule.

I was paying for this one. And after crawling back to my bed, soaked in sweat, I had slept restlessly off and on for hours. I had no idea what time it was when Kylie and Jessica came back, and I didn't give a shit. I wanted to die. I would dedicate my body to science, and they could study the effects of cheap beer on socially awkward college sophomores.

"Do you want anything?" Jessica asked.

"A gun to shoot myself." My head felt like someone was repeatedly taking a sledgehammer to it, and my stomach felt like the lining had been manually torn out by werewolves and replaced with maggots crawling up my throat. And I wasn't being overdramatic. I felt like ass. Like two-day-old roadkill. Like chewing gum on the bottom of a chicken's foot. That'd been hit by a car.

My bed creaked and sank as one of them sat down by my feet. Even that small motion had me gagging.

"We're going to lunch. Do you want to come with us?" Kylie asked.

I didn't even bother to answer that. It hurt to move my mouth, and that was possibly the stupidest question I'd ever heard in my life. I wouldn't go to lunch if a million dollars were offered along with a guaranteed Liam Hemsworth make-out session.

"Then we're going to Zumba class."

The gross national product direct deposited into my bank

account couldn't get me to a Latin dance class. I grunted, wondering why they were so clearly not hungover. Then I remembered that they had spent the bulk of their night getting laid, not getting plastered.

Feeling bitter, I drifted back into a sweaty sleep.

When I woke up, the room was dark and I was disoriented, but the pounding in my skull had abated slightly. The TV was flickering in the corner of our cramped room, and I sensed that Jess or Kylie was still sitting at the foot of my bed, back against the cinder block wall.

"What time is it?" I croaked, my voice hoarse.

"Seven. How are you feeling?"

Holy shit. That was a guy's voice, not one of my roommates'. I half sat up, heart suddenly racing. It was hard to see in the dark, and the sudden motion made my stomach roil, my hair was in damp clumps on my forehead.

Oh my God. It was Tyler, just propped up casually, legs sprawled out, his feet dangling over the side in nothing but socks.

My tongue felt thick, and I was suddenly aware that I wasn't wearing pants. I had collapsed into bed in all my clothes except for the rain boots, and when I had gotten up to be sick, I had peeled off my jacket, abandoning it in the bathroom. Then in bed, I had clawed my way out of my jeans with shaky hands, so that now I was in a tight, wrinkled, wet T-shirt and panties.

With Tyler sitting on my bed watching *Family Guy* like nothing about this was abnormal. A quick glance around showed we were alone.

"Drink this," he said, reaching over and pulling a bottle off my desk. The flashing colors from the TV played across his frame, showing the pull and strain of his bicep muscles as he reached. The black of his tattoo caught my attention, but it was too dark to see what it was.

Propped on my elbow, I was totally embarrassed at how shitty I knew I had to look, but I didn't have the physical strength to jump out of bed and fix it. I didn't have a functioning brain, either, it seemed. When he held some kind of power drink up to my lips, I swallowed a sip. The cool, sweet liquid felt fantastic and cut through the thick phlegm that seemed to have been spray coated over every inch of my tongue and mouth. "Thanks."

"Sure." He set the bottle back down. "You're dehydrated. You'll feel better once you can keep some liquid down."

This was so weird. Like off-the-charts weird. Why the hell was he hanging out in my room while I slept the restless, sweaty sleep of the hungover? The beer seemed to be leaching out of my pores, and I smelled like leftover Chinese food.

"Where are Jess and Kylie?" I asked.

"At dinner." He shifted and the bed creaked. "I'm going to turn the light on so cover your eyes for a second."

I fought the urge to hiss when he flicked on my desk lamp, and my dry eyes dilated. I couldn't prevent a little moan, though. "I'm never drinking again," I said as I fell back onto my pillow.

"Everyone says that. Few live up to the vow." There was more rustling, and then suddenly he produced a saltine-cracker pack. "You should eat a cracker."

I wasn't used to having someone take care of me, and the fact that it was a hot guy who was having sex with my roommate was just creepy. I did take the pack, though, and tore open the plastic so I could nibble on a corner of the cracker. It tasted like shredded cardboard, and I gagged a little. Tyler was right there with the drink again, and having a bad boy as a nursemaid made me start to wonder if I was actually hallucinating. Maybe this was some sort of elaborate roofie-inspired fantasy.

I dribbled the red liquid all down the front of me.

Nope. Not a fantasy.

Just me, rocking the awk.

I wiped my chin.

He stood up, and I was torn between not wanting him to leave because I wanted to know why he was there, and being so relieved that he might leave me in pathetic peace, that I said breathlessly, "Are you leaving?"

"No. Unless you want me to. Do you?" That question came directly at me over his shoulder, dark eyes unreadable.

I shook my head, because I couldn't tell him to leave. That was too rude. And at the same time, I wasn't sure I wanted him to leave.

I took math and science courses because they were easy for me, they made sense. There was logic to them, with a right and wrong answer. Literature could never provide me those absolutes, because you could never really predict what someone was thinking , or what they would say. At least I couldn't.

Yet the mystery of words, of people, was fascinating to me. I wanted to understand, yet I never seemed to be able to assemble the puzzle pieces of behavior in the correct order.

"Is this your dresser?" he asked, tapping his knuckles on the chest of drawers.

See? Never in a thousand years could I have predicted he was going to say that.

"Yes." I watched him yank the first drawer open and root around among my socks. "Um . . ." Thank God he hadn't picked my bra-and-panty drawer.

"Where are your T-shirts? I'll get you a clean one."

For real? This was the guy Jessica had described as so hard-core? Who worked out with weights and came from a bad part of town and had his penis pierced? He wanted to get me a clean shirt.

"Second drawer."

He dug around for a minute, then emerged with one of a kitty daydreaming about math equations. "Cute."

Whether or not that was sarcasm, I wasn't sure. If I had had to guess, he would have made a comment about liking pussy, which I imagined eight out of ten males would have done under these circumstances.

But instead, as he brought it to me, he tapped it and said, "Though this one is wrong. The answer is twenty-seven."

Sitting up, I took the shirt, blinking. I studied the equation his finger was pointing to and did the quick calculation in my head. "You're right," I said, not fully able to keep the surprise from my voice.

"I'm smarter than I look," he said.

Apparently he was. I was mumbling an embarrassed protest when the door to my room flew open and Jessica and Kylie came in, giant mugs of coffee in their hands.

"Look who's up!" Jessica called out. "Yay! Glad you're feeling better."

I wasn't sure that was an entirely accurate assessment of the situation, but I knew from experience she didn't really expect a response anyway.

"Alright, I'm taking off," Tyler said, already heading toward the door. "Talk to you guys later."

"Bye, bitch," Jessica told him.

Kylie gave him a wave.

Then he was gone and I was just sitting there, clutching my kitty T-shirt. "Why was he here?" I asked.

"Because he likes you," Kylie said in a singsong voice, stripping off her shirt and rooting around in the closet in her bra and sweats. "Are you going to the club with us tonight?"

As if. I totally ignored her question and pushed my hair back off my head, my fingers shaking a little. I reached for the drink Tyler had left sitting on the desk and took a sip, formulating my protest so I didn't sound too reactionary. "Whatever. Seriously, why was he here?"

"He didn't want to go to dinner with us. And I am being serious. I totally think he likes you. He has been asking a ton of questions about you to me and Jess. We were wishing we had like a bio on you so we could just hand it to him so he'd quit bugging us." There was a thump as she fell into the back of the closet. "Ow. Shit. I can't find my cowboy boots."

Yanking off my dirty shirt, I pulled the clean kitty one on over my head, hoping it would cover the burn I felt in my cheeks. There was no way Tyler Mann was interested in me. He wasn't. He wouldn't be. He might be curious about who the mute brunette was, but in the same way that you're curious as to why Donald Trump has a chinchilla on his head.

"He doesn't like me," I insisted when my head reemerged. "He's with Jessica." Who I was afraid to look at. I didn't want to turn and see her shooting me murderous glares.

But Jessica laughed. "He's not *with* me. He's just been with me. Huge difference. Huge. I so don't like him that way."

I watched her moving around her desk, swallowed by a giant UC sweatshirt, bear paws stamped on the butt of her yoga pants. She was peering in a hand mirror, inspecting her teeth and looking very unconcerned that Tyler had been hanging out in our room while I slept. I seemed to be the only one who thought it was ludicrous.

"But you've . . ." I started to say, then wasn't sure how to finish my sentence.

"Fucked him?" she asked cheerfully, shooting me a grin. "Yep. He's a good time, and he knows how to use that piercing to my advantage, if you know what I mean."

Actually, I had no idea what she meant. In theory, sure, I could imagine the clitoral stimulation that might occur from a tiny metal ring, but I couldn't actually envision what that felt like. Too far out of my reality. "No, I don't know."

"Oh, shit, I guess not."

The look of sympathy she gave me was so heartfelt, I almost laughed. At the same time, it made me feel a deep sense of longing for all the experiences I had missed out on.

Kylie emerged from the closet, triumphantly holding her coveted boots. "Found them," she said breathlessly, flipping her hair back. "You should totally go for it with Tyler."

"No!" The thought was horrifying. First of all, because I couldn't imagine spending time with a guy who my roommate had had sex with. Second, because I was convinced there was no way in hell Tyler was actually interested in me. Third, because I wasn't sure I was interested in *him*. He didn't seem like my type. While I may not have dated, I certainly had crushed on plenty of guys, both fictional and living, and they tended to be the underdogs, with soulful eyes and a moodiness driven by insecurity. Hello, Grant.

Tyler was too confident to fit into that box of Broken Boy.

Then again, pining for passionate musician types hadn't really played out well for me.

"Why not?" Jessica asked. "If it's me, God, don't worry about that."

"It's just . . . no. The answer is just no."

Kylie had dropped her sweatpants as well, and she stood in her pink bra and thong, hands on her hips. "This could be good for you. Now get dressed, we're going out."

"And the answer to that is no, too." I pulled the covers more firmly up to my chest. I wasn't going anywhere. I was going to lie in bed until Sunday morning.

She gave a cluck of disapproval. "Lame."

"Yep." I ate my crackers and watched them move around the room getting ready, transforming from Zumba enthusiasts to sexy partyers, cleavage out, miniskirts on. When Jessica pulled out the false eyelashes, I knew they weren't playing. This was a commitment. They were in the mood for an all-nighter—strobe-lights-flashing, vodka-flowing, booty-grinding kind of adventure—and I wasn't going to see them until after a post-partying Denny's chow down on ham and eggs at five a.m. Guys would be flirted with but not allowed to touch, and it would be a girl-power night out on the town.

Then I said something stupid. "Is Tyler going with you?"

"See!" Kylie said in total rapture. "You *do* like him!" She spritzed a cloud of perfume in my direction.

Coughing, I sputtered, not even sure why I had asked. "I'm just worried that he might come back here and camp out at my feet again."

"Uh-huh." She rolled her eyes.

Then they air-kissed me, waved, and were off, the door slamming behind them, leaving me alone in a dorm room littered with discarded boobie tops and hair products. The feathered mirror above Jessica's bed fluttered from the draft, and I was left alone with my thoughts and the pretentiousness of Hemingway and Tennessee Williams awaiting me.

Plus a strange yearning for something I didn't understand and wanted to ignore.

Resolutely, I got up to shower and tried not to listen for a knock at the door.

CHAPTER THREE

MY DAD PUSHED UP HIS GLASSES AND SMILED AT ME THROUGH the computer screen. He was sitting in the family room of our house, and he was wearing a Cincinnati Bengals jersey, which looked incongruous (and too big) on him. He had never been a sports lover and was definitely the science nerd, preferring to stargaze than head down to Cincinnati for a baseball or football game. So he looked a bit like a middle-aged man wearing a costume, but I knew that his girlfriend Susan was big into football and he was trying to be open to new things.

He was my dad, but different. Altered.

Even the family room behind him looked different from when I had left home at the end of the summer and Susan had moved in. The house hadn't changed for twelve years after my mother died, the same plaid furniture and oak kitchen table in the exact same spots where she had placed them, a border with faded red apples circled the breakfast nook. The pictures were frozen in the early two thousands, me with gap-toothed grins and as a chubby baby splashing in a bathtub. There was the requisite engagement portrait of my parents with big hair, her hand lay carefully over his in a phenomenally cheesy pose, and their wedding photo, all framed in the same honey oak color as the dinette set. My father had never added another picture to the gallery, and I seemed to have stopped growing at the age of eight.

There was only the past and never the present.

But Susan had replaced the plaid sofa with a nice neutral, modern one that Dad was perched on, and she had painted the existing coffee table and all the picture frames a crisp black. So there were the same photos, with large sweaters and overalls below faces that no longer existed, and while they were same, the framing was different.

Altered.

I wasn't sure how I felt about it. There was no question that the old furniture was dated and ugly, but the more there was of Susan, the less there was of my mom.

Susan herself popped up behind Dad, leaning over the back of the new couch. "Hey, Rory, how are you?" she said, her voice pleasant and neutral.

"I'm fine. I'm just freaking out over this inorganic chemistry exam I have," I told her. I did like Susan, though I didn't necessarily feel close to her. But she had been dating my dad for three years and she had never tried too hard. She hadn't forced herself on me or cheerfully suggested shopping trips or bonding spa appointments. She had stood back and let me adjust to her presence, and she wasn't fake.

It was clear that she cared about my dad and that was cool. I appreciated it and appreciated even more that her being in his life didn't really affect mine. She had moved in right after I had left for school this year, and I hadn't been home for a weekend yet. I knew my dad was stressing about the whole thing, sure I was going to collapse into juvenile angst over his girlfriend, but while I kept waiting to resent it, so far I didn't seem to really care. If she turned my bedroom into a sports museum, though, we were going to have to throw down.

"Oh, God, I can't help you with that. That's your dad's area." Susan was a high school English teacher and cheerleading coach.

For real. My dad, the chemical engineer who got excited about breakthroughs in biodegradable plastics, with a cheerleading coach.

"But I'm sure you'll ace it. You always do."

Usually there was truth to that statement, but I had just wasted an entire Saturday sleeping off the worst hangover of my life. "I'm going to try," I said. "But I think Hemingway is going to have to take a backseat. I can't read and study at the same time and my classes for my major are more important. What are you guys up to?"

"We're having some people over for the game later," my dad said, and he sounded proud.

"That's cool," I told him, and I meant it. He was even more socially awkward than I was, tending to bore the snot out of people with his theories on making plastics from plant materials and the solution to the economic crisis. Without my mom to guide him through the maze of small talk, he had gotten very limited in what he did outside of work and driving me to school and science camps.

After Mom had died, my dad hadn't been able to handle the Girl Scout meetings, sleepovers, playdates, and sending birthday treats to school. Between the grief and his naturally introverted personality, it had been beyond his scope of ability, and he didn't return phone calls from the other moms and forgot to fill out field-trip forms. Eventually I stopped getting invited to parties, and I was dropped off the rosters of all my grade school clubs, so that by the time middle school rolled around, it was just dad and me in a house that never changed.

In high school I had taken control and tried to create a life for myself, with marginal success.

Now Dad was attempting to do the same thing.

Sometimes I wondered what Susan saw in him. But I realized that he was a supersweet, generous guy, even if he was a total dork. He was a lovable dork. And once in an unexpected moment of sharing, he told me that Susan had been married to an abusive guy who spent all their money on his failed fitness club. So in comparison to that, Dad was downright sexy I would imagine. Or at least not threatening.

"But if you need help studying, let me know. We can go through it now together." He put his thumbs up in the air. "Team Macintosh!"

Oh, God. See? Totally adorable dork.

I laughed. "Thanks, Dad. I think I'm okay, though. I'm going to the library because Jess and Kylie are still sleeping. I'm in the dorm lounge right now." No one used the lounge on our floor. It was a forgotten room that smelled like burned microwave popcorn and had threadbare carpet and one square wood couch. There was a whiteboard hanging crookedly on the wall, but nothing was written on it.

"Still sleeping? It's past two. What are they anemic or something?"

Susan laughed and rolled her eyes at me, a knowing look on her face. "Oh, John, it's a good thing you're pretty," she teased him. She gave him a quick kiss on the temple. "I'm guessing they were out partying."

He made a face, pulling away from her kiss. I knew he was embarrassed by the affection. "Didn't you go with them, Ror?"

"No. I was studying and watching a horror-movie marathon." And thinking about Tyler's bizarre little visit.

I could see my answer had my dad torn. He wanted me to study, but he wanted me to have a social life. Even though he would never say it, because we didn't talk about emotions, I knew he felt guilty for not making things easier for me as a kid.

"Make sure you're still having fun," he settled on, a nice generic suggestion.

"Yep."

"So . . ." There was a pause so painful I frowned. I had no idea what he was going to say, and he looked like he had sat on a pin he was shifting around so much, wiping his hands on his knees. "Any cute guys there that you like?"

Yikes. For some reason I had a feeling that Susan had suggested he open up this ridiculous dialogue with me. "Nope. This was voted the Homeliest Campus in America, you know."

It took him a second, but then he made a face. "Ha ha. You know what I mean."

"I do. And no, I haven't met Mr. Wonderful. I haven't even met Mr. Sort of Okay." Then I gave him a smile. "Don't worry about me, Dad. I have plenty of time still to explore unhealthy relationships with self-absorbed jerks. I'm taking philosophy next semester so I have high hopes for that class."

"Perfect," he said, pulling a smile.

I knew he worried about me. He had already been dating my mom by the time they were twenty, and he seemed to think my lack of a boyfriend up to this point was an indicator of impending crazy-cat-lady, old-maid status. Maybe he was right. But

I worried enough about it myself. He didn't need to carry that burden, too.

"Have fun with your friends," I told him, wanting to encourage his social interaction. In that way, I guess I was really no different from him. We worried about each other. When you spent a decade with no one else, it just worked that way.

"Thanks, honey, you too. We'll talk to you soon. Over and out, Captain."

I saluted him. "Yes, sir."

Yep. An adorable dork.

ON MONDAY, I WANDERED AROUND THE BOOKSTORE straightening UC T-shirts and sweatpants, wishing I was anywhere but my work-study job. I had done okay on my chem exam, but I wasn't prepared for lit class, and I had sat through the lecture wondering if the book I had attempted to read was even the same one the professor was talking about.

Tired and pissed off at myself, I moved from rack to rack, pounding hangers down to make the sweatshirts stop exploding in all directions, and contemplated going for tutoring in lit, though I wasn't even sure they offered it. Tutoring was for math and science and foreign languages, not for reading a book. Presumably once you got to college you knew how to do that.

"Is this me?" a voice said from behind.

I turned and there was Tyler holding up in front of him a woman's tank top that read Sexiest Bearcat, a lazy smile on his face as he watched for my reaction. Oh, God. He was the last person on the planet I wanted to see when I was stressed and still wondering why he had been in my room on Saturday.

"It's not your color," I told him, feeling hugely self-conscious that I had barely managed to brush my hair before work, and I'd bitten off my lipstick from irritation hours ago.

"Yeah, you're right. This one would look good on you, though."

I snorted. I couldn't help it. No one had ever accused me of being sexy before, and if I were going to pick spirit wear, it wouldn't be a tank top designed to show off breasts. So not my style.

"Not your color either?" he asked.

"No." I went back to the rack, straightening what I had already straightened, wondering what he was doing there. Mid-semester, the bookstore wasn't all that busy. Usually it was parents and high school students on tour who came in and bought golf shirts and *UC Mom* tees. Somehow I didn't think Tyler was there to buy either of those.

He was just standing there, eyeballing the rack next to me without any sense of purpose. Wearing a plain black T-shirt and jeans that hung exactly the way they should on a guy, he had a bicep tattoo that read *TRUE Family* in a tribal script. For some reason, that softened my irritation with him. It wasn't his fault he made me uncomfortable. He was just trying to be nice. Maybe he felt sorry for me because of what had happened with Grant, and he had come to the bookstore to buy pens and just wanted to say hi, and I was being weird about it. When you knew someone, you went over and acknowledged them. It was the way human beings interacted and I needed to stop looking for more meaning in everything than there was.

"Can I help you find something?" I asked him, striving for casual. But instead I sounded like a fifty-year-old saleswoman, and he called me out on it.

"Yes, can you show me this in a bigger size? And can you help me find gifts for my grandkids?" That was him mocking me, no question about it.

My cheeks heated.

Tyler scrutinized me. "Seriously, Rory, I know you're at work but you don't have to act like we've never met before. I don't think they'll fire you if you talk to me for five minutes. It's work study. You'd have to light the stadium blanket display on fire for them to can you."

"I did that last week and they didn't actually fire me. That's why I need to toe the line this week," I told him dryly.

My sarcasm, which I usually delivered in a complete monotone, had the same effect on him now as it had in the car. He looked stunned for a second, then he grinned. "Well, then I can't risk getting you in trouble. Tell me where the books are. I want to browse the lit section."

"Sure. They're this way." I led him to the other side of the store, where there were racks and racks of books. "Is there a title you need for a class or something?"

"No, I just like to read."

I glanced back to try to gauge his expression. He looked serious. I wouldn't have pegged him as a big reader, but then again, what did I know about him really? I had just seen him slamming back beers and making out with Jessica. I didn't even know what he was studying in school. The only thing I knew about him was that Jess had said he came from a messed-up family, and that he still lived at home not far from campus.

"What do you like to read?"

"Anything. Fiction, nonfiction, genre fiction, literature. Everything." Immediately he picked up *The Alchemist* off the shelf. "Have you read this? It's really good. You have to get used to the narrative, but then it's a cool story. The kid is kind of a pussy, but then he gets it in the end."

I shook my head. "I haven't read it." The fiction section of bookstores always seemed to me like a mysterious world where I wasn't allowed entrance, the intriguing and colorful covers a patch-work of complex stories, glimpses into other people's lives, and where I should have felt at home, because I was generally an observer, not a doer. Yet when I read fiction, I was always knocked off-kilter by the scene changes, the styles of the various writers, the hints that seemed designed to tease and confuse, the theme that I could never ferret out. I read almost nothing other than nonfiction, facts and vocabulary. That was my comfort zone.

"Who is your favorite author?" He had moved on to a book I didn't recognize, with a black-and-white photo of small children on the cover.

"I don't have one. I read mostly nonfiction." I spotted Tennessee Williams on the shelf, the bastard.

"Really?" Tyler looked surprised. "I would have thought you were a huge fiction reader, being so smart and everything. You're premed, right?"

I had no idea where he'd heard what my major was, but I felt compelled to share my limitations with him. "I'm good at math and science. I like facts and figures. Literature is the hardest subject for me because I feel like I never understand what the authors are trying to tell me. It's like they're trying to trick me."

"So you're a logical kind of chick, huh? I should have figured that out. Me, I'd rather read a book than do math problems any day." He dropped his beat-up bag to the floor. "I'm guessing I've read thousands of books at this point."

Clearly I had to toss my preconceived notions about him

out the window. Thousands? The thought made me break out in anxiety-inspired sweat. "Sounds time-consuming. And expensive."

"Oh, but I have a secret weapon." He dug in his pocket and pulled out his wallet. Picking through it, he withdrew and held out a very battered card. "Da-dum. My library card. Sexy, huh?"

I smiled. I couldn't help it. There was something really charming about him, I had to admit. It was like he knew exactly who he was, and he wasn't afraid to show himself to anyone. And while, yes, he was the bad boy who smoked and was tatted up and wouldn't hesitate to punch someone in the face, he also liked to read. I admired that. "Awesome. So are you an English major?" I would have never guessed that, but maybe he wanted to be a teacher or something.

"Oh, hell no. I wish. I can't afford four years of school with no guarantee of a job. I'm getting an associate's degree as an EMT." He made a face. "All the anatomy and phys classes suck. But I know if I can push through it, I can get that piece of paper and have a job right away. Only eight months to go. If I don't fuck it up."

I felt sympathy for his stress. "If you need help studying, you can call me. That stuff is easy for me."

"Seriously?" There was a thoughtful expression on his face, and I wondered if that had sounded too conceited.

So I added, "Now if I could figure out what anything means in *A Streetcar Named Desire*. God, I'm so bad at it. Today in class I felt like I was listening to a foreign language. Symbolism sucks."

"Maybe we can trade off, because I can help you with that. That's my thing." He pulled out his phone. "Give me your number, and we can study together sometime this week."

"Okay, cool." I wasn't sure if that was actually cool or not. It seemed like maybe it was actually a bad idea, but I couldn't pinpoint why that would be bad. Other than the fact that I still felt awkward that he knew I was a virgin, and he had seen me on the floor fending off Grant. But maybe if we hung out, none of that would seem important anymore and I could relax around him.

So I gave him my number and he immediately dialed it, so that I would have his, too.

"How does Thursday look for you?" he asked.

"I should be free." My heart was beating faster than normal, and I wanted desperately to wipe my hands on my jeans.

"Okay, I'll talk to you later." He picked up his bag and turned to go. Then he paused and asked, "Hey, do you sell condoms here?"

I blinked. The change of subject caught me off guard, but I also felt a sudden tight pit in my stomach at the realization that he had, was, and would continue to have sex with my roommate, and possibly any number of other girls. It made me feel rejected and jealous, which was stupid.

Angry at my own reaction, I just shook my head. "No. The closest place is probably Walgreens across the street."

"Thanks." He winked at me, yanking the tank top back off the rack on his way past. "I'm buying this. Catch you later, Rory."

I didn't even want to think about who he was buying that for. Suddenly I wasn't sure that studying with Tyler was going to be healthy for me.

But I also knew I wasn't going to cancel.

I was too curious.

And oddly attracted to him.

WALKING ACROSS CAMPUS WITH KYLIE AFTER OUR MUTUAL calculus class on Wednesday, I kicked the leaves with the toes of my black riding boots, pushing my hands into the pockets of my peacoat. It had been an unusually cold October, and I could almost smell winter in the air. When I had first come to school as a freshman, I had missed the small-town feel of where I'd grown up, an hour out of Cincinnati. Our campus was urban, built in a depression in the geography, so the whole layout felt a bit like a bowl, with the stadium right in the center, buildings rising around it in a circle. But I was used to the constant press of architecture now, and there were still green spaces to hang out in.

"So what should we wear on Saturday?" Kylie said, walking beside me in skinny jeans and fuzzy boots that looked like an acrylic sheep had died to produce them. She had an equally fuzzy cap on, yet half of her chest was exposed to show off her cleavage. It seemed like a meteorological oxymoron to me. Then she added, "I want Nathan to see me and jizz in his pants," and I forgot all about her conflicting wardrobe pieces.

I laughed. "Eew. Why would you want that?"

"I don't mean literally. I just want him to see me and instantly want to bone me."

"I don't think that's a problem. He pretty much looks at you like that all the time." Nathan was actually a really nice guy as far as I could tell. He had grown up with Tyler and Grant, and shared an apartment with a guy named Bill who drove home to Columbus every weekend to visit his high school girlfriend, giving Nathan and Tyler the run of the place.

Sometimes I wondered if Nathan wanted to be more than just a hook-up for Kylie because he was always kissing the top of her head and trying to hold her hand. She brushed him off with teasing words and laughter most of the time, and he took it good-naturedly, but I felt kind of bad for him. Kylie wasn't at the point in her life where she wanted to be committed—she was having too much fun snagging male attention everywhere she could, and I didn't blame her. If I could pull it off without vomiting, I would love to flirt with more than one guy at a time.

"You think so? Well, I was trying to decide which costume I should wear. Last Halloween I was a sexy cop and I was thinking about being a sexy nurse this year, but that seems so expected."

"It does," I said quite honestly. The only options that seemed available to girls for Halloween were sexy fill-in-the-blank. You could be anything from a sexy zombie to a sexy schoolteacher, but if you wanted your tits and ass covered in any real capacity, you were out of luck. Of course, sexy anything suited Kylie. But I still felt like being creative was at least a little bit important. "Why don't you be a sexy Roller Derby girl? You can wear skates, and it will set you apart from all the other girls at the party." I knew that was important to her, to not just blend in with the sea of gorgeous and tanned blondes on campus.

"Hm. Maybe."

"Plus, you can elbow Nathan just for fun. I bet he'll actually think that's hot. Guys like bitches." Why was a mystery to me, but again, it was a logic issue. I pulled my coat tighter and sniffled. I felt like I was getting a cold, and I wasn't sure if I even wanted to go to the party after the football game on Saturday. I certainly wasn't going to wear a sexy anything if I did.

"I bet Tyler doesn't like bitches."

Ugh. I so did not want to talk to Kylie about Tyler. I didn't even want to think about Tyler.

"You should go as a sexy scientist," Kylie said. "And you can offer to experiment on him."

I laughed. "You do know me, don't you? There is no way those words would ever come out of my mouth."

"I know," she said cheerfully. "But I can only live in hope." She hooked her arm through mine. "Shit, it's cold."

"It would probably help if you covered your breasts."

"God, so practical all the time. Prude."

"Slut." This was an affectionate exchange we had established early on in our freshman year when we had in fact realized we did like each other, for no discernible reason.

Kylie and Jessica had been friends in high school in Troy, and they had requested to room together. There had been a dorm-room shortage and so they had randomly placed me as the third in their room, and we'd been together ever since. I had only had a couple of friends in high school and they had been like me, quiet and studious. But I liked to think that the three of us balanced each other out a little, and I had certainly learned to respect differences.

"So if you could have sex with anyone on campus, who would you pick? Because we're going to make this happen. You cannot go through life a virgin—it's just too sad."

"I don't know."

But I was lying.

A face had already popped up in front of me, though I would never have admitted it, even under threat of forcing me to become a literature major if I didn't respond.

CHAPTER FOUR

"I THINK YOUR PROBLEM IS MEMORIZATION," I TOLD TYLER AS we sat in the back of a coffee shop, his cup of black coffee drained, my latte cooling quickly. His anatomy book was spread out in front of us, and I was going over his last exam with him—he'd gotten a 76. "You understand the principles of how the parts function, you just don't have the terminology down."

His head was propped on his chin, and he was sprawled across the table. His leg had been inching closer to mine over the past half hour, and I had repeatedly shifted to the left, wishing we weren't sitting on the same side of the booth. "Has anyone ever told you that you have pretty hair?" he asked, completely ignoring what I'd just said. "Because you do."

My hand had been on its way to my cup, and with his words, I jerked, shooting the cup across the table and onto the floor, coffee dribbling out. "You're not even trying to study," I accused, leaning over to pick up the cup, my palms sweating a little. Where the hell had that ridiculous line come from? I could see his legs under the table and he spread his feet even farther apart, his thigh brushing mine. I swallowed hard.

"Sure I am. I heard every word you said. I need to do more memorization. And it is anatomy." He was watching me, intently, not smiling. "I'm studying your anatomy, so I'm still on task."

For some reason, I felt like he was making fun of me. I couldn't figure out how exactly, but it just felt too rehearsed, trite. "That's the dumbest line I've ever heard," I told him flatly.

The corner of his mouth tilted up. "You're a tough one. I like that."

"I'm not tough. I just don't want to be here all night and you haven't learned anything." I sounded like his mother and I knew it, but I couldn't stop myself. He made me flustered, and I had no tools to deal with his odd, flirtatious behavior.

"I've learned that your hair is beautiful." He reached over and lazily pulled a strand out, stretching it toward him.

The touch made me shiver. I considered my hair my best asset. It was long and thick and glossy, with a baby-soft fine texture. That he would choose to point it out confused me. Torn between wanting to be flattered and feeling that he was just avoiding studying, I yanked my hair away from him. "You need to stop lifting your lines from pornos. Not all girls are going to fall for that crap."

"What do you know about pornos? You have a secret addiction to sex videos?" He still didn't sit up, but he drew his textbook closer to him.

I had backed myself into a corner with that one. "No, of course not! I am just making assumptions about the behavior in them."

"You're too smart to make assumptions."

He was right. I felt neatly put in my place, but at the same time, I felt like he was complimenting me.

"Step outside with me for a second. I need a cigarette and that's why I can't concentrate." He stood up, nudging me to leave the booth. He made no move to collect his books or his bag.

"We can't just leave our stuff here," I said, though I did stand up to move out of his way. "I'll just stay."

"No one is going to steal your textbook. You probably couldn't give it away."

"Someone could resell it."

"For five bucks?" Tyler held his hands out and looked around the coffee shop. There was one guy asleep in the opposite corner and a couple of girls who were both buried in their cell phone screens. "This isn't a crime wave waiting to happen."

Because I knew he was right, I was tempted to force my point just on principle, but I didn't want to look belligerent. I did grab my nearly empty latte and took it with me to throw away. "Five minutes, that's it. We need to go through all your muscle groups."

He turned and I realized exactly where his thoughts had gone by the twitch of his mouth and his raised eyebrows. "Sounds kinky."

I wished. "It's not."

"God, you're so in control," he said, pushing open the front door and digging in his pocket to retrieve a pack of Camel cigarettes. "I can't break you. I keep trying, and nothing."

"What is it that you want me to do?" I asked, genuinely curious. I wasn't sure what I was failing to produce, and while I had no intention of changing in any way, I did want to understand. Maybe it would give me insight into how other people related, into why it was so difficult for me to establish relationships.

Tyler pulled a cigarette out of the pack and stuck it in his mouth. He held the pack out to me in offering, and I shook my head no. Lighting it, he took a deep drag, then blew it out to the side.

"I keep trying to direct our conversations and you won't follow me. You're just like . . ." he pushed his hands down toward the ground. "Firm."

Firm. A guy I thought was actually hot with a capital *H* was describing me as *firm*. I didn't even know what that meant, but it certainly wasn't something a guy would want to date. No wonder I'd never had a boyfriend.

I stared at him as he stood there in the cool night air, wearing nothing but a T-shirt and not looking even remotely cold, his biceps cut and well-defined. When he lifted his cigarette to his mouth again, I saw there was another tattoo on the inside of his wrist. His movements were confident, casual, and as the smoke rose in front of his chiseled face, I suddenly wondered what he looked like naked.

Firm. That's what I imagined he would look like. For a guy, that was an awesome word, with several positive implications. But for a girl, unless he was talking about your ass, not so much of a compliment.

"I have no idea what you're talking about," I told him honestly.

"I know you don't. That's what I find so cool and interesting. You're just you. You're real."

He might as well have said that *real* was a synonym for *freak*. But there was nothing fake about me, that was true, and there never would be. I had no ability to fake it, to lie and giggle and flirt my way through conversations with guys. So maybe that was the truth of it—unless I chose to do that, I was going to be alone because I was too honest. Too unflinching. Guys wanted to be flirted with, stroked, coaxed.

"Thank you," I said, because I wanted him to understand I appreciated that he got me. It made me feel like maybe we could actually be friends if he wasn't put off by my directness and occasional failure to follow social protocol.

For some reason, my response made him grin. "Rory."

It didn't sound like a question, but I still asked, "What?" when he didn't continue. "And your five minutes is almost up."

"You're cute."

Cute like puppies are cute when they're running along and wipe out for no reason, an adorable clumsy ball of not-so-bright. It was a compliment, and I believed he meant it. It just wasn't the one I wanted.

"You're down to thirty seconds. You'd better suck harder."

He laughed. Then he stepped forward, cigarette hands-free in his mouth, and touched both of my shoulders. He rubbed me vigorously, the motion making my head jerk back and forth. "Relax. It's all good, babe," he said, words mumbled from around the filter.

The tangy sweetness of his cigarette rose between us, and I was cold from the wind, yet his hands were warm on my shoulders, heating through my sweater. They were bigger than I had expected, two large masses wrapping almost entirely around my upper arms, and I was aware of how tall he was, how broad his chest. He filled the space, enveloping me without even being that close, and I wanted what I couldn't have. I wanted to be the girl who could flirt, who could hair flip. If I were her, I would go on my toes and pull that cigarette out and toss it to the ground, then kiss his mouth, running my hands over his chest, and he would kiss me back.

In reality, none of those things would happen.

"Do you know what the latissimus dorsi and rhomboids are?"

His right hand pulled away from me and he removed his cigarette from his mouth. Smoke filtered out with his words. "I have no fucking clue."

"My point precisely."

"God, you're hard-core." But he didn't sound at all annoyed.

An hour later, our positions had reversed. I had refilled my latte twice and was jittery with caffeine, and I wanted nothing to do with selfish characters. "If you need to smoke, we can break at any time," I told Tyler, trying to sound generous. "I don't mind."

His eyebrow shot up. "I bet you don't. But forget about it. I can wait until you've at least created an outline for your essay."

I was tempted to thunk my head on the table. "I don't get it. I mean, not a single one of these characters is likeable. Stanley is a douche bag, Stella is a doormat, and Blanche is a drunk."

"The point of *Streetcar* is not for you to want to be buddies with these characters. It's to explore relationships." Tyler was looking at my professor's description of the intended essay on my tablet, his lips moving as he read the instructions. He had the book propped open with his forearm, and I didn't even care that he was cracking the spine. The book was cracked, in my opinion.

"All their relationships are delusional, from what I can tell. Blanche hides in the dark so men don't guess her real age, she and her sister pretend that nothing bad has ever happened, Stanley doesn't do anything but play poker and boss Stella around. If they would just like communicate with each other, they could resolve all their issues in ten minutes."

"That's what makes the book so realistic," he told me dryly. "Real people don't discuss shit with each other."

He had a point. I didn't really discuss my emotions with anyone either. I had spent most of my life being a silent observer. "Oh."

In one fell swoop, I got it. Literature wasn't intended to be about perfect people, it was about flaws, very real and very deep human flaws.

"What's that? Did you hear that?" Tyler cocked his head to the side and cupped his ear. "It's the sound of the lightbulb clicking on over Rory's head."

"Ha ha. Okay, I guess I get it. But I don't know, shouldn't there be like a lesson or something from a story?"

"Why?"

Shifting on my seat, I tried to find the words to express my frustration. "I guess, what is the value of a book if there isn't a lesson?"

"That's the scientist in you speaking."

It was, but I still wanted to prove my point. "For example, Stella is being abused by her husband, yet not only does she tolerate it, she seems to enjoy it on a certain level. Is it healthy to perpetuate that kind of abusive fantasy to female readers? Why would she think it's sexy to have her husband throwing shoes around and breaking things in the height of passion?"

"I think that may have something to do with your, you know, status." He flashed his fingers in a *V* to me.

Really? He was not talking about victory or peace. He was referencing my virginity.

"You haven't, um, experienced how hot getting a little rough can be."

Stunned, my cheeks burned with embarrassment. The image of Tyler picking Jessica up and tossing her onto the bed in a fit of overwhelming lust crowded out my rational thoughts, and I felt nauseated.

"You're right. I don't." I probably never would either. "But hitting a woman is never okay."

"Of course not!" He looked offended. "Hitting her and throwing a shoe are two totally different things. Any sort of direct physical contact is not cool. Neither is forcing her to do anything she doesn't want to." He gave me a long look. "I think you'd know my feelings on that."

He was talking about Grant. Humiliation washed over me, and I was back on the stained carpet, shoving ineffectually at Grant's chest, trying to break his hold. I was grateful to Tyler for his actions on my behalf, but that didn't mean I wanted to be reminded of them. The truth was, he knew far too many personal details about me.

"I'm done studying." I yanked the book out from under his arm and shoved it into my backpack. Snapping the lid shut on my tablet, I jumped out of the booth.

"Wait, Rory, I didn't mean . . ."

"I know." I cut him off, because I would be a hypocrite if I stood there and refused to be reasonable after I had just complained about characters behaving the same way. But that didn't mean I wanted to go into any detail.

"Sit down. Please." His hand reached out and grabbed my wrist.

If he had left it like that, I probably would have jerked away. But he slid his fingers down across my sensitive skin until they were entwined with mine. The feeling was so intimate, so unexpected, that I plunked down on the wooden bench, speechless, all embarrassment driven right out of me.

He squeezed my hand and stared at me intently, his knee bumping mine. "We're good?"

I nodded. "Yeah. We're good." I wasn't sure why or what *good* actually meant, but I didn't really want to leave.

"HEY, RORY, HOW ARE YOU TODAY?" JOANNE ASKED AS SHE passed by me with a cat cradled in her arms.

"Good. How are you? How are the kids?" I was on the floor at the animal shelter Friday afternoon, running a brush across a Yorkie named Licorice. His eyes were watery, the left one cloudy from a cataract. He sat patiently between my legs and closed his eyes each time I stroked the brush through his fur. The longer we sat there, the closer his warm body leaned toward mine.

"Driving me crazy. Back talking and going over on their texting allowance. Then Heather had the nerve to sneak out of her room, steal ten bucks from my purse, and meet up with that loser gang-banger at the bowling alley." Joanne was in her forties, curvy, with blond hair that she still rolled and sprayed in the way she probably had in high school. She was supersweet and great with the animals, affectionate with me. Yet every time I saw her, it seemed like one of her kids was off on a rebellious streak. "I don't know what to do. You're young. What the hell is going through their heads?"

I shook my own head. "I have no idea. I never did any of that stuff. One time I got mad and told my dad to shut up, then I cried and apologized for the next two hours."

She set the cat down on the table and scratched him behind the ears. "I wish you were my daughter." Looking around the room, she added, "Have you seen Lois? I need to give this guy his insulin and his chart is missing."

"I saw her go to the front reception area like five minutes ago." Leaning forward, I gave Licorice a kiss on the top of his fur. Joanne's comment about being my mother, a casual compliment, made me feel melancholy. I'd been feeling weird since I'd left the coffee shop the day before, Tyler giving me a wave and not even a backward glance as we had headed in our two separate directions.

I didn't understand what he was doing, what he wanted from me. Because in my experience, people wanted something from each other. To use them, to gain friendship, for a romantic relationship. I didn't think he had any of those three as his motivation, and it was like a Rubik's Cube that I kept turning around and around with no solution.

That's why I liked animals. They were uncomplicated. You knew in the first five minutes if they liked you or not, and their affection was genuine. I had started volunteering at the shelter midway through my freshman year, and while I only went there once every two weeks because of my school and work schedule, I loved it.

Licorice suddenly closed the gap between us and licked my face. "Thanks, buddy."

My phone buzzed in my pocket, and I sat up a little so I could pull it out. I had a notification of a social-networking friend request from Tyler Mann. Was that my answer? Was that literal or metaphorical?

I would need him to interpret it, and I wasn't about to ask him.

I hit Ignore for now and went back to sliding my fingers through Licorice's silky, thinning fur.

CHAPTER FIVE

AS WE WALKED DOWN THE STREET TO THE HOUSE WHERE THE Halloween party was being held, I was already starting to question my choice of costume. Jessica, Kylie, and another friend, Robin, and I had gone shopping Friday night, and in a rare moment of confidence in showing my inner snark to the world, I had decided to go as a *Toddlers & Tiaras* pageant princess. At the store I'd bought a crown and white ruffled socks and white Mary Janes. I'd borrowed Kylie's homecoming dress from the year before, and it was showing both more leg and more shoulder than I was used to. With curled hair and a sash that I had written across with a glittery fabric pen, I was definitely not going to blend into the background, which was my usual choice. But at least I hadn't bowed to the sexy pressure and wasn't walking across broken sidewalks in fifty-degree weather in sky-high heels the way my three friends were.

Robin, who had lived in the room next door to us the year before, was a sexy kitten. Jessica was a Playboy bunny. And Kylie had spent an hour fretting her way across the costume shop until finally she had settled on a sexy banana costume that had a zipper down the front so her banana could be peeled. I was trying not to judge, but it was hard to understand how she could have eyeballed at least fifty costumes and decided that she wanted to be a yellow fruit. She seemed to be wondering the same thing herself because she was worrying the whole walk.

"The yellow on these shoes is off," she said, lifting her foot up, then grabbing me for balance. "I should have just gone with black, like that little end thingie on a banana."

"I think you're fine," I told her. "You look amazing." She did. She had a banging body, and her hair and makeup were flawless. "Nathan is going to drool, big time."

"You think so?" she said, looking completely unsure of herself.

"Of course."

It was interesting that even someone as secure in herself as Kylie could have moments of self-doubt, and I started to wonder if maybe she wasn't as disinterested in Nathan as she made it seem. Or liked to think.

"Fuck, it's cold out here!" Jessica rubbed her arms and said, "We should have made those assholes pick us up. Tyler has a car. Why are we walking?"

"Because it's only two blocks," I said. "And we wouldn't all fit in Tyler's car anyway."

"I could have sat on Nathan's face," Kylie said, with a giggle. "Then we would have fit."

Jessica snorted. "I hope that Sebastian guy is here, you know the one from my international relations class. He plays soccer with Jake, who lives in the house. Sebastian is so hot, and I would definitely like to get to know him better."

I wanted to say "What about Tyler?" but I didn't want to draw any attention to myself and specifically to myself regarding him. So I kept my mouth slammed shut.

The party was at a house off campus that had formerly been the showroom for a plumber and bathroom remodeler, and when they had pulled out of the business, they had, for whatever reason, left three toilets in the front display window of the old house. The backyard was also a graveyard of toilet parts, with broken tanks and bowls leaning precariously on their sides. The house had been nicknamed the Shit Shack by the guys who lived there, and when we approached the front door, there was a toilet seat hanging from a rusty nail and someone had written *Welcome to the Shit Shack* with a Sharpie on it.

Promising.

Jessica laughed.

Robin made a face, tossing her black hair over her shoulder. "These idiots better have a big keg because this week was ass. I bombed my Spanish midterm."

After the weekend before, I personally wasn't thrilled with the idea of a keg, but as we entered the house, the smell of beer smacked me in the face, and I recoiled a little. This wasn't going to go well. I could practically still taste the vomit in my mouth.

Jessica disappeared immediately, her bunny tail bouncing as she clicked down the hall toward the kitchen, scanning the room with predatory skill. Robin went left, swallowed into a crowd of sexy referees and slutty cheerleaders. Kylie took my hand and said, "Let's get a drink." She started weaving across the sea of bodies clad in a wide range of costumes from Edward Scissorhands to Mario.

I never really understood the girls-holding-hands-at-parties thing. Kylie was very fond of doing it, and while I suspected it was a confidence booster, a sign to everyone that she had a friend at her back, she insisted it was for my safety. But I also thought the trend was some kind of attention-getting faux-lesbian signal to guys. *Hey, look at us. We're good friends and we hold hands . . . get us drunk and we might make out for you.* It made me uncomfortable. Because I was never going to make out with Kylie, and because I didn't think that we needed to throw out sexual promises and innuendos to guys to get attention.

But then again, who was a virgin and who wasn't? Who could have a boyfriend if she wanted, and who spent her time with books and shelter dogs?

Yeah.

Besides, I knew she was feeling insecure about her banana, so I held Kylie's hand and obediently followed her to the keg, deciding I wouldn't mind a beer after all.

"OMG, look at the keg, that's awesome." Kylie pulled a plastic cup off the stack and filled it with the spout of beer shooting up out of the toilet the guys had perched on top of the keg. It was like a frat boy bidet.

Charming.

Praying that toilet had never been used in any capacity other than as a makeshift beer bong, I filled a cup for myself and took a sip of the flat, cheap beer and tried not to sigh.

Half an hour later, I still had two-thirds of my beer, and I was standing there feeling bored and self-conscious. Kylie had long ago abandoned my hand, and she was fending off the third guy to try to unpeel her banana, his hand teasing on her zipper while she laughed and swatted at his wrist. Nathan was across the room, looking bitter and miserable, wearing a flight suit and aviator sunglasses. Every three seconds he glanced over at Kylie, while still maintaining a firm grip on a girl in a gingham crop top and Daisy Dukes. There was clearly some dynamic going on between Nathan and Kylie that I really didn't want to be in the middle of, some pheromone-driven power struggle.

One of the curls was tugged on the back of my head, and I turned around to see Tyler standing behind me. He was wearing jeans and a Metallica T-shirt. "Nice costume," I said, feeling both relieved to see him and nervous at the same time.

"I'm a Muggle," he told me with a completely straight face.

Of course he was. "Oh, yeah? No letter inviting you to Hogwarts, huh? That sucks."

"My parents were disappointed, but I still have my magic wand so it's all good."

I rolled my eyes. "You're gross."

He laughed. "What are you supposed to be? My mom at her prom in 1988?"

"No. I'm a toddler with a tiara." I pointed to my head and the crown.

Reaching out, he pulled the sash out straight so he could read it. "Miss Diagnosed?" He grinned. "Rory, you fucking crack me up."

I smiled. "At least you get it. I've had like three people tell me they're totally confused."

"Your premed wit is on display, babe. Though you don't look like any toddler I've ever seen."

"Too tall?"

"Among other things." He took my drink out of my hand and sipped it, then made a face. "Piss water. Come on, let's go out back. I have a stash of real beer under my jacket. Brandon's watching it."

I had no idea who Brandon was, but I really had no desire to stay in the crowded house and feel superfluous, so I let him take my hand and lead me across the room. Apparently my hand was in high demand tonight. Tyler unceremoniously pitched the keg beer in the garbage can, and I tapped Kylie's arm on the way by.

"I'm going outside."

Her eyes lit up when she assessed the situation, and she gave me a rousing double thumbs-up. "Okay! Have fun!" she sang out, way louder than I would have liked, before turning back to her court of panting guys.

"What the hell is Kylie supposed to be? A rubber glove?" Tyler asked when he let go of my hand to pull open the screen door at the back of the house, waiting for me to pass.

"She's a banana."

He snorted. "That's a stretch. She needs a stuffed monkey to make it believable."

"Oh, that would make it believable?" I asked, amused. "Because that's all yellow spandex with a big zipper needs to be convincing as fruit?"

"Smart-ass."

I couldn't argue that. "What is going on with her and Nathan?"

He shrugged, heading down the rotting wooden steps to the yard, which was mostly dead grass and dirt, with plumbing parts jutting up like toilet tombstones. "I don't know. None of my business."

Such a guy response.

Tyler approached a very short guy with a nervous look on his face as he shifted uneasily in front of a leather jacket. "I'm back. Thanks, bro." He fist bumped the guy, then bent over and retrieved his jacket. Under it was a twelve-pack of Bud Light.

I wasn't sure how that was supposed to qualify as superior beer, but at least it was in bottles. Tyler pulled out three and used his key ring to pop the caps off. He handed one to the other guy and one to me. "Brandon, this is Rory. Don't be a douche bag in front of her."

"Hey," he said to me, his eyes shifting, looking everywhere but at me. He took a long swallow of the beer, holding it at the very top of the bottle.

"Hi." And that's where it ended. I sucked at small talk.

Shivering from the breeze, I scanned the yard. It was dark, but the light from the back porch cast a yellow glow over the twenty or so people standing around, talking, drinking, laughing. Suddenly, a heavy jacket landed on my shoulders.

"Stick your arms through," Tyler ordered, his leather jacket swallowing me as he wrapped it around my body.

"I'm fine," I protested because it felt odd, too familiar, to wear his clothes.

"Just do it. You girls are never weather-ready. I swear to God, it makes no sense."

I thought about protesting, but he was right. I was wearing a strapless minidress, and his jacket was warm and smelled like cigarettes and cologne. Feeling very girly, I put one arm through, then transferred my beer to the other hand and repeated the process. "I was going to be a Sexy Bearcat, but someone had already bought the tank top."

He paused with a cigarette halfway to his mouth and smirked. "I would have paid money to see that."

Never in this lifetime.

"Isn't anyone worried about the cops showing up?" I asked, well aware that we were right out in the open, being illegal. The

Shit Shack was surrounded by dilapidated houses and sketchy wig and liquor stores, but it still seemed to me like it wouldn't be that hard for a cruiser to drive past and decide to liven up his Saturday night with a college-party bust.

Tyler, of course, looked unconcerned. "How old are you?"

"I turned twenty two weeks ago."

"Damn, you're older than I actually thought. But if the cops come, pitch your drink in the bushes, then cut through the back lot to my car."

"How old are you?"

"I'm twenty-two, so I'm legal."

For some reason, hearing that he was more than two years older than me made him even more unnerving. I had at least thought we were numerically in tandem. "I thought you were a sophomore."

"I am. I worked for two years after high school to save up money, though eight bucks an hour at a shitty convenience store doesn't add up to much."

"I guess not." It was a reminder to me that I was lucky that my dad was paying for the tuition my academic scholarship didn't cover. I only did work study for spending money.

Tyler sat down on a powder blue toilet, his legs spread apart. He patted his knee. "Sit down."

"No!" I was *not* going to perch on his knee on a toilet.

He blew a cloud of smoke out in my direction and was about to say something when Jessica came up behind him. She smiled at me, then leaned over, pressing her breasts against his back, and draping her hands over his shoulders onto his chest. While she whispered something in his ear, I glanced over at Brandon, who looked as uncomfortable as I felt. Taking a huge sip of my beer, I tried to be nonchalant as I watched Tyler nod at whatever she was saying, her bunny tail rising to the sky above her perfect ass.

Oh, God. I felt anxiety rising in my throat like a clam gone down wrong before sliding back up. I didn't want to see them make arrangements to hook up later. But Tyler leaned forward and pulled something out of his front pocket. He passed it back to her, and she slipped it down the front of her costume into the haven of her boosted breasts. She gave me a big grin, then gave Tyler a loud smacking kiss on the side of his head. He made a face and pulled away, waving her off.

"What was that?" I asked after she left, laughing at his dismissal, because I wanted to throw up and I had to know, even if I sounded pathetic or bitchy or rude.

"Vicodin. Jess wants to get high tonight since her intended fuck buddy isn't here."

I should have raised my hands to catch my jaw dropping, but I didn't have time. I stared at him, mouth gaping open in shock. I thought *he* was her fuck buddy. And since when did my roommate use Vicodin? Not to mention, why did Tyler have it?

"What?" I stuttered, the bottle of beer slipping in my hand. "Oh, shit!" I gripped it harder and prevented it from hitting the ground. But then I felt so stupid and so freaked out about what I'd just heard, that I just started walking away. I wasn't even sure where I was going.

"Where are you going?" Tyler was right behind me.

"Bathroom." I didn't look at him, but I could practically hear his frown of disapproval.

"Okay. You want me to go with you?"

"To the bathroom?" I shot him a look of disbelief. "No. I'll be right back. I promise." I would. I was wearing his jacket, and besides, I didn't have any way to get back to the dorm. Plus, I really didn't want to embarrass myself any more than I already had. I just needed a minute alone to get my shit together.

Someone was in the bathroom, of course. The door opened and it was Jessica.

"Hey!" she said brightly.

I pushed her back into the bathroom and locked the door behind her.

"What, Rory? Are you okay?" Her brow furrowed and her bunny ears bounced as she shook her hair back.

I set my beer down on the sink and studied Jessica. "What's going on? What did Tyler give you?"

"Just a happy pill. I like the way it makes my skin itch."

Clearly my face registered the horror I was feeling, because she took both of my hands into hers. "Oh, come on, don't make a big deal out of this. I do it like once a month. It's no different than getting wasted a few times a month."

"It chemically alters your brain."

"Which is why it feels so good." Jessica laughed. "Seriously, this is not a problem. I just didn't feel like drinking tonight, but I wanted a little high. This is a legal drug, you know."

She had a point there. And I couldn't imagine that one pill would do more than was intended when a doctor prescribed it. It would just make her feel loopy and numb, which I guess was what she was going for. I felt a little relieved but not exactly okay. "Just don't take more than one at a time, okay? Promise me."

Jessica nodded. "Yeah. Of course. I'm not looking to OD. Are you okay? Did something happen with Tyler?"

"No. Nothing happened," I said truthfully. I didn't understand the whole casual attitude toward sex partners. It seemed like a bigger deal to me than that, and it made me feel . . . lonely. Not to mention, I wasn't sure how I felt about him walking around with pills in his pocket that I'm guessing he did not have a prescription for. "Do you know where Tyler got the Vicodin from?"

"He steals it from his mom," Jessica said without hesitation. "But not because he wants to pop it. I don't think I've ever seen him actually use. But his mom is a serious drug abuser and she's OD'd like four times. He takes it to keep her from taking too many at once." She leaned around me to look in the mirror, fluffing her hair and adjusting her ears. "I also think he wants to make sure his younger brothers don't get into it."

"Oh." That was awful. That was downright messed up. "How old are his brothers?"

"I don't know. It's not like I've ever met them. I've just gathered this information from what he and Nathan have said to each other."

For some reason I enjoyed knowing that Tyler didn't share his personal life with Jessica, which was really petty. "So no Sebastian tonight?" I asked, feeling more sympathetic toward her.

"No. He went home for the weekend apparently, which is a drag. But don't worry about me if you want to leave with Tyler. I can get a ride back or hang with Kylie."

I studied her face, but she was just making duck faces at herself in the mirror. Someone pounded on the locked door. "So you really wouldn't care if I hooked up with Tyler?" Even though I didn't intend to, or more accurately, not that he intended to, I just was amazed that she wouldn't care. I kept seeking clarification or looking for the moment when jealousy would rear.

"Of course not, for like the nine millionth time. Why would I care? I think it would be so good for you." She turned and shook my shoulders. "Just do it. You'll feel so much happier!"

I made a face.

The pounding came again.

"We're coming! Shut the fuck up!" Jessica yelled in the direction of the door. "Do you need to pee?" she asked me.

"No."

"Are you wearing Tyler's jacket? It's ruining the look of your outfit."

"Yeah, but it's warm," I said as I followed her out of the bathroom.

She glared at the girls who were waiting outside the door and they made pouty faces back. "Bitches," Jessica muttered.

I figured they just wanted to use the bathroom, given that what was in that keg was basically wheat-colored water, but I wasn't going to argue with her. Having Sebastian missing seemed to have given her a bit of an attitude, which I could understand. You pictured the night going a certain way and when it didn't, it was hard to recover your enthusiasm. I wasn't sure how I had pictured the night, but I had never been enthused about the party to begin with, so I was struggling with my emotions, my feelings of jealousy and hopelessness that even if Tyler was interested in me, it was for one thing only. And even that was most likely out of curiosity or a sense of challenge.

Tyler was standing at the back door, arms crossed over his chest, clearly waiting for us. "Are you okay?" he asked me.

"She went to the bathroom, not strolling through the ghetto naked," Jessica said, rolling her eyes. "God, you're being weird, Ty. But she's all yours now for the rest of the night. I'm going to find Robin."

She retreated back into the kitchen, pushing past two guys chest bumping. It left Tyler and me alone in a small alcove that served as a mudroom, gym shoes all over the floor and winter coats and North Face all-weather jackets hanging on a series of hooks, giving the small space a crowded intimacy.

"Is it true?" Tyler asked, with a wicked smile that did warm things to parts of my body I had been attempting to pretend didn't exist. "Are you all mine now for the rest of the night?"

"In what way?" Because I needed specifics.

"In every way."

The words were direct enough to scare me. For a week his attention to me had been escalating, and was unexplained. Friendship? Or future bed buddy? There had been teasing innuendos, but never forthright, never totally obvious. Any of them could have been explained as a joke. Now here it was, his moving from friendly study buddy to flirt with a purpose.

When he moved closer to me, head descending toward mine, hand slipping around my waist, I panicked. "What are you doing?"

"I'm planning on kissing you. If that's okay."

"I haven't decided," I answered truthfully, backing up a little and sinking into puffy coats as I retreated to gather my thoughts.

His amusement came out in a soft exhalation and he smiled. "Rory, you seriously kill me. I don't know a single other girl who would have answered like that."

Tell me about it. "I'm sorry. But it's the truth."

"I don't want you to be sorry. I *like* that about you." His hand slipped inside his jacket, to touch the small of my back, gently urging me to move forward toward him. "But you know what I do want?"

"What?" Though I could take an educated guess.

"I want you to kiss me."

"And that's it? Because I can't promise anything else." I wanted to be clear on that point. I wasn't sure how far I was willing to go, and in a world where sex partners were passed out and around like a mutual pack of cigarettes, I didn't want to find myself in a situation I wasn't cool with.

"That's it. For now, anyway. But don't worry. Only what you want, I promise."

Though his eyes seemed to indicate that I would want a whole lot by the time he was done with me.

"What about Jessica?" I asked, because it also seemed important to hear his feelings on my roommate. The soft down of the coats was surrounding my shoulders, and I could feel a hook poking me in the back of the head, but I couldn't bring myself to move. It felt safe.

Though it didn't feel as safe when Tyler evaporated the space between us by raising his other hand and burying it in my thick curls, his hips pressing against mine. He looked serious, his voice quiet, but firm. "Jessica and I were in agreement to use each other and now we're in agreement to stop using each other. You heard her. She doesn't care. We're friends. Nothing more, nothing less."

I was out of rational reasons why I couldn't do the one thing I wanted to do more than anything else. There was nothing left to discuss or negotiate, and I was well aware I was most likely the first girl who had done either. But this was it—I was in or out and the choice was mine to make.

So I nodded. "You can kiss me."

CHAPTER SIX

SOMETHING PASSED OVER HIS FACE, MAYBE A FLASH OF RELIEF, but that could have been my imagination.

"Thank you," he murmured, a satisfied smile in place, before his mouth descended onto mine.

Then I couldn't see or think. I could only feel the press of his body against me, his breath a hot rush past my ear as his lips brushed over mine. It wasn't what I was expecting. It wasn't a determined or aggressive or erotic kiss. It was delicate, worshipful, teasing.

But that only made it all that much sexier. I found myself curling my fingers into the front of his Metallica shirt, needing to steady myself. The guys I'd kissed in the past, which admittedly was not exactly an extensive list, had been amateurs. Tyler was a pro. The pressure of his hand in my hair, stroking carefully, felt intimate but not demanding. His thumb moved across my waist, back and forth, back and forth, raising goose bumps on my arms under his jacket, as every inch of my body became aware of him and his mouth taking mine.

The little kisses he started with became deeper, longer, until I was heating up from the inside out, my lips swollen, my breath frantic little bursts between moments of intense contact. He pressed me harder into the coats and I clung to him, shocked to realize that his thigh was between my legs and I was wrapped around it like he was a seesaw.

Suddenly I heard laughter and a pointed cough. I remembered where we were.

Turning my head, I broke away, panting. He was breathing hard, too, his eyes dark and glassy with desire. "Let's get out of here. We can go to Nathan's apartment."

I hesitated. A week ago I had been painfully getting loaded on that dingy sofa with Grant while Tyler was in Bill's bedroom with Jessica. I couldn't go there. I couldn't do that. Not yet. Because if I went to Nathan's, then sex, while not expected, was at least an option. Shaking my head, I said, "I'm not ready to have sex with you, Tyler." I felt like an idiot for saying it out loud, but it was the truth and I couldn't pretend otherwise. My emotions were too jumbled, my body too tense, with both anxiety and lust, to go where I knew he wanted to take it.

"That's not what I meant. I already promised you we'll only do what you want. I just want to be alone so we can talk." The corner of his mouth turned up. "And I'm not opposed to making out. We'll go old school."

How could I say no to making out?

I nodded.

If he had been feeding me a line, promising me that we'd be together or have a relationship or anything else that smacked of bullshit designed to get a free pass into my panties, I would have said no. But he'd been pretty straightforward with me, and he wasn't offering anything more than exactly what he had said—making out and talking. I could live with that. It might never be offered again, and I was going to damn well take it.

"Excellent." He leaned forward and kissed my neck. "Mmm, you smell good. Now let's get the fuck out of here."

A girl dressed like a sexy Ernie gave me a knowing smirk as Tyler pulled me by the hand down the hall. I refused to be embarrassed considering she was dressed in an outfit no self-respecting stripper would even wear, her ass spilling out of denim shorts, an orange-and-blue striped bra barely covering her breasts, and a fuzzy orange Ernie face strapped to her head.

We found Nathan standing under the keg, mouth open as the arch of beer shot up from the toilet and straight down into his mouth. "We're going to your place, man."

Nathan turned long enough to see our hands clasped together and to nod. He pulled back and swallowed, making a gargling sound. "Where's Kylie?" he asked me.

"Sorry, I haven't seen her. If I can't find her I'll text her that I'm leaving. Do you want me to tell her you're down here?"

But he shrugged. "Doesn't matter to me."

Sure it didn't.

We did actually find Kylie and Jessica together on the couch talking to a group of girls. I was opening my mouth to explain what we were doing, but Tyler beat me to it. "We're going to Nathan's. See you tomorrow when I bring Rory back."

Wow. Way to be discreet. Now not only did Kylie and Jessica know, but so did everyone within the immediate area. I shouldn't care, but I did. I wasn't sure how I even felt about any of this, I didn't want to deal with other people's reactions and opinions.

Mortified, I stood there and blushed. Fortunately, Kylie stood up and hugged me. "Have fun," she whispered, her voice excited. "Make him use a condom."

I didn't bother to correct her assumption. We could talk about all of this tomorrow when we didn't have ten girls gawking at us. So I just nodded.

Jessica hugged me, too. And then we were leaving, Tyler pausing in the backyard to scoop up the remains of his beer from Brandon, who was still guarding it intently.

"Who is Brandon?" I asked him as we went out the front door and started down the street.

"He's some guy I met in the EMT program."

Somehow I didn't think I wanted Brandon to hold my life in the balance in an emergency situation, but I stayed silent. It wasn't my business to be judgmental of a socially awkward guy, given I might be considered his female counterpart.

Tyler had let go of my hand to light a cigarette, the beer tucked under his arm as he bent forward to cup a hand against the wind. I kept my fingers neatly encased in the sleeves of his jacket to ward against the cold and debated how to say what I was feeling. Finally, I just blurted it out. "I'd prefer you didn't make it so obvious I'm going home with you."

He glanced over at me, smoke rushing past, obscuring his face. "Why?"

"Because I don't want people to think I'm a slut."

"Why do you care what people think? You know who you are, Rory."

I did. And maybe that was my fear. Not that people would think I was a slut, but that I was pathetic for thinking the hot bad boy would genuinely be interested in me. I wanted them to know that I was as smart as my IQ proved, that I knew he was just curious about me, nothing more. That I was an anomaly he wanted to explore and potentially categorize. Because that was what we all did—we searched for labels for people until we found one we thought might fit, and then we sighed in relief that we had placed them.

It shouldn't matter to me what people thought, but maybe if they thought I was a pathetic idiot it would matter because deep inside I was afraid that maybe I was. I was okay being a lot of things, being a fool was not one of them.

"It's complicated," I told him.

"So I'm supposed to be like a dirty little secret?" he asked, words light, but an edge behind them I'd never heard.

I hadn't thought of it that way at all, or from his perspective. "No, of course not. I mean, I just kissed you in the hallway. I wasn't exactly trying to be super discreet. But I don't think anyone needs to know where I'm sleeping." Or who I was or wasn't sleeping with.

But now that I heard my own words, I realized it did sound hypocritical because I had kissed him in public.

"Got it. I won't tell anyone you're slumming." There was a vulnerability there that shocked me, despite his hard tone.

I'd hurt his feelings. I could see it clearly.

Stunned, I reached for his hand, but he was still holding his cigarette. It amazed me that anyone was capable of hurting him, least of all me.

He stopped at his car and popped the trunk. He tossed the beer in the back and went around the driver's side without looking at me.

When I slid into the passenger seat, I said, "Tyler," without any idea what I was going to say next. But then when he looked over at me, eyes dark, hands gripping the steering wheel tightly, jaw clenched, I found the words. "That's not what I meant. If anything,

I'm worried that people will think I'm a joke for thinking you would be interested in me."

Brutal honesty. If he laughed or said he wasn't interested at all, then I would save myself some time and possibly my virginity. I saw no point in playing games. God knows I'd always sucked at sports, and this was the same thing. I had no clue what I was doing, but I could only be me.

He made a sound of exasperation, tossing his cigarette out the cracked open window then cupping my cheek with his callused palm. "This is no joke."

Then he kissed me, and it was even more intense than at the party. It was hot and demanding, his tongue pressing between my lips to tangle with mine. His free hand slipped inside the strapless dress, brushing over my nipple. I gasped against his mouth, shifting on the seat so I could get closer to him. Passion exploded between us, and he moved too, dragging my leg over his thigh, the motion shoving the skirt of the dress dangerously high on my thighs.

My head fell back as he moved his lips down my neck, lightly sucking the delicate skin into his mouth, and I tried to keep my eyes open. I wanted to see the dark strands of his hair, the sharp angle of his cheekbone, as he moved over me. I shivered when he pulled his jacket farther apart on me, so that he could move down, lower still, to slide his tongue over the swell of my breast, now peeking up from the dress.

I'd never been so aware of my body, so aware of every inch of another person, and I listened to the sound of Tyler's breathing, the hitch and rise of his desire, the sharp intakes of air, the blast of heat from his lips as he groaned, before closing his mouth over the tightness of my nipple. He was pressing against me in various places, and the scent of him, so different from mine, so earthy and male and strong, had me digging my nails into his biceps as I clung to him.

The rustling of our clothes and my own soft moans surrounded me and it was all so warm and damp and wonderful that when his fingers crept up under my dress, I didn't stop him. The sash from my costume had lodged itself around my throat, but I didn't bother to move it as I sighed in delight, his lips and stroking fingers everywhere. His rhythm on my nipple matched that of his thumb under my panties, and before I could even consider, think, stop it, I shuddered against him, biting my lip to prevent from crying out.

Shocked, breathless, I felt my cheeks heat up as I stared at him, sucking in air. He had stopped moving, and lifted his head up to give me a cocky smile of satisfaction. "That didn't take long."

I shook my head, feeling mildly embarrassed. "I didn't mean to . . ."

He laughed and sat up so he could brush a kiss across my lips. "You're a nut. Why else would you be doing any of this if you didn't mean to?"

"I don't know." I just wanted to be a little more sophisticated.

Tyler readjusted my dress so my chest was covered again and he withdrew from under my skirt. "You have goose bumps. Let me turn the car on."

I didn't really think the shivers were from cold, but I didn't argue with him. Tugging my dress down closer to my knees where it belonged, I watched him light up another cigarette. There didn't seem to be a pattern to his smoking. I'd seen him go hours without having one, but then times like tonight, he seemed to light another almost as soon as he put one out. The addiction seemed behavioral, not physical.

Maybe I stressed him out.

He did start the car, but he made no move to pull out of the parallel parking spot and go to Nathan's. "What kind of doctor do you want to be?" he asked out of nowhere.

I blinked at the unexpected topic change. "I want to be a coroner."

"What?" he asked, glancing over at me in surprise. "Like autopsies and shit?"

I nodded.

"Damn. And you look so sweet all the time."

"It's very logical," I told him, like that was supposed to explain everything. But I didn't really feel like having a conversation about my career choice when I was still pulsing with desire and was wondering what he intended to do and what I intended to let him do.

"I suppose it is. But gruesome." He looked behind him and put the car in drive and pulled out onto the street. "Come on, let's take you back to your dorm."

"What?" I reached back for the seat belt to click it in before I remembered there wasn't one. For some reason that upset me, and I wasn't sure why. Maybe it was a need for protection, literal and otherwise. "I thought we were going to Nathan's." *I thought you wanted to have sex*. And I thought maybe I just would have said yes, given how he'd made me feel in under three minutes over a gearshift.

"If we're going to stick to just making out, I don't think it's a good idea."

We had actually surpassed making out already, in my opinion. I didn't know what to say. Did he just not want to have sex with me? Because what other explanation could there be? Maybe my

future career had turned him off. I knew that not everyone understood why I would want to slice open corpses.

"Did I do something wrong?" I said, then hated myself for
saying it. God, that was such a lame, pathetic girl thing to ask. But
it was out, and I couldn't take it back.

"No, of course not." He sounded surprised. "I just promised you
I would only go as far as you wanted to go, and honestly, Rory, I have
a boner the size of the Empire State Building right now. I think maybe
we just need to take it easy. I don't want you to regret anything."

"Oh." I wasn't sure what else to say. I wanted to trust that his
actions were out of respect for me. But then why did I feel so
rejected?

Was it that he didn't want me to regret it, or that he didn't want
to regret it?

We drove in silence and I studied him without shame, wanting
to remember this moment, this car ride, feeling like it might be the
last time I saw him. My finger came out and traced the tattoo on
his bicep, following the lines of the tribal letters spelling out *TRUE
Family*. He glanced at me in surprise but he didn't say anything.

"What does this mean?" I asked. "Something besides the
obvious?"

"It's mine and my brothers' initials. Tyler, Riley, U, and Easton.
The four of us make a family and my parents can go fuck themselves. We don't need them."

"That's beautiful," I said, and I meant it, though it was sad that
his parents didn't factor into the equation. If I were to get a tattoo
to represent my family, I wasn't sure what it would be. A little book
with two names on it? Or an angel on my shoulder watching me,
for my mother?

"That's one way to put it."

I realized he had stopped at the circle by the front door to my dorm, which meant he was not planning to park the car. Not planning to walk me to my room or even to the door. Not that I expected him to. But that didn't mean I didn't want him to.

Nor did he bother to put out his cigarette. It was a noxious smoking cloud between us as he leaned over and gave me a quick kiss. "Get some sleep. I'll talk to you tomorrow."

It felt like a dismissal. For a second, I just stared at him, longing, wanting, and my expression must have been more obvious than I realized, because he swore.

"Jesus, don't look at me like that." His finger came out and wrapped one of my curls around itself. "You're so fucking beautiful, you're killing me."

He did look agonized, though I didn't understand why, and when he tugged on the curl, it was hard, not teasing, shocking me into action. I started to peel off his jacket. But he shook his head. "It's cold out, don't worry about it. Good night."

He might as well have taken his foot to my back and shoved me, he sounded so ready to be rid of me. I suddenly felt sick and I threw open the door, repeating my actions of the previous Saturday night, but with a whole different set of confused emotions. This time when I bent over and removed my room key from my pageant sock, I glanced back to see he was rubbing his face with both hands, like he wanted to erase away whatever he was thinking.

Ironically, I didn't want to erase anything. I wanted to hold on to it, to savor it, to remember it late at night alone in my dark room.

Ripping his jacket off, I ran up all four flights of stairs to my room, unwilling to wait for the elevator.

*   *   *

THE DOOR, THROWN OPEN TOO HARD, SLAMMED INTO THE WALL and woke me up. I was about to pry my eyes open and yell at Kylie and Jessica to quiet down when I realized they were talking about me.

"I can't believe she actually did it, that she went home with Tyler," Kylie said, her words slurred, a loud thump indicating she had dropped her purse on her desk. The desk lamp came on, casting a weak glow through the room, making it likely they would notice that I was, in fact, in the room.

Staying still under the covers, I kept my eyes closed and tried not to move, breathing as slowly as possible. I was curious to hear what their true opinion about it was. Especially Jessica's.

I had fallen asleep almost immediately after Tyler had dropped me off, which had surprised me, and I had no idea what time it was. I had woken up so easily I suspected I'd been asleep for a while and we were cruising toward morning. They obviously thought I would still be at Nathan's, cozied up with Tyler. Hardly. I had fallen asleep all alone, as usual.

"I know. I didn't think she would go through with it either. She was kind of freaking out on me in the bathroom."

That was an exaggeration. I had just been making sure Jess wouldn't care. Her voice now sounded tired and almost as slurred as Kylie's, making me think that she'd gone on to drink some beer after the Vicodin pill.

"Damn it, my feet are swollen."

I could hear Jessica sink down onto her bed, which was positioned to form an *L* with mine. I knew she was going to notice me any second. Probably the only reason she hadn't was because my bed was under Kylie's loft, and I was in the shadows. "I wish more people understood how fucking smart and sweet Rory is."

Aww. That was nice to hear. I was about to roll over and announce my presence when Kylie said, "No, shit. I really think this thing we've set up with Tyler is going to help her confidence."

I stiffened and stifled a startled exhalation of air. What did that mean? I did not like the sound of *set up*.

"She'll be able to put herself out there more once she's gotten over this whole 'I'm a shy girl virgin' role. Because I don't think that's her. Well, the virgin part was, I guess, until tonight. But the shy thing, that's what I mean." Kylie was fumbling around on her desk, knocking stuff over and shoving her chair against the wall. I could easily picture her, trying to unzip her banana, drunk, losing her balance and colliding into everything within a three-foot range.

"Totally. I'm glad Tyler finally got his head out of his ass. I was starting to wonder what the hell was taking him so long. I was starting to wonder what he was doing. He never put that much effort into getting me into bed."

Kylie snorted. "Like it was hard with you."

Jessica laughed. "Good point. But seriously, he was being weird about the whole thing. You'd think he'd be all 'time is money' and try to get the deal done as fast as possible."

Now my heart was racing and my fingers twitched beneath the covers. It took every ounce of willpower I had to keep my eyes closed. Time is money? There was a deal between my roommates and Tyler? To do what?

I had a sneaking, awful, craptacular feeling I knew exactly what that deal was.

"For a hundred bucks, you'd think he'd be motivated."

Oh. My. God. I sucked in my breath. I couldn't help it. My

roommates had paid Tyler to have sex with me. For whatever creepy, misguided reason. And he had been willing to take it.

I went still again, praying they wouldn't notice me, spots dancing behind my eyes from clamping them shut so hard. I would die, I would literally die from pure mortification if they knew I had heard them. I couldn't deal with it.

Tyler didn't like me. He wasn't even attracted to me. He had feigned interest in my life, had studied with me, had taken care of me after I puked from drinking, because he had an end goal in mind. It was all intended to bring down the defenses of a naïve virgin so that she would drop her clothes and let him use her. For money.

Use me. For a lousy hundred bucks.

For a second, I thought I was going to throw up and I actually gagged, horror and bile and disbelief clogging my throat like backed-up sewage, and I couldn't stifle a little cough.

"Rory?" Kylie asked in amazement.

I let my eyes flutter, knowing there was no way out of it. "Hey," I said, putting as much sleepiness into my voice as possible. "You just get back?"

"Yeah." She leaned over me, sticking her face right into mine. She searched my face, looking excited. "How was it?"

"Good," I said, because it had been. Until it hadn't. Tyler had gotten me off and so in that regard, he had earned his money. I didn't want to go into anything else with them. Ever.

She hugged me, an awkward embrace, given she was shitfaced and I was lying down, her breasts dangling in front of me. "Yay! I love you. You know you and Jessica are my best friends ever."

"Me, too," I said, because I couldn't form a coherent sentence. I rolled back over toward the wall and closed my eyes, wishing I could shut her words out as effectively as the sight of her.

"I can't believe he brought her back home," Kylie whispered to Jessica in what was definitely not a whisper by sober standards. "He could have at least let her sleep there."

"Douche bag," was Jessica's opinion.

All I could think was that he was definitely more than that, none of it good.

When I was ten years old, I was invited to Ashley Goldman's birthday party, and while I was excited, I was shocked, too. We weren't friends and she was the most popular girl in fifth grade. It made me suspicious to get the invitation, like it was either a mistake or I was going to be a joke of some kind, but my dad kept insisting that Ashley must like me and want to be friends, that it was a chance for new beginnings and some other such bullshit. The day of the party, I was so nervous I had diarrhea all morning and begged my dad not to make me go. But he did, and when I, gift out, stupidly optimistic, timidly approached Ashley, she ripped it out of my hands and tossed it on the table with, "I only invited you because I had to because your dad is my mom's boss."

I spent the whole party in a corner of the backyard playing with the Goldmans' cocker spaniel and hating my father for his good intentions.

That was how I felt now.

An hour later, when I was still wide awake and my roommates were passed out, deep in sleep, I got up and went into the bathroom we shared with our suitemates. Stripping off my pajamas, I got into the hot shower in my panties and let the tears come. As the water streamed over me, I scrubbed my face, too ashamed to be fully naked, wanting a protective layer between me and the memory of Tyler's touch.

I sobbed, for the little girl I had been, who had never understood why I didn't just fit in, and for the realization that I never would. That my life was meant to be walked alone, with a thin plastic barrier pulled taut between me and everyone else, my thoughts never capable of running parallel with the majority of human beings. In the world of Stellas and Stanleys and Blanches, I was destined to be Harold, the guy who's never in on the joke and wants everyone to like him, and never has a freaking clue what is really going on. When Harold finds out that Blanche is no virgin, and in fact she's the opposite of pure, he's stunned, and we all think he's stupid.

That was me. Totally stupid. Really, was it so shocking to think that a guy like Tyler didn't have the purest of intentions? No. It wasn't.

But that didn't make it hurt any less.

I sat on the floor of the shower, knees to my chest, hair in wet, damp hanks on my forehead and my cheeks, and I stared at the water swirling down the drain, wishing it would take me and my humiliation with it.

CHAPTER SEVEN

THE PLAN WAS TO LET KYLIE AND JESSICA THINK THAT I HAD actually had sex with Tyler. I figured if they thought the deed was done, they would let it go with him, and he in turn would let it go with me. The goal was to never hear from him again, and I figured he wouldn't tell my roommates the truth. He would just take the money and disappear, which couldn't happen soon enough for my taste.

It didn't take long to put the plan into effect. I was studying at my desk the next morning, unable to stomach going back to bed after my shower, my eyes gritty, head throbbing from lack of sleep when Kylie sat up in bed, yawning.

"Oh my God, last night was crazy," were her first words. Her second, which came after she threw a stuffed penguin at Jessica to wake her up, were: "Tell me how it was with Tyler."

I was expecting their curiosity, and frankly, I had some curiosity of my own. I didn't think I was ever going to really get an answer that would satisfy me, certainly not without telling them I knew the truth, but I still wanted to scrape and poke at the layers of their comments to see what was underneath.

"It was . . . quick," I said, because that wasn't being deceptive. What had happened between us was over in minutes.

Kylie made a face. "Did you come?"

I nodded, flicking my pen back and forth across my palm. I didn't want to remember that moment, holding on to him, his mouth on my breast, my body tight and tense and aroused. Yet at the same time, I wanted to relive it over and over, which meant I had zero pride and no self-esteem whatsoever. I shouldn't want to repeat it.

"Well, that's something at least." Jessica peeled the covers back, kicking them to the bottom of her bed. "God, I'm sweating balls. Why did he bring you back here? Was it like right after?"

"Yes. And I don't know. He said he thought it was best." I studied both of them, trying to read their expressions. They didn't look anything but annoyed with Tyler and mildly hungover. "I guess he just got what he wanted, right? No reason for me to hang around."

They exchanged an uneasy glance. "I'm sure that's not it," Jessica protested. "Maybe he had to work today or something. The important thing is that you had a good time."

"I did." But there was no warmth in my voice, and we all heard it.

Kylie started down from her loft. "You don't regret it, do you?"

I thought about it, fiddling with the strap on my cami. I hadn't bothered to get dressed yet. I felt and looked like ass. But did I regret what I had done with Tyler?

"No," I said truthfully. "I don't regret it." I regretted that he had felt like he needed to be paid to mess around with me. I regretted that my roommates felt like someone needed to be paid to want to stick his dick in me. That didn't boost my confidence about my desirability and it reminded me of Grant's parting words—that no one wanted me. Yet I didn't actually regret kissing Tyler, which made me question my sanity.

"Oh, thank God," she said, holding her perfect yellow manicure up to her T-shirt. "I would feel so shitty if you regretted it."

"Why?" I asked, sharper than I intended. I didn't think that she was about to confess, and she didn't.

"Because we like totally encouraged you."

"Why?" I repeated.

Kylie looked nervously to Jessica, who definitely tended to be more articulate. They were clearly picking up on the vibe that I was upset, and I tried to soften my mouth, my forehead. I was angry, but I wasn't going to hold anything against them. Yes, I was furious that they had set me up to potentially be humiliated or used or mistreated, but strange as it was, I knew their hearts were in the right place.

But I needed time to cool down, to process what had happened.

Jessica pulled her hair off her lip where it had been stuck, most likely in lip-gloss remnants, and reached for a water bottle she had on the floor. "Rory, the thing is, you're this amazing person, and no one ever really gets to see it because you hold yourself back from everyone. We thought that maybe if you got physically close with someone, that maybe you'd be able to get emotionally close with some-one, too."

Stunned, I stared at her. "You think I hold back?"

She nodded. "I know you do. Maybe it's because of your mom . . . but anyway, we shouldn't have pushed you. I hope we didn't encourage you to do something you didn't really want to because I will hate myself if we did."

Did I hold back? Was observer equal to emotionally withdrawn? It wasn't that I didn't want to be involved . . . I didn't think. Thoughts swirling in my head, I assured Jessica with a tightness in my throat, "No. No, you didn't. Don't worry. I'm not upset with you."

They were my only two friends, and I wasn't about to lose them, not even under these circumstances.

ON TUESDAY IN THE FOOD COURT AT THE UNIVERSITY CENTER, I saw Kylie, over by the pasta and pizza restaurant, locked in a heated conversation with Tyler. While my cheeks burned, I hoped she was telling him what I had told her, that I'd had sex with him, so he would understand I had lied for a reason, and that he was off the hook, free and clear. Because my plan to have him stop talking to me had been an epic fail so far.

Sunday he had texted me.

Had fun with u last nite.

Surprised, I tapped the lame response

Thanks, me too.

Want to come to Nathans? We're watching football.

I have too much studying to do. Go Bengals.

Bengals suck. Watching the Giants.

To which I didn't reply. I didn't give a shit about either football team, and I didn't have any studying to do, unless you counted reading ahead to the next book in lit, and there was no way I wanted to do that. I just wanted him to leave me alone.

Monday he texted again.

Whatya doin 2nite?

Working.

Only until 5, but he didn't need to know that.

Want to hang out after?

I have a chem lab report to write so I shouldn't.

Again, I wasn't lying.

I pushed my quesadilla around on my plate with a tortilla chip and stabbed at my guacamole. Jessica and Robin and Nathan were talking away about a movie I hadn't seen, and I was puzzling out all the things about Tyler that didn't make sense. Why was he still texting me? If his goal was strictly to collect the money, then why had he put so much effort into being friends with me? Why would he still bother at this point?

But most of all, why wouldn't he have taken me to Nathan's and nailed me when I clearly had been willing? He had insisted we were just going to make out. That I could stop him at any point.

It wasn't logical. But I kept learning over and over that people did not behave in any logical way. They were random and unpredictable, and didn't always choose the quickest route to accomplish a goal.

Kylie and Tyler were making their way over to the table, and I hit the button to turn on my e-reader, forcing myself to stare at the words on the screen. It was a book I'd never heard of by an author I'd never heard of, and the language was so choppy, I basically gave up by the third line. But I still kept staring because I did not want to talk to Tyler.

A hand squeezed my shoulder and I looked up.

"Hey," he said, smiling at me.

"Hey."

"Whatcha reading?" He leaned over and swiped one of my tortilla chips.

As he crunched, I stared up at him, wanting to probe his mind, wanting to know what was going on there in his gray matter. But I figured every girl on the planet had found herself wishing she had a free pass inside a man's mind at one point or another. Maybe it was self-preservation that we didn't have such powers. It might be holy-crap creepy in there.

"I have no idea," I told him honestly.

He laughed. "We studying this Thursday?"

My hesitation was obvious. "I don't know if that's a good idea."

Tyler pulled out a chair and sat down on it backward, so he was leaning over the back watching me. "What's going on? Why are you acting weird?"

"I always act weird."

"No, you don't. You are usually honest and straightforward. Now you're just avoiding me." He leaned closer, his voice dropping. "Why did you tell Kylie we had sex?"

"I never told her that," I protested, because I hadn't.

"Then you let her assume. Why? You told me it was no one's business what happened between us. In this case, what didn't happen."

I glanced around, nervous. No one was looking at us, but it wouldn't be that hard to hear what Tyler was saying. I played with my stacked bracelets, pulling them up my arm and letting them fall. "I don't want to talk about this here." I didn't actually want to talk about it ever. I couldn't tell him the truth, and anything else I might say to try to justify my behavior was going to sound like a lie, which it was.

He made a sound of exasperation and then shoved the chair back. "Then let's go somewhere private and talk about it."

"I have class," I protested. But I couldn't help but wonder why it mattered to him, why he was so clearly frustrated. Why he still wanted to see me.

Without another word, he stood up and slammed the chair back into the table, making me jump. Everyone at the table stopped talking and turned as he stalked off, hand raking through his hair. The minute he shoved through the front door he was digging in his pocket. For a cigarette, I was sure.

"What is his problem?" Nathan asked me.

I shrugged. The truth was I really didn't know what was going on. I wished I did. It just seemed like if he had been doing a favor for my friends, or had needed the money, or was looking for the ego stroke of bagging the virgin, he wouldn't react like this.

"Well, what did he say?" Kylie insisted, her smoothie hovering in front of her lips.

"He wanted to leave, and I said I had class and he shoved his chair. That's it."

"He's been acting moody all week," Nathan commented. "I wonder what's up with him."

"Yeah," Kylie said, looking at me. "I wonder what's up with him."

Jessica's and Robin's eyes were on me, too. Nathan was frowning at me. So many eyes staring at me, it was unnerving. I didn't like being in the spotlight.

"How would I know?" I asked defensively. Honestly, I was the one who knew the least about what was going on. They were all in on the Get Rory Fucked Fund. Well, I didn't know that Nathan knew, but it seemed likely enough, given how much Kylie was into him. "I have to go to class." I stood up, grabbing the plate with my barely eaten quesadilla.

"Rory," Kylie started, but Jessica shook her head at her, an indicator to let me go.

So I left, with a wave and a half smile.

Tyler texted me on Wednesday and I didn't answer.

He texted on Thursday and I didn't answer.

By the time he texted on Friday I felt like my skin was too tight and my legs wouldn't stop bouncing up and down every time I sat. My fingertips felt cold all the time, and there were dark circles under my eyes from not sleeping. Everything I had heard Kylie and Jessica say and everything Tyler had said to me kept spinning around and around and around in my head like a violent whirlpool.

I spent extra hours in the lab, face covered in protective goggles, drowning in a lab coat. On Friday, I went to the animal shelter even though I wasn't scheduled to work. They could always use an extra hand, and I didn't want to be in my room or in the cafeteria with everyone.

What I didn't expect was Tyler to show up at the shelter. I was on the floor playing with a few beagle puppies when I heard Joanne. "Rory? Your friend is here."

I glanced up and her eyebrows were raised in question, and she looked concerned. Behind her was Tyler, his hands crammed in his front pockets. I lost my balance and fell back onto my butt. Puppies leaped all over the front of me, and I tried to control them, hands blocking multiple tongues determined to lick my face.

"Tyler, what are you doing here?" I hadn't thought he would track me down. I thought he would get tired of me not answering his texts and stop.

Clearly, I was wrong.

"It's dark outside and I didn't want you walking back by yourself. I'm here to give you a ride."

I wanted to trust that he was genuine. I did. My frozen insides thawed just slightly.

Joanne's expression changed. "You know what, I tell her that all the time. I can't stand that she walks around in the dark by herself. All it takes is once for something awful to happen. We appreciate you picking our Rory up . . . She's a sweet girl, isn't she?"

Tyler smiled. "Yes, she is."

I rolled my eyes. "Thanks. And thanks for the ride. I'll get my bag."

As I led the three stumbling puppies back to their kennel, Joanne gave me a grin. "He's cute," she mouthed so that Tyler couldn't see. I shook my head, wanting to laugh. Could she be any more obvious?

I was nervous to be alone with Tyler, but part of me was glad to just get it over with. Every single day my anxiety had been growing, not lessening. We walked silently to his car, me buried in my military jacket, footsteps squeaky as my rain boots bent with each step. It wasn't raining, but I liked my rubber boots. There was something defiant about them. Like I was encased in something solid.

"I'm sorry I still have your jacket," I said, feeling guilty as I realized he was just wearing a T-shirt, a metal cross dangling down over his chest. It was an elaborate piece with lots of scrolling and a detailed crucified Jesus on it. "I should have brought it to you." Not that I knew where he lived, but I guess I meant I could have taken it to Nathan's.

But he shrugged. "It's no big deal. I don't really get cold that easily."

I had noticed that. Somehow it made him sexier than he already was.

The minute we were in the car, as I moved a pile of dirty papers off of the passenger seat, he spoke. "So, do you really want me to just go away? Is that the message you're giving me? Because I can do that. But the truth is, I'd rather not do that. I like hanging out with you."

I liked hanging out with him, too. I could admit that. Maybe it made me pathetic, but the truth was, I had fun with him. He was funny and smart and compassionate. Hot. I couldn't discount that. What I saw when I was with him, I couldn't reconcile with a guy who would coldheartedly agree to seduce a girl for money or laughs or whatever sick reason you'd expect a guy to say yes to something like that. He wasn't going to take naked pictures of me and blackmail me online with them. He just wasn't. I knew it. I wasn't sure how I knew it, but I did.

Then again, sometimes we see what we want to see. We make people better in our heads than they actually are.

I wasn't sure what was the right thing to do, but I couldn't lie. "I like hanging out with you, too."

"Then let's do that. We can just be friends, or more, or whatever you want. Your call. Just don't disappear, okay?"

I nodded.

His phone rang and he glanced at it. "Shit, I need to answer this. Sorry."

"No problem." I bit my lip and stared out the window as he started the car.

"Yeah, what's up?" he said into his phone.

Then he sighed at whatever the response was. "Okay, don't worry, I'll be there in ten minutes. Just lock yourself in your room with U, okay? Just stay out of her way and you'll be fine. I'm on my way home right now."

As I glanced over at him, concerned at the tone of the phone call, he pulled a U-turn at the intersection and started back down the way we'd come. "I need to stop at home for a minute. Do you mind? That was my brother. My mom is freaking out and he's scared."

That didn't sound good, especially given what Jessica had told me about his mother's drug use. "No, no, of course I don't mind. How old is your brother?"

"He's only ten." The worry radiated off him, as palpable as the smoke that wafted off his cigarettes.

"Oh, God. What is she doing?"

"Who knows?" Tyler fumbled in his pocket for his pack of cigarettes. When he drew them out, he propped them against the steering wheel and tried to retrieve one. His hand was shaking.

I took the pack from him. "I'll get it for you. You just drive."

"Thanks."

Pulling one out, I also extracted the lighter that was jammed in the pack. I had never lit a cigarette before, but how hard could it be? Sticking it in my mouth, I flicked the lighter and held it up to the tip. It ignited and smoke clouded my vision. I gave a tentative suck to ensure the flame's survival, but I kept the air in my mouth before blowing it back out so I didn't inhale any of it.

When I handed it to Tyler, he was grinning at me. "Sexy."

"It's cancer in a stick," I told him flatly, tucking the lighter back in the pack and dropping it next to the gearshift. The taste in my mouth was disgusting. It was like I'd licked the remains of a campfire.

"Doesn't make you sucking on it any less hot."

"Uh-huh." But I didn't lecture him. I sensed he needed the distraction, that he was worried about his brother. I couldn't imagine what his mother was doing—that just wasn't a part of my experience—but I hoped it wasn't anything serious.

The neighborhood we were driving to was lower income, blue collar, the houses old, the paint peeling. They were lined up close to each other, with sagging porch roofs and scrubby shrubbery.

"Here it is. Don't be too jealous." Tyler pulled into the gravel drive of a white house with flaking black shutters. One was missing altogether and it gave the house the appearance of a woman who had put makeup on one eye and had forgotten to do the other. Lying facedown in the bushes was a statue of the Virgin Mary, her robe muddied. The 5 in the house number was hanging upside down from a rusty nail.

"Do you want me to wait here?" Not because I wanted to sit in the car, but because I wanted to be respectful.

"Nah. It's cold out here. And maybe if you're there she'll behave herself." He studied my face. "Unless you don't want to. You don't have to."

There it was again—that vulnerability I had seen on his face after the Halloween party. I knew it was legitimate. I wasn't wrong about that. "No, I'll go with you."

When we got out of the car, he threw his cigarette down in the driveway and I saw it wasn't the only butt there. Hundreds littered the crumbling blacktop, and as we ascended the rotting front porch, I saw an old plastic chair and, on the floor next to it, a large glass ashtray overflowing with butts that had been rained on. It smelled like stale smoke and beer and mud. Mail spilled out of the box attached to the house, and Tyler ignored it as he opened the front door.

We had barely stepped into the narrow vestibule, my feet sinking into filthy beige carpet, eyes adjusting to the dark, when something flew past Tyler's head and hit the wall with a smack.

Beer exploded all over him, and he pulled me behind him.

"Turn the light on so your aim is better," he said mildly. "All you did was waste a full beer."

I knew then that whatever I had been expecting, it was probably going to be much, much worse.

CHAPTER EIGHT

THE LIGHT DID COME ON, AND I SAW THAT A WOMAN WAS LYING on the couch in nothing but an oversize T-shirt, her stick-thin legs bent at an awkward angle. Her brown hair was cut in layers, and she had bangs that seemed straight out of an eighties movie. Even in the dim lamp light, I could tell that her skin was broken out and there were dark circles under her eyes. She was glaring at Tyler and as she struggled to sit up, she pointed a finger in his direction.

"I know you stole my shit," she said. "You need to get the fuck out of this house and never come back."

"No, I'm not going anywhere until you give Riley guardianship of Jayden and Easton." The way he spoke as he moved into the living room, bending over to pick up empty beer cans on the way, I figured this was a dialogue they had frequently.

"Fuck you. They're my kids. What kind of a son tries to take his mother's kids away from her?"

"One who knows his mother is a drug addict." With his free hand, he took mine and led me past the couch into the kitchen, making sure that I was on the far side of his mother. There was corded tension in his neck muscles, and he was gripping me tightly. While his words were mild and calm, he seemed aware of everything that was going on around us, and while I was a little scared, mostly I felt sad that this was how he had to live. That every day must be a constant assault of words, and home was never a safe place. His mother didn't even seem to notice I was with Tyler, and I had to admit, I was grateful. I'd never heard a mother swear at her child like that and it was unnerving.

He dumped the cans in an overflowing trash can in the kitchen and flicked the light on. He turned the hall light on, too, and knocked on the first door. "It's me, unlock the door."

Tyler pulled me into the shadows of the hallway, away from the living room. He tried the knob and popped his head in. "What was she doing? Yeah?"

I couldn't hear the responses, nor could I see into the room. What I did see was Tyler's mom stumbling toward him, her hand raised.

Without thinking, I let out a cry.

Tyler turned just in time to get clocked. His mother just hauled off and punched him in the face.

"Oh my God!" I blurted out, unable to stop myself. I had never been that close to anyone getting hit before, and I couldn't comprehend that it was his mother who had done it. His mother. I stood behind him, helpless, patting my pocket for my phone, wondering if I should call the cops.

But Tyler just took the hit and gave a sigh of exasperation. He reached out and took hold of her wrist as she raised her arm to land another blow. "Stop," he told her, and his tone was gentle, not angry. It was like he was speaking to a spooked animal. "Let's go sit down."

She sagged, the fight in her seeming to disappear. She let him lead her back to the couch. "Who are you?" she asked me, her eyes glassy, as she sank into the floral cushions. Her hand felt around on the floor for her beer. She spilled it on the retrieval and sucked the liquid off her arm before taking a long drink.

"I'm Rory."

"You Tyler's girlfriend?"

I could feel him tense next to me, but I was determined not to make this harder for him than it already was. He had gestured for his brothers to come out of their bedroom, and two boys, one in his late teens, who clearly had Down syndrome, and another, small and wiry with dark features and curly hair, moved into the kitchen, silently.

I shook my head. "We're friends." It was the least complicated description of what we were, since I wasn't really sure what that was anyway.

"Well, don't get pregnant," she told me. "It will fuck up your life. Trust me on this one."

What was I supposed to say to that? Appalled, I just stared at her, the smell of cat dander and dirty clothes and beer clogging my nostrils. The stench of rotting food radiated from the kitchen, and I saw his brothers were both in the refrigerator foraging for food, like they'd been trapped in their bedroom for a significant amount of time.

Tyler sighed. "Mom, for once, can you just shut the hell up? God."

She sat up straighter. "You're the worst one of them all! I got fat when I was pregnant with you, and then your father cheated on me with that whore at the gas station, and then every day since then, you've been such a pain in my ass." She gestured to me, sloshing beer out of the can. "I got one kid trying to take my other kids from me, I got this one stealing my drugs, and then I have the retard and the mistake."

"Don't call them that," Tyler said, and his voice was hard, edgy.

"Why not? It's true. Retard, retard, retard," she yelled in the direction of the kitchen.

His brother turned, his lips pursed. "Yeah, Mom?"

"Don't answer to that!" Tyler said, clearly angry. "That is not your name. Your name is Jayden, and you are not a retard."

"Yes, I am," Jayden said, sounding confused. He was wearing an Angry Birds T-shirt and he nervously pushed up his wire-frame glasses. In his hand was a moldy hunk of cheese.

"No, you're not. A retard is someone who is stupid and you are not stupid, do you understand me?" Tyler reached out and took the cheese from him. "Don't eat that, buddy, okay? I'll go to the grocery store in a little bit. Easton has some bread and I know there's still peanut butter. Make yourself a sandwich, alright?"

"Okay, Tyler." He went over to Easton, who was cramming a handful of dried cereal into his mouth.

Easton had a deer-in-the-headlights look, like he was waiting to get hit, which maybe he was. He also wasn't Caucasian. He was biracial, and I thought of how it must feel to hear his mother's words, calling him a mistake. I couldn't even imagine.

Clearly she didn't like not being the center of attention. She stood up and walked into the kitchen, running her hand through her ratty hair, her huge shirt dingy and thin enough to show the outline of her panties underneath. "Yep, I have a fabulous life.

Husband in jail. Four shitty, asshole sons. How could I get so lucky?" she asked, voice dripping with sarcasm.

It was out of my mouth before I could stop it. But the logical option was so obvious to me that I said it before I could prevent it. Besides, she had infuriated me. Who stood there and called her kids assholes? "I don't think luck is part of the equation. It's a failure to make good choices."

Tyler let out a laugh. "True that, babe." He finished clearing off the tabletop, which had been littered with dirty dishes.

Her eyes narrowed at me, and I realized I should have kept my mouth shut. "You go to college with Tyler? He thinks he's smart now that he takes classes and obviously you do, too, with your cute little hair and your rich-girl clothes. But if you were smart, you wouldn't be with a loser like him."

Tyler's laughter cut off.

Instantly I knew she had chosen the perfect way to slice him deep.

And I understood why he had made the comments he had, about being my dirty little secret.

This was his life, and he was ashamed of it.

"Don't call him a loser," Jayden said, coming to his brother's defense in a way that made my heart swell. "He's not a loser. He's awesome."

I could see Tyler's tattoo on his arm, and I fully appreciated what that meant. They had one another, a band of four brothers, living in filth and tension. I knew almost immediately he would never call the cops, either, because then Jayden and Easton would be taken away.

For whatever reason, Jayden's remark seemed to set their mother off. She swept her arm across the counter, sending glasses and cans and an ashtray flying across the room, dropping to the floor with a series of crashes and bangs. "I hate you all! I hate my life!"

Easton jumped out of the way of an errant can with a dexterity that showed this wasn't the first time he had leapt for cover.

When Tyler reached for his mother, clearly intending to pull her arms down, she slapped and kicked at him, landing several hard blows. Then suddenly she crumpled against him, and he held her while her anger dissolved into hysterical sobbing.

"It's okay," he told her, stroking the back of her hair. "You're fine."

Tears welled in my eyes at the sight of him comforting her, his muscular arms holding up the woman who couldn't hold herself up.

"What would I do without you?" she asked, voice anguished. "You know I don't hate you. I love you boys, all of you."

"I know. I know." He petted her, and led her to the kitchen chair.

She crumpled onto the table, head on her arms, tears streaking down her gaunt face. "Where are my pills?"

"They're all gone. You took them all." Tyler pulled out his cigarettes and lit one. He held it up to her mouth. "Take a hit."

She did, sucking deeply, head still prone on the table. Smoke blew from her thin mouth, her eyes sunken and hopeless. She reached out and hit the button on the radio, and heavy metal music blasted into the room.

There was a knock and a woman entered the kitchen from the back door. "Hey."

"Aunt Jackie's here," Easton announced in the way that little kids have of stating the obvious.

"Get some fucking pants on, we're going," Aunt Jackie told Tyler's mother. She was bundled up in a giant red sweatshirt, and she was wearing jeans that were at least three sizes too small. She had camel toe, and her cigarettes and cell phone were clearly outlined in her front pockets. She was a good hundred pounds heavier than Tyler's mom, who had stood up and stumbled down the hall.

"Really, Jackie?" Tyler asked in disgust. "You're not helping."

"Don't back talk me, brat," she told him. She was in her forties, and she had seen some hard living, her skin leathery, hair thinning on top. "Look out for your brothers."

"I always do," he told her, taking the butter knife from Easton, who was managing to get more peanut butter on the counter than on his slice of bread. Tyler efficiently spread the peanut butter on the bread, then handed it to his brother, who took an enormous bite.

"Dawn! Let's go!" Jackie shouted, ignoring Tyler.

His mother came back into the room wearing jeans and a T-shirt, her nipples clearly poking through. She was carrying a ratty flannel shirt. "Okay, I'm ready."

"Put some real shoes on," Tyler told her.

I glanced down and saw that she was wearing threadbare slippers that might have been pink at one time but were now a faded salmon.

"I'll be fine." She kissed him on the cheek, but her eyes were already darting to the door and she had a twitch in her eye and her mouth. Her hand was shaking noticeably.

Then they were gone, door slamming shut behind them, and I noticed that Easton's shoulders visibly relaxed.

"Well, the good news is she won't be back until Sunday most likely," Tyler said, putting a lightheartedness into his tone that I knew he didn't feel.

"Huzzah!" Jayden said, raising his bread in the air. "Can I turn this music off?"

"Please do." Tyler pulled the keys out of his pocket. "I'm going to the grocery store. Is there anything you want?"

"Pop Tarts," Jayden said.

"Milk," was Easton's response.

"Jesus," Tyler muttered under his breath, and I knew that he was thinking exactly what I was thinking—that a ten-year-old shouldn't have to ask for milk. Louder, he said, "Okay, be back in an hour. Lock the door."

He stubbed out his cigarette in an overflowing ashtray and pulled the nasty garbage bag out of the can and pulled it tight. Then he gestured for me to follow him out the back door.

I wasn't sure what to say to him, but he had barely gone two feet when he said, "I'm sorry. I'm so sorry. I should have never brought you here. But when Easton called, I wasn't sure how bad she was, and I didn't want to take the time to drive you back. But I should have. I'm sorry." He was fast-walking down the back steps, and in the dark I couldn't see his face.

"It's okay," I told him, because it was.

"No, it's not!" Tyler took the bag of garbage and threw it at the rusting metal cans next to the garage. It hit with a loud bang, knocking the can over, the lid spinning and coming to a stop a few feet away. "God! What the fuck was I thinking?" He reached out and kicked the can, twice, his boot making an angry dent. "Here I've been trying to impress you and then I bring you here. I'm a fucking idiot. What about my life could possibly impress you?"

His face was agonized, his anger and frustration and humiliation all written there clearly for me to read. I was struggling not to cry, because I knew that he was struggling not to cry tears of anger. I had never seen anything like what had just happened. I knew in theory that mothers could be awful and drug addiction was rampant and people lived in dirty houses, but I had never seen it. Never smelled it. Never heard those kinds of words designed to hurt outside of movies.

I went over to him by the garbage cans and I put my hands on his cheeks, drawing his face toward mine, going up on my tiptoes so I could see into his eyes with more clarity. "Actually, I've never been more impressed with you than I am right now."

He stared down at me, jaw working.

I kissed him. I closed my eyes and guided my mouth up to his, pouring all of my emotions into the touch. I wanted him to understand that I understood, that I thought he was amazing for the way he dealt with his life. That the fact that he still found reasons to grin and laugh were testament to his true nature, that his desire to take care of his brothers spoke volumes about his character. There was no one in *Streetcar* like Tyler. He was trying to make the best of his life.

Even if he had taken money to have sex with me.

Okay, so maybe I couldn't exactly award him sainthood, but I knew right then and there that if Tyler wanted to keep seeing me, I wanted to keep seeing him because there was more to him than he showed our friends. Which meant that no matter what the motivation, he would not be a bad person to lose my virginity to. I was still curious, I was still seeking those experiences that everyone else was already talking about, and Tyler wasn't a liar or a cheat or someone who would enjoy having me fall for him so he could then dump me.

Whatever his reasons for saying yes to Jess and Kylie, in a completely insane way, I was grateful.

Because I was standing there, and for the first time, really, I felt like I was of worth, of value, to someone. I was comforting him and that made me feel important. That I had something to give.

"Rory," he murmured against my lips. "God, you feel so good. Why wouldn't you talk to me all week? It was driving me crazy." He wrapped his arms around me and held me tight against his chest.

Dropping back down to the soles of my feet, I ran my fingers over the stubble of his beard. He needed to shave. "Because I was afraid. I didn't think that you really liked me." That was true. "I kept waiting to be the punch line."

"Why?" he asked, puzzled. "Why would you think that?"

"Because guys like you don't like girls like me."

The corner of his mouth lifted up. "And girls like you don't like guys like me."

"Except apparently in our case." This was his last chance to bail.

But he didn't. He just kissed me, softly. "Because we're amazingly awesome, that's why."

"I agree. Now let's go to the grocery store."

He stiffened. "You're going to the grocery store with me?"

"Sure, why not? I don't have any other plans, and I like the grocery store. It's very organized. It soothes my mathematical soul."

He laughed and it was a sound of relief. "Well, then, okay. Let's go."

In the car, he started the engine and said, "I should explain a few things."

"Not if you don't want to." I knew it was hard to talk about private things, especially when it came to family.

"No, I want to. I don't want you to think that I haven't thought about other options for my brothers. But the truth is, there aren't any. I'm sure you noticed that Easton doesn't have the same father as the rest of us. The thing is, my mom never said anything to my dad. Hell, maybe she didn't know, I don't know. But no one knew Easton wasn't my dad's until he was born. When my mom came home from the hospital she got of the car and my dad ran her over with it."

"*What?*"

"Yeah, I don't know how he didn't kill her, honestly. I was standing on the front porch waiting for her and I saw the whole thing. He just drove over her like she was a Coke can. I was twelve."

"Oh my God." I couldn't even comprehend. I just stared at Tyler's profile as he drove.

"My dad wound up in prison and my mom had a lot of injuries. It messed up her back and her elbow real bad, and that's how she started using prescription drugs. Before that she always drank, but not as much as my dad. He was a real violent drunk. But once she got on the pills to help with the pain, she became a full-blown alcoholic. My dad got out of prison briefly but violated his parole by robbing a liquor store, so he's away for probably ten years this time."

Reaching over, I linked my hand with his and squeezed it. He gave me a half smile. "So there's not much money and she's always up and down, but the thing is, never once has she hit Jayden or Easton. She only hits me and I can handle it. She used to lay into Riley, too, but he had a hard time controlling his temper. One time he hit her back so he decided it was time to move out. He's twenty-five and he works in construction and he lives in a buddy's basement. He's helping me pay for school so that I can get a decent job and we can get an apartment. Between the two of us, we can take care of the boys. That's the plan. I don't want to involve the courts, though, because they'll put them in foster care first. I can't do that to them, because who the hell knows what will happen? If we just play it cool and move them out to a place with Riley, she probably won't do anything about it. We're laying the foundation, you know? But I can't move out. It would set her over the edge. She needs a punching bag, and I'm it."

There was more to it than that. He didn't say it, but I could hear it. He couldn't abandon her. He couldn't leave her alone without anyone, and I felt my respect for him grow.

"That's not very fair to you," I said. "But I completely understand why you're doing what you do. It must be nice to have brothers who care that much about you and the other way around. It's lonely being an only child."

"Yeah?" He shot me a teasing look as we entered the supermarket parking lot. "Were you just too much for your parents to handle? Wild child Rory?"

I laughed. "Yeah, right. Actually, when my mother was pregnant with me they discovered she had uterine cancer. She chose not to do radiation so that hopefully she could deliver me. The doctors thought she was insane. They urged her to have an abortion, but she refused. I was born six weeks early, then they gave her intensive chemo and radiation. She went into remission and everyone said it was a miracle." I shrugged. "But she couldn't have any more kids, obviously. Then when I was seven, it came back."

"Holy shit. That sucks."

"Yeah. I felt guilty, you know, that I killed her. If she hadn't been pregnant, it wouldn't have grown so fast." I realized that I had never told anyone that before. I had never said it, because I had never wanted to acknowledge the guilt I felt. I had wondered if my father felt that way too, if he regretted having me, because if it weren't for me, his wife would still be alive.

"Cancer wasn't your fault, Rory. Hell, if she hadn't gotten

pregnant, maybe she wouldn't have caught it at all the first time, and she wouldn't have had even those seven years."

"Yeah, maybe you're right."

As we walked into the grocery store, my small cold hand wrapped in his big callused one, I marveled at the strange places and people we could draw comfort from, when we didn't even know we needed it.

CHAPTER NINE

I HAD NEVER GROCERY-SHOPPED WITH ANYONE ELSE BEFORE. By the time I was around sixteen and had my license, my dad and I had taken to shopping separately, filling the kitchen with our own personal preferences. My dad gave me fifty bucks a week to pick up what I wanted, and I gravitated toward yogurt and vegetables to snack on, and on occasion, lean meats to cook for my dad and me. Rarely, if ever, did I buy something out of a can. Tyler bought only cans.

As the pile of processed and packaged foods like SpaghettiOs and jellied cranberries grew higher in the cart, I asked, "Do you have a problem with fruits and vegetables?"

He shrugged, grabbing crackers and the Pop Tarts Jayden had requested. "No. They just require effort. Like chopping and shit. Plus they go bad fast."

"Like chopping and shit," I repeated. "So cutting the stems off strawberries is more time-consuming than opening up a can of sugary cranberries?"

"Yes," he said, like this was obvious. He was leaning over the cart, dwarfing it with his broad shoulders, and there was nothing domestic about the way he looked, tattoos and Iron Maiden shirt, his jeans sporting a few holes in the knees.

The store was right down the street from his house, and it was a business that had a firm grip on its demographics. Beer, potato chips, and marshmallows were on special right as you walked in, and there was no fancy sushi counter, no floral department, no extensive wine department like the grocery store by my suburban house. The floors were dirty, and the deli smelled like the slicers hadn't been cleaned in longer than I cared to think about.

Maternal instincts I didn't even know I had were suddenly springing up, and I found myself saying, "Come on. We're swinging back through produce."

As I put a bag of baby carrots in the cart, I told him, "You don't have to cut these. Just eat them."

"Why?" he asked. "They don't taste like anything."

"Trust me," I told him, suddenly feeling proud of myself. I had never really thought about it, but I could cook. I made dinner for me and my dad all the time at home, and I could Google a recipe faster than anyone. This was something I could contribute to another human being, other than the assurance that someday I would put my intelligence to use. After med school. This was *now*. "I'm making dinner tonight."

"Rory, you don't have to cook for me." He actually looked alarmed at the thought.

"Why, you don't think I can do it?" I asked defensively, scanning the racks for garlic bulbs.

"I'm sure you can do it. It's just . . . you saw my house. Nobody cooks in my house. I'm not even sure we have more than one pot."

"Well, tonight I'm cooking," I told him. "So deal with it." I marched down aisles, adding ingredients I would need, including a bag of chicken breasts and disposable plastic food containers I could use to keep chopped fruits and vegetables for his brothers to eat during the week.

"I'll be right back," he said, as I waited in the deli line for Swiss.

When I turned back around, plastic bag of cheese slices in my hand, I saw he had added a case of beer and three packs of cigarettes to the cart.

"I'm done shopping," he said with a grin.

"Nice." I couldn't help but smile at him in return. "They probably won't let you buy that with me standing next to you, though. They'll try to card me, too."

He scoffed. "Are you kidding me? Have you looked around? This isn't exactly a quality establishment. Not only will they not card you, they won't even card me. Plus I bet if you go in the back room you can get a tattoo."

I laughed. "I'll pass."

He was right. They didn't card him. The cashier didn't even look at us as she dragged our items over the belt. I started to pull my wallet out of my purse as I saw the total climbing past forty dollars.

Tyler's hand came out and covered mine, preventing me from taking out my money. "Rory, you are not buying this food," he said quietly. "And if you try, I swear to God, I will lose my shit. You're doing too much already."

My hand stilled and I fished around under my wallet. "I'm getting a breath mint," I lied, pulling the little box out. Sometimes pride saw us through a lot, and I knew he needed his.

It was the right response. He gave a smirk as he pulled his wallet out and counted bills. "You planning on making out with someone later?"

"That depends on you."

"Oh, yeah?" He raised an eyebrow.

"Yeah. If you behave yourself."

"Wow. Getting sassy, aren't you?"

"I am, aren't I?" I asked in amazement. "I didn't know I knew how to do that."

Tyler snorted. "You're cute, do you know that?" He turned to the bored cashier, who was sixty-five and chewing gum, her arms crossed over her ginormous breasts as she waited for Tyler to give her his money. "Isn't she cute?" he asked the cashier.

The cashier's eyes swept over me, cracking her gum. "Adorable," she said, in a completely monotone voice.

"Tyler!" I said, mortified.

But he just laughed and paid for the groceries, including the bottle of disinfectant spray I had managed to put in the cart without him noticing.

"LIKE THIS," I TOLD TYLER AND HIS BROTHERS, SHOWING THEM how to bring down the knife at an angle to pop the stem off each strawberry. I had chicken in the oven and carrots cooking in a glaze on the stove top, potatoes boiling beside them. The strawberries were supposed to be for dessert, served with the shortcakes I had bought. Or put in the cart. Tyler had bought them.

Jayden and Easton were standing beside me, intently studying my motion and trying to emulate it. Tyler had already set his knife down. "My fingers are too big to do this," he declared and popped the top off a beer on the counter's edge.

I thought he just had zero interest in cooking, but I didn't say anything. He had been busy watching us and giving commentary on what we were doing as he cleaned the kitchen. When we unloaded the bags, he'd found the cleaner and had proceeded to scrub the kitchen table and counter, and mop the floor with it. He'd taken out the last of the trash after tossing everything that was bad out of the fridge. I hoped I hadn't embarrassed him. That wasn't my intention at all. But he didn't look upset. Nor did he look like he'd never cleaned before. I had a feeling he did this more often than anyone would ever suspect but that it was a losing battle. With the filth gone, and the stench replaced by pine cleaner and baking chicken, the room was a lot more pleasant. But it was still a dingy, worn kitchen, with cracked linoleum, peeling floor tiles, and walls that probably hadn't been painted in thirty years. A yellow phone was still on the jack, its cord entwined around itself, trailing down the wall, forlorn and forgotten. I'm sure it didn't work, but no one had ever bothered to take it down.

"Am I doing this right?" Easton asked anxiously.

"Don't cut off your finger," Tyler called from the back deck, where he was flinging the trash.

"You're doing awesome," I told him. "And the best part of being the person who cuts the fruit is that you get to sneak some." I popped a strawberry in my mouth.

Jayden did the same. "Holy crap, that's good!" he said.

Tyler laughed at Jayden's enthusiasm.

When we sat down at the table five minutes later, the chicken, mashed potatoes, and glazed carrots on four mismatched plates, Jayden was downright ecstatic. "I really like you," he told me with pure adoration in his voice. He had that awesome guilelessness that people with Down's have, and I smiled at him.

"I like you, too, Jayden."

"Hey, careful there now, buddy," Tyler told him. "Rory's here with me, you know." He leaned over and kissed my temple. "I think what my brother means is, thank you for dinner."

"Yeah, thanks, Rory," Jayden said, his mouth full of mashed potatoes.

"You're welcome." I felt ridiculously pleased.

Easton was studying his carrots like they were going to bite him. "You don't have to eat those," I told him. "I didn't know what you like or don't like."

"At least try them," Tyler urged, rubbing Easton's head back and forth, causing his fork to vibrate on his plate. "You don't even know if you like them or not because I honestly don't think you've ever had a carrot."

"Yeah. Don't be a dick, Easton," Jayden told him.

Tyler let out a loud laugh. "Dude, you have a fucking potty mouth."

"Do you hear the irony in what you just said?" I asked him, taking a bite of chicken.

"Nope," he declared, even though he clearly did.

Easton licked a carrot suspiciously. He seemed to deem it acceptable, putting it into his mouth, but he carefully set his fork back down and chewed methodically. Jayden and Tyler were shoving food into their mouths like it was going to disappear if they didn't inhale it.

"Did you get me a job application?" Jayden asked Tyler.

"No, sorry, man, I forgot."

"I need a job, Tyler. How else am I going to get my tattoo?" He tapped his bicep, which admittedly was not in the same condition as Tyler's. He had the soft muscle tone most Down's kids seem to have.

"What do you a want a tattoo of?" I asked him. Jayden was easy to talk to, easy to like.

"The same one that Tyler and Riley have. *TRUE Family*." He tapped his arm again.

My heart pretty much collapsed in my chest in a giant mass of liquid Jell-O. "That would be cool."

"U thinks a tattoo will help him with the ladies," Tyler said, with a wink at his brother. "Right, bro?"

Jayden caught on that Tyler was teasing him, and he said loudly in annoyance, "Well, it worked for you! You got Rory, didn't you?"

"You think Rory only likes me for my tattoos?" Tyler gave me an amused look and picked up his bottle to take a long drink.

"Why else would she like you? It's not like you have a big dick or anything."

I dropped my fork and my jaw. Hello.

Tyler's beer shot out his nose at Jayden's pronouncement and he thumped at his chest, choking and laughing. "What do you know about how big my dick is or isn't?" Then he held his hand up, still wheezing and chuckling. "Never mind. Don't answer that. We shouldn't be talking about this shit at the dinner table. It's not good manners."

"It isn't?" Jayden asked.

"No. Genitalia has no business at the dinner table. Right, Easton?"

His little brother shrugged, still chewing the same carrot. It had to be like baby food in his mouth by now.

"Why does Tyler call you U?" I asked Jayden.

"Because my mom always calls me 'Hey, you,' so we shortened it to U." Jayden didn't seem at all bothered by that.

Me, on the other hand, I wanted to cry again.

"That doesn't seem very nice," I said.

Jayden just shrugged. "It's easier to spell and it fits in the tattoo. It makes it perfect." He looked proud of that fact.

"Yeah, without the *U* we don't spell a damn thing," Tyler told him, leaning over the table to fist bump with him. "We need you. Ha ha. Get it? You? U? God, I'm funny."

"You're stupid," Jayden told him good-naturedly.

"Are you sleeping here tonight?" Easton asked, pureed carrot sliding out onto his lip as he spoke. The question seemed innocent enough, but there was fear in his dark eyes.

"Yeah." Tyler studied his brother carefully, before putting his hand on his shoulder and squeezing. "After dinner I need to take Rory home, but then I'll be right back. Promise."

"Will you read *Harry Potter* to me?"

Easton seemed younger than his ten years to me, both in appearance and mannerisms, and I wondered how he did at school. I couldn't imagine things were easy for him.

"Sure," Tyler said easily.

"I don't have to leave yet," I blurted out, then shoved more potatoes in my mouth, embarrassed at how that sounded. I didn't normally invite myself to places. "I mean, I don't want to interrupt your night. You can just take me home whenever."

"Okay," Tyler said, and I couldn't tell what he was thinking.

"Can you spend the night?" Jayden asked, leaning over and licking the remaining glaze off of his plate. Every last bite of food was gone.

"I . . ." My cheeks burned. If I said either yes or no, I was possibly going to look bad to Tyler. I would look desperate if I said yes, rude if I said no. I felt backed into a super-awkward corner. Besides, as it was I wasn't sure if I was ready for sex at all, so I certainly didn't want to do it with his brothers in the next room. Or hell, for all I knew, the same room. But Tyler wouldn't either. Right? Did he even want to have sex with me? Or did he just want to be friends who kissed each other?

The silence was deafening.

Tyler said to Jayden, "Only if Rory wants to. And you can't expect her to make you breakfast." Then he looked at me, eyes burning with desire and something else that I couldn't quite gauge. But it didn't look like a friends-only stare. "I would really like it. But I'm selfish that way. You should definitely feel like you can say no."

"No, I'll stay," I said, striving for casual. "I would like that, too." Actually, I wasn't sure if I was going to like it or not. It wasn't exactly my element, but at the same time, I didn't want to leave. I wanted access to this other side of Tyler, the one no one at school had seen. I wanted this view of siblings, a tight bond, even in such dysfunctional circumstances.

"Cool." Then Tyler shoved his chair back suddenly, taking his plate to the sink. His hand immediately went for his pocket to pull out a cigarette.

I stared at him, realizing that if he were a gambler, smoking would be his tell. It gave away when he was nervous or uncomfortable. He wasn't any more at ease with us sleeping together than I was, and for some reason, that instantly made me feel better.

"What?" he asked, when he realized I was watching him.

I shook my head. "Nothing." Maybe people weren't so hard to figure out after all.

Ten minutes later, when Jayden and I were sitting on the couch together, plates of berries and shortcake on our laps as we watched *SpongeBob* on TV, I could see Tyler and Easton out of the corner of my eye in the kitchen. Their chairs were drawn close together, heads bent down over the library book Tyler had produced from his room. As Tyler's voice carried across the room, a steady murmur as he read the story, his arm snaked over the back of Easton's chair, and the boy's slight form leaned almost imperceptibly into his brother's strong embrace.

It was then that I realized it would be very easy to fall in love with Tyler Mann.

And that if I didn't want to get my heart broken into a million pieces, I needed to be very, very careful not to do that.

CHAPTER TEN

I TEXTED KYLIE AROUND TEN, KNOWING SHE WOULD WORRY about me. I was still on the couch and Tyler was in the bathroom. I had a feeling he was cleaning it because he'd gone in with the spray bottle and had been in there for twenty minutes.

Staying with Tyler tonight.

Where?

His place.

We're at Nathan's and you are not here. I'm freaking. Are you sure you're ok? Where are you?

His house. His mom's house.

What?!?! For reals?

Yes.

Whoa. No one goes there. Is it gross?

I didn't want to admit that it was. Or had been. That seemed disloyal.

No. It's fine.

O-kay.

I was guessing Nathan and Kylie and Jessica were having a discussion about where I was and why. My roommates probably didn't understand why Tyler and I were still hanging out with each other now that we had supposedly already had sex and I had avoided him all week, but I wasn't about to enlighten them. Besides, I didn't exactly know what we were doing either.

Tyler came and plunked himself down next to me on my free side. Jayden had curled up with a blanket to my right, and Easton was in a velvet chair with a calico cat that had matted fur. Tyler put his hand on my knee and gave me a smile. "You doing okay?"

"Yep."

"I have to work tomorrow at nine," he said. "I hope that's okay. I should have thought of that before. We'll probably have to leave here around 8:15 to get you back and me to work on time."

"That's fine. That way I'll be up and I can study before Kylie and Jess get back."

"Nerd," he said teasingly.

"That's me." It was a label I had never minded wearing. It was the truth and that was that.

"Want to go to bed soon?"

My palms went clammy and I started sweating. "Sure." What was meant to sound nonchalant came out like a squeak. The anticipation was killing me and I just wanted to get it over with. I wanted to be done with the whole awkward first-time experience and be able to enjoy myself.

But Tyler squeezed my thigh. "Don't look so terrified. I'm not going to try anything. That would be like luring you here under false pretenses or something."

Did I look scared? God, how embarrassing. I was both relieved and disappointed at his words.

"Besides, I don't have any condoms and you heard my mom—getting pregnant will fuck up your life. She's living proof." He seemed to think this was funny.

I wasn't as amused. First of all, because I thought what his mother had said was horrible and I couldn't imagine poking fun at it, but I realized he had to either laugh or be angry. But secondly, he had been in the bookstore looking to buy condoms less than two weeks ago. I'm sure he had bought them at the drugstore, and I was guessing they came in a three-pack, at bare minimum, with probably as many as twenty-four in one box. Assuming he was short on cash, which was likely, he would have bought the cheapest—the three-pack. But still, that meant he no longer had them. Which meant they'd been used. And not with me. Three times. At least.

So with who?

I didn't think it was Jessica, because she was already campaigning for me at that point. But whoever it was, I wasn't happy about it.

"Good point," I told him coolly.

He stood up and said, "Sorry I can't offer you a toothbrush or anything, but I can give you some basketball shorts to sleep in."

"That'll work." I followed him down the hall to the second bedroom on the right, a small eight-by-eight box with a twin mattress on the floor. He flicked the light on, and I saw it was loaded with a sheet that had pulled free of the mattress, three pillows, a blanket, and balled-up clothes.

After shutting the door firmly, he peeled off his T-shirt and added it to the pile, which he then shoved over onto the floor. For the first time, I had a view of his bare back and I realized the tattoos weren't constrained to his arms. There was a giant elaborate cross between his shoulder blades, with a very heavy-metal look to it. It spanned from one shoulder blade to the other and vertically down his spine. It was also clear how much he worked out because the muscle definition was droolworthy, and I found myself even more jealous of the unknown girl who had gotten to have sex with him when I wasn't even going to be able to. It seemed so not fair.

"Do you mind if I take my jeans off?" he asked, finger on his fly.

"No." Annoyed, more at myself than at him, I kicked off my boots and carefully set them in the corner, my crossbody bag next to them. I yanked off my sweater and folded it, leaving me in a cami and skinny jeans. I crawled into bed, fixing the sheet and refusing to look at his near nakedness.

"Is something wrong?" he asked.

I should have said no. Most people would have. But being silently petulant wasn't me. I had absolutely no right to be upset with him if he had slept with someone else, and I knew that. Logically.

"No. But if I said I have condoms, would you want to have sex with me?" I asked, adjusting two pillows behind my head and taking in the sight of him, realizing I'd be an idiot not to. His thighs and calves were muscular with a fine sprinkling of dark hair. There was another tattoo, a fiery red dragon racing down his left calf. When he turned fully toward me, his expression fierce, I tried not to glance at his black boxer briefs.

Tried and failed. What could I say? I'd never seen a penis in person (aside from Grant's) and I was curious. But there was only a bulge visible beneath the cotton.

"Are you saying you have condoms?" he asked, voice tight.

His briefs jumped and I realized that he was growing an erection while he stood there. Oh, God. I stared. I couldn't help it. "No. That was a hypothetical."

He made a strangled sound in the back of his throat. "Then why would you ask me that? And maybe next time you could warn me if it's purely hypothetical."

I just shrugged. Honestly, I wasn't sure. Other than maybe in some backward way I was fishing for a compliment. "Why didn't you buy some at the grocery store?"

"Because I didn't think sex was on the menu tonight." He pulled a pair of shorts out of a pile and slid into bed, handing them to me. "Are you pissed because I didn't plan this better? I didn't know you were going to spend the night. Hell, I never dreamed you would agree to spend the night. Yesterday you weren't even answering my texts." His warm body filled the space next to mine and he lay on his side, watching me with his head propped up by his arm.

"I'm not pissed." I wasn't. I was irrationally irritated, and even that was dissipating. What he had said made total sense and I knew it. If he had bought condoms at the store I would have thought that was presumptuous. It was hard for a guy to win sometimes.

"You clearly are pissed."

"No." I shook my head. Under the blanket I struggled out of my jeans, tossed them behind my head onto the floor, then pulled on the shorts.

"I wish you'd just rail at me," Tyler said, reaching out and playing with the ends of my hair. "That I know how to deal with. This . . . I don't get."

"I can't be a drama queen. That's not me," I told him.

"That's not what I mean . . . it's just, I can't tell what you're thinking half the time. You're so quiet."

I wanted to explain to him that some stories were loud, and some were quiet. His was filled with verbal arguments, slammed doors, heavy metal, and bad mufflers. Mine was one of hushed hospital hallways, the soft breath of a dying mother, whispered words of sympathy, and an achingly empty house where the most noticeable voice, the one of laughter and encouragement and cheerfulness, had been silenced.

But I just told him, "The expression isn't 'I talk, therefore I am.'"

Not everything needed to be said. Including my unwarranted jealousy of his past.

He laughed and his warm breath blew over my shoulder. "You have a point. If that were the case, Kylie would be a philosopher and we both know that's not even remotely true."

That brought a smile to my face. "No, probably not."

Tyler continued to play with my hair, pulling a strand all the way out and letting it fall over his hands in a waterfall of auburn waves. I hadn't slept in the same bed with another person any more than I had grocery shopped with anybody, and it gave me an intriguing perspective on him. Lying horizontally, he didn't feel so much bigger than me, so much more powerful. For the first time ever, we were able to look directly into each other's eyes without him bending down or me looking up.

We were perfectly aligned.

"I guess we should have turned the light off before we got into bed," I said.

"Then how would I see how beautiful you are?"

It should have sounded like a line. It was a line. Yet he looked so sincere that I couldn't help but believe that to him, I was beautiful. I felt beautiful under his gaze. A guy didn't touch with the gentleness he had if he didn't appreciate what he was looking at.

His wrist was visible as he lifted my hair up and let it drop over and over, the motion relaxing me, and obviously him. My body was growing warm under the blanket from his heat radiating toward me, and he smelled like cigarettes and toothpaste.

"What is this tattoo?" I asked, tapping his wrist with my index finger. It looked like an infinity symbol, but it was overlaying something else.

"It's a mistake. Got it when I was fifteen. It's supposed to be the Batman symbol."

I pursed my lips, suddenly wanting to laugh. "Oh?"

"I know. Totally stupid. But I was fifteen, what can I say? And it was only ten bucks because some douche bag was learning how to be a tattoo artist. I hear he works at the cell phone store now."

"It doesn't look like the Batman symbol at all."

"Thank God. His lack of skill actually benefited me." Leaving my hair alone, he locked his fingers through mine. "I'm guessing you don't have any ink."

"No. But not because I don't find it fascinating. I just haven't felt passionate enough about anything to put it permanently on my body. I'm not a very passionate person." My father used to joke that I was adopted from a Vulcan family.

His eyebrows shot up. "Not very passionate? Given what I saw in the car, I don't believe that."

Yeah, that was me blushing. "That's different."

"Let's see."

Tyler kissed me, and it, too, was different from this angle. I could feel his body everywhere along mine, and because now we were essentially the same height, our kiss was deeper, more invasive, and he gave a low moan in the back of his throat. Our bodies found a rhythm together, rocking and moving in tandem, hands stroking everywhere we could as his tongue plunged urgently into my mouth.

This was what I had been imagining. What I'd been waiting for. This was hot and wet and desperate, tangled legs and swollen lips and gasps of pleasure on his twin mattress.

Tyler broke away and set me back away from him. "I have to stop. I want to take your clothes off so badly, damn."

I was breathing hard and as I wiped my lips, I almost told him to hell with safe sex. But as soon as that thought popped into my head, it was like a bucket of ice water was dumped over my desire. I wasn't going down that road. Ever. No matter how much my body seemed to think otherwise.

"Maybe I am passionate about certain things," I told him.

He laughed. "Your passion is about to kill me. Fuck." Standing up, he pointed his finger at me. "I'm turning the light out and we're going to sleep. Stay on your side of the bed and try not to be so damn hot, understand?"

I made a face, using my fingers to peel my upper lip back to my nose in a move I hadn't attempted since second grade.

He laughed. "That will do it, thanks."

"You're welcome."

The light went out. The mattress groaned and sagged in the dark as he rejoined me on the bed, punching at his pillow, as far away from me as humanly possible on a narrow twin bed. I tried to hover near the wall. He kissed the back of my head.

"Good night, beautiful."

"Good night."

I lay in the dark and listened to the sound of his breath as it slowed and evened out, and I marveled at where I was and who I was with.

It didn't make sense. It wasn't logical.

Yet there was no place I'd rather be.

*   *   *

WHEN I WOKE UP, TYLER WAS WATCHING ME. HE GAVE ME A soft smile. "Hey."

"Hey." I was stiff from staying in one position the entire night, and I was instantly worried about bed head and morning breath. Rolling my neck, I covered my mouth as I yawned and tentatively snaked my arm out to stretch it. I let my hand land on his warm chest.

"You stiff?" he asked, giving me a soft kiss. He looked sleepy, his beard stubble even more pronounced after just eight hours of sleep.

I thought about the process of hair pushing itself out of our follicles while we slept and was amused at the imagery. Sometimes I wondered if I was the only one who found science so entertaining.

"Roll over, I'll rub your shoulders. This mattress sucks."

Was he for real? He was going to give me a back rub? That was definitely high on the Hot List. I complied and rolled over because the idea was totally appealing. Every muscle in my neck and shoulders had kinked. I visualized an intricate Celtic knot beneath my skin. When his hands landed on my flesh, I sighed in pleasant anticipation of a relaxing massage of my muscles.

We seemed to have a different concept of what relaxing was. Tyler dug into my shoulders with an iron grip, rubbing so hard that my teeth rattled as I jerked back and forth on the bed. I was definitely awake now, if not looser.

"Thanks," I said, wanting to laugh. Generosity fail. But it was the thought that counted.

Twenty minutes and one McDonald's drive-thru later, we were pulling up in front of my dorm. Tyler gave me a long, lingering kiss, one that made me forget completely that I hadn't brushed my teeth. "You busy tonight?"

"No."

"Want to watch a movie or something? We can hang here in your room."

"Cool. Text me when you're done working." I went to the front door, still sleepy, in desperate need of a yoga class, wearing the rumpled clothes I'd been wearing when I left the shelter the day before, blissfully happy.

The feeling continued when Tyler had no problem watching ID TV with me and listening to a medical examiner explain how he had used the clues left on a murder victim's body to solve the crime.

We were snuggled up on my bed, Tyler's back propped against the wall, me sprawled across the mattress, head and upper body in his lap. His fingers lazily stroked across my arm.

"So that's what you want to do?" he asked. "Comb over dead people?"

"Yes." I knew that most people thought my particular interest in forensics was bizarre and that I must be missing a compassion gene in order to be able to slice into people. But the opposite was true—I wanted to give answers about the dead to the living. If I had an iron stomach and a logical mind with great memorization skills, what better way to put them to use than conducting autopsies and giving families peace of mind? Or at least closure.

Maybe it would have been more strategic to keep my future plans on the down low, or at the very least, not expose Tyler to the reality of it on a TV show filmed in a morgue, but that seemed dishonest. This was me.

"You are one bad-ass chick, Rory. You look so sweet and naïve, but damn, your pretty face hides an amazing mind."

The praise made me feel a little giddy. I smiled up at him. "Thank you. And the human body is fascinating, what can I say?"

His eyebrows went up and down. "I can't argue with that."

I laughed, enjoying the easy feel of lying on him, my face next to his stomach, his arms wrapped around me. I realized that very rarely did I touch anyone. Kylie was a hugger and she laid one on me every few days, and I returned it, liking that clear indicator of true friendship. My dad occasionally patted my head or moved me forward with his hand on the small of my back. I had kissed a guy or two. But that was it. Since my mother died, I hadn't been touched. I hadn't realized I had missed it.

But now it felt like the nerve endings of my skin were awakening after dormancy. With more than a million sensory receptors distributed throughout my skin, every single one seemed to have been lazily stroked into awareness by Tyler. My Meissner's corpuscles were registering every touch and greedily responding with shivers, goose bumps, and a rise in serotonin.

It felt freaking awesome, and I never wanted to go back to a world where I existed behind a metaphorical glass wall watching everyone else interact with each other. No matter what happened, if Tyler changed his mind and decided tomorrow he no longer wanted to hang out with me, I would have that knowledge moving forward. I would be different. Not that I wanted to think about the future or an end or anything. I just wanted to enjoy the moment.

"Fuck me, that is that guy's large intestine lying on the table." Tyler cocked his head slightly, a grimace on his face as he paused in the act of lifting his bottle of water.

"It's in the way," I told him. "There are a lot of organs packed into our chest and abdominal cavities."

"That's the sexiest thing you've ever said," he teased.

"Really? Then I guess I need to step it up."

"I'd like to hear that. Talk dirty to me, Rory."

I opened my mouth, wanting to accept the challenge. But nothing came out. My mind went totally blank. We both laughed.

"That's about what I thought," he said. "I guess I'll have to be dirty enough for both of us."

"Okay." I stared up at him, wondering if tonight was the night. If he had bought condoms. If he was going to yank my shirt off over my head and make me feel more of what I had in the car.

He seemed to know exactly the direction my thoughts had taken. "Kylie said she was coming back in like ten minutes, remember?"

Damn. "Yeah."

"Don't look at me like that," he warned.

"Like what?" I asked.

He snorted. "Yeah. The innocent act isn't working. You know exactly what you're doing."

I did. It made me feel sexy and powerful when his head descended, his intent clearly to kiss me.

The door flew open. "I'm back," Kylie announced. "What are you guys doing? Gross, is that a dead guy on TV? What is he doing with that saw? Sick."

Tyler rolled his eyes. "I don't know how she doesn't pass out," he said. "Air is always leaving her mouth, but there can't possibly be time for her to inhale between words."

Tapping his leg in reprimand, I sat up, too content to truly be disappointed at the interruption. "Yes," I told Kylie. "That's a saw. He has to get through the rib cage to the heart. It's a very extensive process and requires bone cracking."

Ironic, wasn't it, that the physical heart was so hard to reach, yet my emotional heart seemed to have been found with very little effort on Tyler's part.

CHAPTER ELEVEN

"GIRLS' NIGHT!" KYLIE SHOUTED, ARMS UP OVER HER HEAD AS she dropped down low on the dance floor on orders from Flo Rida.

I wasn't going to attempt that move, knowing I'd end up on my ass. And not in a good way. I just bounced from side to side, pretending that I knew how to dance. The reality was, I had a respectable sense of rhythm, but my arms never seemed to coordinate with my legs. I tended to look like a heron searching for a fish when I attempted dances that had choreographed moves.

Fortunately, it was a typical Saturday night at the club just off campus, and everyone was too drunk to notice what I was or wasn't doing. I did enjoy dancing, just not when someone was recording it on a phone. Kylie, Jess, Robin, and I were out for the night, and on strict instructions from Kylie, no guys were allowed. After a week of seeing Tyler every day, I was mostly okay with that. He was working anyway, and I didn't want to be one of those girls who started seeing a guy and then ignored her friends completely. Then when he turned out to be an ass, she called and cried on you for two hours. Then got back together with him and promptly blew you off again.

I would not be that girl.

So I was out with my friends because one, I enjoyed their company, and two, if I wound up sobbing over a bag of Doritos, which was a very real possibility, I wanted legit sympathy.

Though I would have preferred hitting the mall for some purse—and scarf—shopping or going to the movies, here we were at Republik, sharing a pitcher of beer and fending off drunken frat boys who moved in on us like a school of fish, undulating waves of them, splitting around us and homing in on a target, which was usually Kylie. Actually, there wasn't much fending off going on. Normally the rules of a girls' night were strict in that there could be nothing beyond a minute or two of casual flirting with a guy. No disappearing. No hookups. None of which had ever applied to me, but the point was, we were supposed to stay together and drive men insane with desire from our rebuffs and cumulative girl-power friendship.

That motto seemed to have left the building with Kylie and Robin's sobriety. They were both dancing with a minimum of two guys at any given moment, and Robin had already made out with one guy and let another do a shot off her boobs. It wasn't even eleven yet.

I was cool with all of that. I knew that Kylie was struggling to figure out what she was doing with Nathan, and we all needed to blow off steam before finals in a couple of weeks. But what I was not cool with was the fact that Jessica and Kylie were throwing random guys in my direction with encouraging nods and tongue wiggling.

On my own, I wasn't attracting much attention, which worked

just fine for me, but my roommates seemed determined to throw one hapless friend of a hot guy after another at me. I actually felt sorry for them since they were bound to be disappointed that they were stuck dancing next to the one girl in the group not wearing a miniskirt or a drunken smile of welcome. In a pair of jeans, chunky striped sweater, and ballet flats with a bow in my hair, I wasn't exactly sex personified.

"What's your name?" one yelled into my ear, adjusting his baseball cap and looking determined to make the best of having drawn the short stick.

"Rory," I shouted in his direction.

"Tori?"

Sure, why not? I nodded.

"I'm Mike." He stuck his hand out.

Which was kind of funny, considering we were packed onto a sweaty dance floor with red lights strobing over us at random pulses guaranteed to give someone a seizure. But I took his hand and quickly shook before letting him go. He was wearing a John Deere T-shirt and giant gym shoes that landed on my foot when he moved as awkwardly as me.

"Shit. Sorry."

Kylie came up behind me and gave me an over-the-shoulder bear hug, shouting into my ear, "He's cute! You should totally go for it!"

Feeling like I was wearing a blond throw blanket, I ignored her, starting to get annoyed. It wasn't that unusual for my friends to suggest I flirt with a guy. What was unusual was that they were doing it now, when they knew I was spending a ton of time with Tyler, who they had *paid* to de-virginize me. Which he hadn't. Not yet, anyway. While we had found plenty of time to make out, there was always a reason it didn't go any further, whether it was time, privacy, or lack of condoms.

So he hadn't complied with their request, but they didn't know that. They thought I had slept with him, was sleeping with him. Wasn't that what they had intended? So now why were they determined to make me see the charm in a random redneck?

"Do you want a drink?" Mike asked when Kylie bounced off of me and grabbed the hand of Mike's friend, forcing him to spin her.

I shook my head. "No, thanks. I'm actually seeing someone, and . . ."

Jessica cut me off. "It's just a drink! And you're fucking Tyler, not dating him. There's a big difference."

Okay, now that pissed me off. That was a brutal blow on the dance floor. Breath coming in anxious bursts, I apologized to Mike. "I'm sorry, I need to go."

He looked simultaneously horrified and intrigued. I don't think he had viewed me as a girl who would screw for the sake of screwing, and while I might have been diminished in his moral opinion, I had shot up in the ranks of his interest. Given the chance, I suspected he would double his efforts to talk to me now there was proof that I put out. "No problem. I'll be here."

I wouldn't. Without even acknowledging Jessica, I left the dance floor and went straight out the front door of the bar, ditching my coat at the coat check. I needed fresh air. I needed to not lose it completely. Knowing Tyler was usually bored at work and would answer me, I pulled my phone out of my purse and tapped out a text.

Can you pick me up at Republik when you get off work?

He was done at midnight and it couldn't come soon enough for me.

His response came right away.

Sure. What happened to girls nite?

Disaster. Thx. C u ltr.

Jessica burst out of the club behind me.

"Rory! Rory, what? What's wrong?"

Turning I screamed at her, "What's wrong? What's wrong is that you think it's perfectly okay to tell I guy I was not even remotely interested in that I have a fuck buddy! Which, for your information, I do not. I'm still a virgin!"

Kylie came out in time to hear this pronouncement. "What? You said you had sex with Tyler!"

"I didn't say that. You just assumed it. Yes, we've messed around. No, we haven't had actual penetration." The doorman shot me a freaked-out look. I lowered my voice, shivering in the cold but too furious to go back into the crowded club and act like nothing was wrong. "This is more than sex. We're spending time together."

They gave each other a nervous look, and I knew what they were thinking. That this wasn't the deal, and what the hell was Tyler doing?

"I'm sorry, I didn't mean to embarrass you," Jessica said. "And maybe we weren't being subtle in there, but the thing is, we're kind of worried about you. We don't want you to get too invested in Tyler."

"Why, because you think he's using me? For what?"

Kylie shook her head. "He's just not . . . a relationship kind of guy. And you're a relationship kind of girl."

"How do you know that? I've never had one! So who is to say who is capable of a relationship and who isn't? Or is it just that you don't think Tyler could ever want a relationship with *me*?"

It hurt, because that was my fear too, the one that snuck up on me from time to time in the dark and briefly snuffed out my happiness. Tyler wasn't calling what we had a relationship but it was *something*. A friendship with an attraction at the very least. I had to believe that. I did believe that. But they pricked my confidence with their words.

"That's not it. We just want you to be careful," Jessica said. "He has a lot of experience."

Unfortunately, I remembered quite clearly that some of that had been with her. Was she somehow jealous? Was it different now that it wasn't all about a quick hookup they were in control of? God, I hoped not. "You shoved me at Tyler," I reminded them.

"We didn't think . . ."

"That he would be interested in me for more than five minutes," I said flatly.

My lip started to tremble and tears welled in my eyes. I couldn't help it.

"Oh!" In horror, Kylie saw that I was fighting the urge to cry. "No! That's not what we meant . . . Oh, shit, this is awful!" And she burst into drunken tears.

Which made me start crying.

Which in turn had Jessica struggling not to cry. She sniffed a lot as Kylie and I sobbed, my vision blurring from my tears. I wasn't even drunk. I just felt like I was on emotional overload.

"We're sorry, Rory, God, this isn't how I thought this would go at all," Jessica lamented. "I thought you would be, you know, like *initiated* by Tyler, then you'd feel more confident and go on and find a nice guy."

"Tyler is a nice guy." I sucked in a few deep breaths and tried to get a grip on myself.

Kylie wiped at her eyes, smearing mascara all over her cheeks.

"Is he?" Jessica looked dubious about that declaration. "I picture you more with a nerd. Like a guy who is going to be the next Bill Gates."

I managed to stop the flow of tears and hugged myself to stem the shivering. "I appreciate that you guys care so much, but honestly, I want to hang out with Tyler. It's fine, okay? I'm not stupid. But I'm having fun."

"We just don't want you hurt."

"I know. But maybe you can just let me make my own choices, and if I screw it up then you can buy me ice cream and give me advice, okay? I'd really rather pick my own guys. No more attempted fix-ups." Especially if they involved money changing hands.

"Well, I can't argue with that," Jessica said. "I have to admit, I wouldn't like it if you tried to fix me up with someone."

Kylie nodded. "I just love you so much. You're my BFF and I just want you happy."

That made tears fill my eyes again. Which made her start crying again.

Jessica swiped at her eye. "Oh my God, stop. You're both killing me. And I think I need a group hug."

I did, too. I didn't object at all when they crowded me into a hug, and we all sniffled in the cold, my teeth chattering, Kylie's bare arms covered in goose bumps.

"What the hell is going on?" Robin asked.

We split apart and saw her standing in the doorway, looking disheveled. The bouncer had actually moved another three feet away from us, and he was shoving his hands in his pockets, studiously pretending he hadn't heard any of our drama.

"I just had a moment," I told her.

"I thought you guys left me alone. I was freaking. I am way too drunk to be left alone."

"We wouldn't leave you," Kylie assured her.

I felt a little guilty that my intention had been to leave. But I had known Kylie and Jess wouldn't leave Robin, and I wasn't going to feel guilty for calling them out on throwing guys at me. I went for my phone to let Tyler know that the crisis was averted, and he didn't have to pick me up.

Only there was no phone in my purse.

"Where's my phone?" I asked, frantically pawing through my purse. "I can't find it!"

"Did you leave it in the room?" Jessica asked, going into her own tiny wristlet bag.

"No."

Kylie and Robin were doing the same thing as Jessica, scrambling for their phones. It was a chain reaction of paranoia, but while they all looked up relieved a second later, mine was still missing. I glanced around the sidewalk but I didn't see anything. "Shit!"

"Are you sure you brought it?"

"Yes. I just used it!" Where could it have gone in the ten minutes since I had texted Tyler? We had been standing on the sidewalk the entire time.

"Oh, crap, here it is," Kylie said, leaning over and retrieving my phone from a giant puddle of dirty water in the street. She held it gingerly out from her body, and it dripped onto the sidewalk.

"Great." I took it from her, my hand instantly covered in cold water. I wiped it on my jeans and tapped the screen. Nothing happened. I popped the battery out and tried to dry it before rein-serting it. The screen was still black. "Oh my God, this is so annoying."

"That totally sucks," Jessica said. "But can we go back inside? I can't feel my fingers or my nipples."

"Yeah." I was freezing myself. But now I couldn't text Tyler back and tell him not to show up. "Jess, can I borrow your phone? I need to text Tyler."

"No! This is Girls' Night." She yanked the door open and a blast of warm air and loud music hit us.

"No, I mean I need to let him know . . ." I trailed off as she whirled away from me right out onto the dance floor.

Damn.

"Kylie, can I borrow your—"

She was gone too, laughing as a guy dragged her away to booty grind.

"Robin, can I borrow your phone?" I asked.

"Sure."

Thank God.

She handed it to me and I scrolled through her contacts. There was no Tyler Mann. "Don't you have Tyler's number?" I asked, doing a second pass in case I had missed it.

"No. He and I don't hang out."

That was no help whatsoever then because I didn't know his number. I relied on my now-dead phone to contact him.

I was trying to get to Kylie when Mike, the guy in the John Deere T-shirt, stepped in front of me, blocking the hole on the dance floor I had been trying to navigate through. He gave me a lecherous smile.

"Hey there, sexy."

Ick. "Excuse me, I'm trying to get to my friend."

"Kiss me and I'll let you through."

Really? Okay, I realized that he probably could have said that to any number of girls and they would have giggled and done it. But you would think that he could tell by the look on my face I was not going to be one of them.

"I don't think so. I'll just go a different direction." Not that he had any right to block my path, but I didn't feel like standing around arguing with him. I turned around and started to move to the perimeter of the dance floor, figuring I could shove my way along the side to reach Kylie.

He grabbed my elbow. "Come on, Tori, let's have some fun. You're a girl that likes to have fun, right?"

I could hear in his tone he was thinking about what Jessica had said. I could also see that Tyler had walked into the club and was scanning the room, probably wondering why I wasn't answering my phone. Shaking loose of Mike, I moved over to Robin who was just a couple of feet away from him, planning to tell her that I was leaving.

Tyler spotted me and nodded in acknowledgement right as Mike grabbed my hand again and leaned over to try to kiss my neck.

Oh, shit.

Never having had guys hit on me, I wasn't sure how to deflect the interest, since pulling away clearly wasn't working. But knowing Tyler was watching made me more determined than ever to ditch the guy because I didn't want it to look like I was enjoying the attention. I wished I had Jessica's ability to stop guys dead in their tracks with a vicious glare. Instead I just turned and held my hand out to block his maneuvers.

"Stop!" I demanded, annoyed with this guy, annoyed with the

whole night. I wanted to escape the pounding music and the jostling.

Suddenly Mike was gone, shoved back about four feet by Tyler, who had an extremely angry look on his face.

I smiled at him, putting my hands on his chest. "Thanks for coming," I told him. "I dropped my phone in a puddle and it's dead."

"I was worried about you when you didn't answer me." Tyler looked relieved as he kissed my forehead. But then his expression went stony when Mike tapped him on the shoulder.

"What?" he asked in a deceptively calm voice.

"Tori was with me. Go find your own chick to hit on."

"That's not even her name, you stupid fuck. Now back off or we're going to have problems." Tyler was holding on to his anger by a thread. I could see it in the set of his jaw and the twitch of his fists.

I slipped my hand into Tyler's, suddenly unnerved and wanting Mike to see that I was clearly with someone who was strong and capable of protecting me. The environment felt unsafe, humming with tension. I realized that this was not the kind of club Tyler would normally be in, and Mike and his friend who had appeared behind him seemed to sense it, too. The confident sneers on their faces showed they thought they were at an advantage here.

"Why should I back off?" Mike asked, issuing a clear challenge.

"Because she's with me and I have officially lost all patience with you, dumb ass." Tyler imperceptibly shifted me behind him, letting go of my hand. "Now get the fuck out of my way or I'm going to move you out of my way."

Again, his voice was very calm, like he wasn't the least bit concerned that this wouldn't end in his favor. I didn't doubt for one minute that Tyler had been in confrontational circumstances before, and I also knew that he had impressive control over himself. He was no hothead. He wouldn't be the guy to start it, but he would be the guy to finish it. I shivered, uncomfortable with the situation, worried that it wasn't going to end well. I did not want to be bailing Tyler out of jail for assault.

Before Mike could respond, a guy behind him stumbled right into him, making Mike drop his beer. Without hesitation, he turned around and shoved the guy hard, knocking him to the floor, which in turn caused the guy's friend to shove Mike, knocking him into his own friend.

Tyler shook his head and gave me an annoyed look. "Come on, let's get the hell out of here. Where are the girls? Let's grab them before punches start being thrown."

Too late. Mike swung wildly, and the other guy nailed him in the jaw. The guy who had hit the floor came up off the wood with a vengeance and hit Mike's friend in the gut. They went sailing backward and into the crowd like a couple of bowling balls. People and beer went scattering in all directions.

"Shit," was Tyler's opinion. He pulled me quickly through the crowd and deposited me by the coat check. "Stay right here. I'll get Jess and Kylie."

"Robin is with us, too," I told him, nervously scanning the dance floor for my friends. All I could see was a mass of bobbing heads and jostling bodies under the strobe lights. The bouncers shoved past as I got my coat from coat check, watching Tyler get swallowed up in the melee, punches clearly being thrown in multiple directions. The cops would be called if security didn't get this under control in the next minute or two.

The noise level had increased as girls started screaming and bodies hit tables and the floor. The DJ brought the music to a screeching halt and turned the overhead lights on, momentarily blinding me. Jessica came bursting out of the crowd, then Robin, Tyler blocking them from blows with his forearm, his other hand cutting a path through the crowd. They both look relieved to be out of the mess, and Jessica grabbed my hand and pulled me closer to the front door of the club.

"Let's wait outside."

"Where's Kylie?"

"Tyler will get her."

He was already making his way back with a determined look, and I let Jessica pull me outside into the cold, my jacket sliding down and almost hitting the ground.

"What the hell happened in there?" Jessica asked. "Stupid idiot boys."

I shook my head. "Some guy fell into another guy and spilled his beer." Biting my lip, I watched the door as person after person came flooding out, intent on escaping the fight. I heard the distinct sound of sirens coming from down the street. Worried about Kylie and Tyler, I bounced on the balls of my feet.

Robin's teeth were chattering, and her hair was whipping around her face in the crisp, late-fall breeze. She was wearing only a miniskirt and a one-shouldered stretchy top. I was handing her my coat to put on when Tyler hit the sidewalk, dragging Kylie behind him.

"Car is that way," he said, pointing to the right. "Go before the cops get here."

Kylie was stumbling along, her dress hiked up to her thighs, her mouth bleeding. "Oh my God!" I said, trying to reach for her to see what had happened.

"In the car," Tyler said, nudging me forward.

Jessica pulled me until we were all fast-walking, Robin wearing my coat like a cape. The car was only a block away, and we all fell in, a pile of colorful satin tops and mounds of hair. Kylie had taken the front seat and she turned around, wiping at her bloody lip. "I got punched. By a dude."

"Are you serious?" I asked, horrified.

"She took it like a champ," Tyler said, pulling out of the parking lot. "Didn't even hit the ground."

"Why did he hit you?" Jessica asked.

"It was an accident. He was aiming for the douche bag next to me."

"Did he apologize?" I asked, wondering what I would do if I got punched. Cry. No doubt about it.

Kylie grinned, her lip already swelling. "No worries, Tyler made him sorry. Thanks, Ty," she told him.

"No problem. Now where is Robin's car?"

"We walked," Jessica told him.

Tyler sighed. "You shouldn't be walking alone at night."

"Thanks, Dad."

He glanced at us in the rearview mirror. "Rory, where's your coat?"

"Robin is wearing it."

"Where is Robin's coat?"

"I didn't wear one. Nobody wore one but Rory."

"So the only one who brought a coat was the one wearing sleeves?" Tyler shook his head. "At least Rory has some sense."

That was what every girl wants to hear—that a hot guy thinks she has sense. Wanting to roll my eyes, I knew I should appreciate the intended compliment, but I was feeling decidedly less than sexy suddenly. I couldn't take a punch like a champ.

"Except when it comes to you," Jessica said, with a grin, giving me a nudge with her elbow.

Ha ha. I was so not amused.

"Was that idiot bothering you all night?" Tyler asked, glancing at me in the rearview mirror, making no indication whatsoever that he'd heard Jessica. "Is that why you wanted me to pick you up?"

"No."

"We had a fight with each other," Kylie told him. "We cried on the sidewalk in front of the club. It was awesome. Best Girls' Night ever. We laughed, we cried, we drank, we danced. Got punched in the face." She gave a happy sigh.

I sat in the back and looked out the window. Maybe now Jessica and Kylie would trust me when I said that Tyler was a nice guy. He was. He had risked getting arrested to collect us from that club, and I honestly wasn't sure what would have happened if he hadn't been there. So why did I feel so weird?

"I'm not real crazy about Girls' Night, to be honest with you," he said, lighting a cigarette.

Kylie laughed loudly.

When Tyler pulled up into the circle in front of our dorm, he put the car in park with the engine still running. He got out as I slowly stepped out onto the street, feeling awkward and unsure of what to do. Maybe I shouldn't have texted him. Maybe that had been presumptuous. Maybe he was genuinely and truly annoyed with me for dragging him into our night of ridiculousness.

As the girls waved and tottered toward the entrance, Tyler

moved in close to me and put his arm around my waist. "Well, that was interesting."

"I'm sorry," I told him, genuinely meaning that. "I shouldn't have texted you."

He frowned. "What do you mean?"

"I overreacted and I ruined your night. You could have been arrested in that club because of me." Tears rose in my eyes and my lips started to tremble. I clamped my mouth firmly shut.

"You did not ruin my night. I'm glad I was there to get you all out of that frat-boy hell. If I never hear another Usher song for the rest of my life, though, I'll be happy." Tyler bent down and kissed me. "What were you girls fighting about, anyway?"

You. But I just shook my head. "Stupid girl stuff. There may have been alcohol involved."

He snorted. "Yeah, no shit. Though you seem sober enough."

Too sober to be feeling as weepy as I did. "Yeah, I'm fine."

Except that I wanted him to invite me to come home with him. I wanted to press my body against his and have him wrap his muscular arms around me, my cool leg lying on his warm one, his soft hair tickling my skin.

"You should go up and get some ice on Kylie's lip. She's too drunk to do it, and tomorrow she's going to look like one of the Real Housewives from all the swelling."

"True." Disappointed, I stepped back.

Tyler gave me a quick kiss. "Tomorrow we need to go get you a phone. I don't like not being able to get in touch with you."

That should have been a statement that made me feel good, important to him. But for some reason I was feeling that he had put me in the same category as his brothers—someone he needed to take care of. Not someone he thought was hot.

"It will probably work when it dries out."

"If it doesn't, text me on Jessica's phone."

My hot roommate's phone. Feeling a self-esteem crisis coming on, I gave him a smile. "Okay. Thanks, again. Talk to you tomorrow."

Then I strode toward the door, wanting him to stop me. Wanting him to grab me and passionately kiss me or insist we spend the night together or say something completely and utterly romantic that girls dreamed of and no guy ever said.

He didn't, of course.

And I went up to my room to pry some ice out of our mini-fridge for Kylie's lip and tried not to ruin the only relationship I'd ever had by being needy.

It was a damn good thing my phone was dead or I was fairly certain I would have.

CHAPTER TWELVE

KYLIE AND NATHAN WERE SNUGGLED UP IN NATHAN'S ROOM, and Tyler was out on a beer run when Grant showed up. I went to answer the knock on the door, assuming it would be Tyler. Someone must have accidentally turned the button on the doorknob and locked it, because the door to the apartment was almost never locked. But when I opened it, Grant was standing there, slouched, shaggy hair down over his eyes, hands deep in his front pockets.

My smile disappeared and a pit of tension formed in my stomach. "Oh. Hi."

"Hey." Grant moved forward to step into the apartment and for a second I forgot to shift out of the way, stunned to see him standing there so casual, a sheepish smile on his face.

When I blocked his entry by not moving, his eyebrows went up as he turned sideways, his body closer to mine than I would have liked. "Can I come in?"

That pulled me out of my paralysis. Whereas before I didn't move, now I did too quickly, stumbling over my feet as I jerked backward out of his way. "Sure." It wasn't my apartment. I had no right to tell him he couldn't come in, and I guessed that Nathan had invited him over to watch the football game along with everyone else. I couldn't exactly ask Nathan though as he and Kylie were having some kind of reunion sex in his room. Kylie's split lip had prompted Nathan to call her and beg to see her, and she had forced me along with her as moral support.

Not that I had minded, because I knew Tyler would be there.

But not Grant. I hadn't expected that. Ignoring him, I shut the door and went back to the small kitchen, where I had been cutting up cheese for crackers and heating pizza rolls for the game viewing.

Unfortunately, he followed me into the kitchen. "Where is everyone?"

"Tyler is at the store. Kylie and Nathan are in his room."

Grant made a face. "No Jessica?"

"No." I remembered then what he had said to me that night about passing that kiss on to Jessica. I busied myself carefully spacing out pizza rolls on a cookie sheet I had found in the drawer under the stove.

"Hey, listen, um, about that night . . ."

Great. "We don't have to talk about this," I told him. In fact, I'd rather do anything but talk about it.

"I just want to say sorry. I was totally fucked up, and I mean, I thought you wanted to . . . I thought you were kissing me back."

He sounded so pained and uncomfortable with the whole conversation that I momentarily felt sympathy for him. I had kissed him back. There was no arguing with that. When I glanced over at him, he looked even thinner to me now than he ever had. I wasn't sure if he had lost weight in the weeks since that night or if it was just my perception now that I was used to Tyler. "I was," I told him honestly. "I just didn't want to take it any further. I'm sorry I wasn't clear about that up front. But I think I made it clear later."

Chewing his fingernail, he nodded before giving a deep rattling cough. His chest heaved painfully. When he could finally speak, he said, "Then I'm sorry. But what I don't get is why you didn't just tell me you had the hots for Tyler. We could have worked together."

"What do you mean?" I put the tray inside the oven and went to pull out my phone—which was fortunately now working—to set an alarm for fifteen minutes. I didn't bother to tell Grant that I hadn't had the hots for Tyler before that night. I didn't even have them right after that night. It was a week or so later before I really started to appreciate how attractive and charming Tyler was.

"The thing is, people like you and me, we're not going to score with Jessica and Tyler all on our own. It's just reality."

I stared at him, not at all enjoying the sound of that.

"I mean, look at what had to happen for Tyler to notice you. He had to come in and 'rescue' you." Grant made air quotes with his fingers. I had never noticed how watery his eyes were until now, how bruised the skin was under them. "You make him feel manly. He wants to take care of you, like a puppy somebody ditched by the side of the road."

Did he have any clue how insulting he was being? How absolutely and completely rude that was to say to me?

Yet part of me knew that he was right. So maybe Tyler didn't equate me with a puppy. But it was my naïveté that had first caught his attention, and the fact that I had needed a protector. It had been brought to my attention the night before at the club, too. I didn't want to hear Grant saying it out loud. It made me feel like I'd won Tyler's affection by default, by being weak.

"So how does any of that help you? Jessica doesn't fall in for charity cases."

"No, but I bet you anything she likes it rough. If you and I had planned this, you could have told Jessica where Tyler could overhear it that we had consensual sex, but it was rougher than you liked. That there was hairpulling and slapping. Jessica would have been turned on, and Tyler would have felt instantly protective."

I stared at him, appalled. "You've given this a lot of thought, haven't you?" I didn't want to give it any thought. The idea of saying Grant had pulled my hair was too close to the truth of what had happened, and I was disgusted.

"Yes. We wouldn't have even had to have sex. We could have just said we did."

"Because you don't really want to have sex with me, do you?"

He shook his head. "You don't either."

I didn't. But I didn't want to hear that. I didn't want the confirmation that he had been willing to use me as a lousy substitute for Jessica, even if I had already known it. I didn't want to feel that I was unattractive just because a disgusting human being like Grant wasn't attracted to me.

Besides the creep factor and the total deception in his idea, it didn't allow room for the fact that I had been then and still was a virgin, which presumably would have been revealed to Tyler, making it obvious Grant and I had lied. Of course, he didn't know that. Nor did it matter because I decided I truly hated him, and while I wouldn't leave him to die in a burning building, I wasn't going to lift a finger to help him otherwise.

"Sorry I wasn't any help to you," I told him with massive quantities of sarcasm.

"Maybe you could put a good word in with me to Jessica."

"I'll do that." Never. Unable to look at him, I tore open the box of crackers and let a whole pile slide onto a plate.

"Okay, cool."

Someone clearly didn't recognize verbal cues. But then I guessed that wasn't really such a huge surprise. He hadn't understood *no*, so why would he get sarcasm?

"I know she likes pills. Let it drop to her that I can get her some."

I definitely wasn't going to tell her that. Grant getting Jess hooked on prescription drugs was not happening on my watch. My knife sliced into a cheese wedge, as I fought to keep my mouth shut. Where the hell was Tyler?

"And let me know when Tyler gets bored with you. I'll see what I can do to help you out."

Oh, would he now? How effing generous of him. Afraid I was on the verge of stabbing him with the paring knife, I picked up the plate of cheese and crackers and skirted him, heading into the living room. I was putting the plate down on the oak coffee table when the front door opened and Tyler came in, carrying two twelve-packs of beer.

"What the fuck is going on?" he asked immediately, glaring at Grant, depositing the beer on the coffee table.

Grant shot me a smug look, like this somehow validated all his points.

"Pizza rolls are in the oven," I told Tyler, brushing my hair off my forehead. "And apparently Nathan invited Grant over."

There went Tyler's fingers, straight into his pocket, searching for his cigarettes.

"I was just telling Rory I'm sorry about what happened," Grant said. "She's being cool about it."

Tyler slid his eyes over to me, seeking confirmation of this pronouncement. I chewed my bottom lip, not sure how I felt. In the end, I just nodded, because that felt like the only way to disprove Grant's victim theory. Grant had made me feel unsure of myself with Tyler and that made me angry. I didn't want to be the stray he felt sorry for.

"Okay," Tyler said carefully. I suspected he was going to ask me about it when we were alone. If we were alone. We really didn't get much time to just be together without someone interrupting.

His lighter flicked on.

"Hey guys!" Kylie said, bursting out of the bedroom, a huge smile on her face. She was wearing Nathan's sweatpants and T-shirt, and she was waving her phone at us. "Check this out!"

I leaned forward to study the screen, grateful for the interruption in the awkward silence. It was her online social-networking page, and she had changed the profile picture to one of her and Nathan, temples touching as they smiled in tandem for the camera. Under her hometown, it said that she was "in a relationship" with Nathan Turner. That was new. They had never once made it Facebook Official before.

"Wow, that's awesome," I told her.

"We're legit," Nathan said with a grin, looking sleepy and very pleased with himself, and no doubt Kylie. "No more beating around the fucking bush."

Then he and Kylie looked at each and busted out laughing when they realized the possible double entendre of his words.

"Well, I hope you don't give that up completely," she said, reaching out for his hand.

"Hardly." He gave her a long, lingering kiss that made me

jealous. "But now I get to say you're my girlfriend and that just rocks, I'm telling you. You're gorgeous, fat lip and all."

She giggled and they snuggled, and I couldn't stop myself from glancing over at Tyler. I wanted to be in the same position as Kylie. There was no denying it. I wanted Tyler to feel pleased to call me his girlfriend. I wanted him to announce it online, where anyone could see it, in black and white, at any given time.

But there weren't even any pictures of Tyler and me together. We weren't there yet. If ever. We were something, but we weren't official.

He wasn't looking at me. He was reaching for a piece of cheese, ash from his cigarette drifting down onto the coffee table, which he ignored. "I think I just threw up in my mouth," Tyler told Nathan.

Not exactly what I was looking to hear.

It shouldn't matter. I should be happy with what we did have. When had I let myself forget the danger and get too close? I went into the kitchen to retrieve the pizza rolls out of the oven with a balled up T-shirt I had found lying on the counter atop a pile of mail. There were no pot holders. There weren't even any kitchen towels.

When I brought the rolls out on a plate, Tyler was turning on the TV to watch the pregame whatever. I wasn't exactly into football, but I was willing to give it a shot. Or at least I had been. I was feeling decidedly less generous about the whole thing. It was a repeat of the night before, me seeking something, but not really sure what.

Tyler tore a pizza roll in half with his teeth and said, "Thanks, babe." His eyes went to the TV.

Whatever I was looking for from him, that wasn't really it.

But then he reached for my hand, pulling me down onto the couch, tucking me into the space next to him, his arm around my shoulder, our hips touching.

Better.

THE COFFEE SHOP WAS WARM, THE SIGN FOR SEASONAL gingerbread lattes hanging behind the register, the gas fireplace in the corner turned on for the first time since last winter. When I was little, I had loved the smell of coffee. It was the scent of Saturday and Sunday mornings, of pajamas and pancakes and my parents smooching against the kitchen counter. It didn't matter if it was the sweltering heat of August or the bitter cold of January, there was always coffee brewing, and I enjoyed standing in front of the pot watching the drip, drip, trying to puzzle out how water could so readily pick up the flavor of the beans in such a short amount of time. It was amazing to me how quickly things could change.

When my mother died, my father stopped drinking coffee.

Maybe he had never really liked it. Maybe he had only drunk it because it was her addiction and it was there in front of him, but he didn't like it enough to pursue it. Maybe it reminded him of her. I didn't know. I never asked and he never said.

We had left a lot unsaid.

But as Tyler and I studied in the coffee shop, I breathed deep and inhaled the rich aroma of the beans, knowing that when I got back to the dorm, my hair, my coat, my backpack would all carry the slight hint of coffee.

I supposed that was the same with my mother. A slight hint of her still clung to me.

It was a reassuring thought.

"There's only two weeks left of classes, then finals," I told Tyler. "But if you ace your final, you can still get a B in Anatomy."

"And you can get an A in lit if you really want to," he told me, his notebook open to the page where he had scribbled notes to himself in an extremely slanted hand. He also tended to doodle, inking skulls and funny faces all around the margins of the paper.

"I *want* to," I protested. "That's not the issue. It's if I *can*."

"Don't be defeatist. It doesn't fit your personality." He tapped my book. "Read two chapters and we'll discuss it."

I made a face. "I should probably do my calculus instead."

"You can do calculus in your sleep."

"Is that why I wake up so tired sometimes? I'm doing calculus in my sleep? Have you seen me do that?" I ignored the novel about horses and the Great Depression and who knew what else in front of me.

He shook his head with a smile. "You're a little punk sometimes. How come I'm the only one who sees that?"

Because no one else ever bothered to look. "Maybe you're wrong," I told him, tilting my head and smiling so he would know I was teasing.

"Nope. Maybe sometimes, but not about this." Tyler pulled his phone out and held it up. "Smile for me."

Oh, yikes. He wanted to take my picture. For the first time. I sat up straighter, aware that my lip gloss was totally gone and my nose was probably shiny. Plus I hadn't brushed my hair since that morning, and it was so thick and wavy it probably looked like a mophead.

"No, stop worrying. Just smile, like you were."

"I can't now. I'm too aware." I tried to relax again, but I couldn't quite recapture the feeling of easiness.

Tyler was still staring at the screen of his phone, held in front of him. "You know why we get along, Rory?"

"Why?" This could be very, very interesting. Or it could be nothing. I sat, tense, waiting to hear his thoughts.

"Because we both see beyond what other people see about us. We both know that sometimes the best things are below the surface. When I look at you, I see this amazingly smart, funny, generous, and beautiful girl. Did you know that?"

"No," I whispered, my heart swelling.

"It's true."

The flash on his camera phone went off.

And I knew that I had fallen completely and totally in love with him.

CHAPTER THIRTEEN

IT SNOWED THAT NIGHT FOR THE FIRST TIME, BLANKETING campus in the dewy softness of wet flakes, drifting down to land without a sound, fresh and pure. We walked from the visitors' parking lot, where Tyler had left his car, to my dorm, me shivering but lifting my head to the sky, appreciating the beauty of nature. It was light outside from the snow, deceptively so, given it was nine o'clock, the air still and hushed.

Flakes fell on Tyler's hair and his eyelashes, and I thought he was so gorgeous when he turned and smiled at me. "This will melt by morning," he said.

"Probably," I agreed. "But for right now it's awesome."

Like us.

My roommates were gone. Jessica had left for the weekend. Her cousin was getting married and she was a bridesmaid. Kylie was tucked up in Nathan's bed, where she had been nonstop since Sunday.

Tyler and I were alone.

And I had condoms. I had bought them that afternoon, as an insurance policy, knowing we were going to be alone. They were sitting in my top desk drawer, and I had opened it to stare at them about five times, anticipation swirling through me in the form of both giddy excitement and arousal.

Tyler kicked off his damp boots by the door and shook his hair so that the snowflakes scattered. "Damn. Even I have to admit it's cold out there. Come here and warm me up."

He pulled me close to him and we kissed, the familiar feel of his lips pressed against mine tugging at my insides. I knew I was in love with him, and I knew that I wanted to feel him completely, intimately. I wanted to share with him what I hadn't ever shared with anyone else. The mood felt right. We were in sync, our talk at the coffee shop giving me the confidence to show my hand—or at least the condoms.

So when he peeled my coat off and dumped it on the floor, I kissed him eagerly, running my hands down over his chest, and yanking his shirt up to feel the smooth hardness of his muscular body.

"Rory," he murmured after we had stood there making out, our hips bumping into each other, breathing getting louder, lips moist and swollen. "Are you sure no one is coming back here?"

"Positive."

"Come lay down." He led me to my bed, and he yanked his shirt off over his head before he pulled my comforter back and nudged me down onto the mattress.

"Wait," I whispered. "In my desk drawer."

"What?"

"Go in my desk drawer," I repeated, pointing past my head as he hovered over me.

He did, and he made a small sound in the back of his throat. "Shit, Rory. Are you sure?"

"Yes." I had never been more sure.

Taking a deep breath, he pulled the box of condoms out and set them on the bed next to my head. Then he kissed me, hard, with an intensity that almost swallowed me. We had never been naked together, Tyler always staying in his jeans, me almost always completely dressed, his hands infiltrating from necklines and waistbands and under hems to touch me. But now he dragged my shirt up and off over my head, my hair spilling out across the pillow. As he kissed me, he undid my bra and slipped it off with an ease that surprised me. No fumbling. But I didn't have time to worry about the implications of that because when his bare chest touched mine for the first time, I gasped, amazed that the simple brush of his warm flesh against my nipples could be so stimulating, so tingly.

When he undid my jeans and dragged them down with jerky motions, I felt a momentary twinge of self-consciousness, the cool air rushing over my bare thighs and stomach. But then he was touching me again and it didn't matter, nothing mattered but him and the way he made me feel. I reached out and ran my hand along the length of him through his jeans, searching to understand what was going to happen, seeking to give him the same mind-numbing pleasure he gave me.

He swore. "Oh, baby, yeah."

Then he did something I had been curious about and both looking forward to and dreading. His head went between my thighs, and he peeled my panties down over my hips and used his tongue to coax out the most delicious ecstasy I had ever felt. Within a minute, I was digging my fingers into his shoulders and letting out a soft cry, completely stunned at the tidal wave that had just rolled over me.

He smiled up at me over the contours of my body, and I felt overwhelmed, my chest heaving, my fingers shaking as I clenched the comforter, and I said the first thing that came into my head, the thing that was rising in me so quickly I couldn't contain it.

"I love you," I said, as he tore open the box of condoms and pulled out a strip of foil wrappers.

I didn't mean to say it. But it came out. And I meant it.

He froze, his body going completely still. "You don't mean that."

"Yes, I do," I said quietly, because I did. I shouldn't have said it, but I couldn't deny it. That was a lie I couldn't tell.

Tyler shook his head. "You shouldn't."

"Why not?" I asked curiously. I reached for him, tracing my fingers along his jaw as I stared up at him, in wonder at my own emotions, at the beautiful realization that I could in fact love another human being, and that it could feel this good.

His jaw clenched beneath my touch, and his eyes were agonized. "Because . . ."

For a second it seemed he was going to tell me something, but then he collected himself, and pushed back, sitting up. "I can't do this. I'm sorry, but I just can't."

"What?" I asked, stunned.

He was pulling his shirt on, patting his pocket for his keys. He stood up, looking panicked.

When he stood, I realized that he was fully dressed and I was laid out, completely naked, my panties around my ankles. Embarrassment and confusion made my cheeks and body burn. I pulled my underwear back in place and sat up, dragging the comforter in front of my nudity. "Are you leaving? Why?"

His fingers were already prying a cigarette out of his pocket, and he just shook his head at me. "I'll talk to you tomorrow."

Shoving his feet into his boots without lacing them, he left, the door shutting with a loud *snick* behind him, leaving me alone in my empty room. The lamplight from my desk shone behind me, causing my shadow to reflect on the dirty brown threadbare carpet. I could see my messy hair, the outline of my bare shoulder, the lump of the comforter against my chest. Tears squeezed out, silently sneaking down my cheeks.

Then I shot into action. No. It wasn't going to end like this. He wasn't going to leave me here, mortified and wondering what the hell was going on after I had told him that I loved him. Shaking, I pulled on my sweater, not bothering with my bra, and dragged on my jeans. Grabbing my swipe card off my desk I ran out of my room, no coat, no shoes, no dignity.

After almost wiping out on the stairs, lungs aching, I burst through the front door of the dorm and spotted Tyler stepping off the curb to the parking lot. "Tyler!"

He turned and I ran toward him, bare feet sliding in the fresh snow, the shock of the cold making me gasp, teeth chattering from the weather and the trauma of what had just happened.

"Rory, what the fuck are you doing? Where is your coat?"

"How could you do that to me?" I asked, careening to a halt in front of him. "How could you leave me like that?"

He looked away, taking a drag of his cigarette. "I'm sorry, I shouldn't have . . . I just couldn't . . ."

That wasn't any better. I smacked his bicep, surprising even myself with my vehemence. "Do you know how unattractive that makes me feel?"

His eyes widened and he shook his head. "I didn't mean to make you feel that way."

"Well, you did!" I was sobbing now, and I hated myself for it, but I couldn't stop the wrenching sounds from escaping me. "You know I've never had a guy interested in me. You know that I want to be with you. Why would you string me along like this? God, just knowing that my friends paid you to have sex with me and you still can't make yourself do it . . . Jesus, I just want to die from humiliation!"

I hadn't meant to tell him what I knew, but it hurt too much to contain it. I hit him again, feeling betrayed to the depths of my soul. I hated him for making me believe this was something more, and I hated myself for believing it.

His hand grabbed mine, stopping me from pounding into him a third time. "*What*? What do you know about that?"

"I overheard Jess and Kylie when they didn't know I was awake. I know they gave you a hundred bucks to make sure I wasn't a virgin anymore. But clearly you can't even force yourself to be with me."

"I never took the money," he protested, looking horrified. "I never wanted the money, honest to God. You have to believe me! I just went along with their idea because I was genuinely curious about you, I swear, and it was the only way I knew I would get their support. Otherwise, I figured they would try to talk you out of spending time with me."

I hesitated, eyes watery, nose running, further confused. "Bullshit."

"No, it's not!" He tried to take my hand, but I pulled away from him. "I've always been interested in you, from the first time we met, back in August at Nathan's. You were wearing this little floral dress and you looked so scrutinizing, like you saw through everyone's shit, and I was curious. You seemed so different, so interesting. Genuine. Then when we started hanging out, I realized how much I liked you and I knew I couldn't have sex with you right away because I knew you were a virgin and I didn't want you to have a reason to be done with me sooner than later. I was worried that you would get what you wanted, satisfy your curiosity, then be gone."

Was he insane? "You thought I was using you to learn what sex felt like?" I was appalled.

"Well, weren't you?"

"What? No, of course not!" Not really. Maybe sort of, at first. But then it was more than that. "I was curious about you, too."

"Even thinking that I had been paid to have sex with you?"

"Yes." I nodded sharply. "Because it didn't add up. It wasn't logical. If all you cared about was the money then you would have moved as quickly as possibly, maximizing your profits. You wouldn't have bothered to talk to me as much as you did, and you wouldn't have taken things so slow. It didn't add up."

He gave an agonized laugh. "Thank God you're so logical, because you're totally one hundred percent right. It was never about sex for me, it was always about me wanting to be with you, getting to know you."

A flicker of optimism cut through my agony. "So then why couldn't you have sex with me tonight? It sounds like maybe we're both on the same page." Why, why, why? I desperately wanted him to convince me that I hadn't imagined his attention, that he really did care, and I wasn't an idiot to fall in love.

"Because I've been selfish this whole time. I don't have anything to offer you. You are way too good for me. I'm just a guy trying to make life work and I'm dragging you down into my bullshit. It's not right and I hate myself for being so fucking selfish that I'm letting you do this, letting myself do this." He hurled his cigarette off into the snow in anger.

He wasn't the only one pissed off. "Don't tell me what's right for me! You can't decide that for me!" My finger poked him in the chest. "I want to be with you. I have made the choice to spend all this time with you. You didn't force me to do it." My body shook from cold and indignation.

"Rory . . ." His hands raked through his hair and his voice was pleading. "Please . . . just let me do the right thing. For once, just let me do the right thing and stay out of your life."

My heart instantly melted. My anger evaporated. "Tyler," I said softly, going up on my frozen tiptoes to cup his cheeks. "When do you ever *not* do the right thing?"

"What do you mean?" he asked gruffly, head turning slightly into my touch, his eyes tearing into me.

"I mean that you are honestly one of the best guys I have ever met. The question is not whether or not you're worthy of me, the question is if I am worthy of *you*."

"Of course you are," he murmured, hands reaching to snake around my waist, pulling me closer to him. "The truth is, Rory . . . I've fallen in love with you. I love you. And that scares me. I don't want to do the wrong thing. I don't want to be your first and have you regret it later on when you're a doctor and I'm still working at the convenience store."

"You're going to be an EMT," I told him, tears welling again, not from upset this time, but from the overwhelming joy at hearing he loved me. I hadn't even realized how badly I had been wanting to hear him say the words until he had. "And I may not have a lot of experience with relationships, but the one thing I do seem to comprehend is that when there is mutual love and respect, it's usually a good thing, so I'm not getting what you're so worried about. Didn't you just hear me say you're the best man I've ever met?"

For one long moment he just stared at me, then he leaned down and kissed me, hard. "I never stood a fucking chance, did I? You had me the minute I first saw you and I heard you telling the guy next to you that you were premed and that the *Human Centipede* movie is physically impossible."

That alone amazed me. I hadn't even thought he had noticed me, not really, until the night with Grant. "I knew the night you punched Grant. No one had ever stood up for me like that."

"I wanted to kill him. Literally kill him." Tyler squeezed me harder, pulling my body up against his.

"I don't want to talk about him. I want to hear again that you love me," I said, wrapping my arms around his neck. "And I want you to come back upstairs with me."

"Done and done." He kissed me. "I love you."

"I love you, too."

"Now let's go finish what we started."

That worked for me. But when I went to walk, I winced from the sharp pain in my frozen feet. A glance down showed they were bright red. Tyler noticed, too.

"Holy fuck, Rory! Where are your shoes?"

I shrugged. "I was in a hurry."

"Oh my God . . . I'm sorry. I'm so sorry." Then Tyler reached down and swept me into his arms. "I'm sorry, it's my fault." He

kissed me, cradling me in his arms as he walked. "Do you forgive me?"

I snuggled against him, shivering, but thrilled. "Yes, for leaving
without explaining, I forgive you. But running outside without
shoes was my own fault and you can't take the blame for that. It
was my choice."

Given how it had turned out, I wasn't even sorry. Yes, my feet
were burning, but Tyler was coming back upstairs. Tyler was carrying me, in what was definitely the romantic highlight of my life
so far. And Tyler loved me.

Nothing else mattered.

When we got to my room, after ignoring the stares of the three
girls on the elevator, as Tyler set me down onto my still numb feet,
he laid me back on the bed and pulled the blanket over me. "Where
are your socks?" He went over to my dresser.

"It's better if the epidermis adjusts to room temperature slowly,"
I said. "I'll be fine in a few minutes." My feet were already starting
to itch and tingle painfully.

"You sure?" But then he shook his head with a grin and stripped
off his coat and T-shirt and came back to the bed. "Of course you're
sure, who am I kidding? One of the many things I love about you."

The springs creaked as he settled next to me, staring intently
down at me. "I do, you know. Love you."

"I love you, too."

"I want you to enjoy this," he said, hand creeping under my
sweater. "I've never been someone's first, so I hope I can make it
good for you."

His vulnerability always amazed me and only deepened my
feelings for him.

"I know I will," I told him sincerely.

I did.

Tyler took his time stripping off my clothes, peeling down his jeans, sliding our bodies along each other, kissing me everywhere, erasing all the tension and anxious anticipation I felt, so that by the time he pushed inside me, I was ready, in every way that mattered.

There was a sharp sting, and he paused, holding himself over me on his muscular arms, sweat beading on his forehead. "Are you okay?"

I nodded, unable to speak, the sensation new and startling. Nothing could have prepared me for what it would be like, to hold him inside me, and as he moved, I stared up at him and heard the timbre of my voice change, the gasps turn to deep, desperate moans while he stroked me into more pleasure than I had known existed.

"Rory." My name on his lips was raw and intimate.

When he finally fell back next to me, our bodies still joined, his skin slick with sweat, our breathing still exaggerated, I wasn't sure what to say, but for the first time, I realized that words don't always tell everything. That my fingers brushing across his hip, my lips caressing his jaw, could speak for me.

"I don't ever want to be with anyone but you," he murmured into my hair, kissing my temple.

I could feel my smile in the dark. "Are we Facebook Official then?"

"We're more than that. We're the real deal."

"True," I said, sliding my foot over his. "We are."

CHAPTER FOURTEEN

"HI, DADDY!" I SAID CHEERFULLY TO THE IMAGE OF MY FATHER on my computer. "How are you?"

He smiled at me, in the kitchen this time, no sign of Susan. "You sound like you're in a good mood."

I laughed and prayed I wasn't blushing. It was Sunday, and I had spent basically every minute in my twin bed with Tyler when he wasn't at work. I felt like I was bursting with love, excitement, and newfound knowledge. I crossed my legs and hoped none of the above was written all over my face.

"Yeah, I, uh, want you to meet someone," I told him. I gestured to Tyler to get in front of the computer with me. He did, coming behind my chair and bending over and giving my cheek a kiss. I giggled. God, I wasn't normally a giggler. So ridiculous. So freaking happy. "This is my boyfriend, Tyler."

Saying *boyfriend* made my insides feel like marshmallows in hot chocolate, ooey and gooey.

It didn't seem to have the same result on my dad. His mouth

fell open and his eyes widened. I realized that maybe I should have eased him into the idea, but I always talked to him on Sundays, and I had no intention of letting Tyler go home a minute sooner than he had to. Hence the introduction.

Tyler gave a wave at the screen. "Hi, Mr. Macintosh. You have a really cool daughter."

My dad's brow furrowed. "Yes, I know. Thank you."

"Nice to meet you. I'll let you talk to Rory." Tyler went over to my bed and picked up the Cormac McCarthy book he was reading.

I smiled sheepishly at my dad, who was looking like he'd taken a blow to the head. "So what's new with you, Dad?"

"Uh, nothing. Just the usual. Work, home," he said, sounding distracted. "Hey, hon, I just remembered I need to do something. Would you mind calling me tomorrow?"

When you're alone, was clearly implied.

"Sure. Love you."

"I love you, too." I disconnected the call and looked over at Tyler, who glanced up from his book.

"That was short."

"I guess I should have warned him," I said, feeling bad. But not bad enough to ruin my mood. I was basically on an endorphin high, and I was well aware of it. "But I'll call him later, it will be fine."

Tyler tossed his book aside. "Want to take a shower?"

Goosebumps rose on my skin as I sat at my desk, watching him. "You mean, like together?"

"Yes, together. I'm not saying you need a shower. I just want to take one with you." Then he grinned. "Though I probably need one. I've been getting a workout."

I blushed, knowing exactly what he meant by that. "Okay," I

said, even though the thought of standing naked with Tyler terrified me. It was so . . . personal. Which I knew was stupid, given what we had already done, but it seemed different. There would be lights on and I would be totally exposed. But despite feeling suddenly shy about it, I wanted to experience everything with him.

After locking the door to my suitemates' room, and the door to my room, Tyler turned on the water before kissing me. "Now don't go getting any ideas—this isn't about sex. I need some recovery time, so don't be all up in my business in there," he said, giving me a mock-strict look of warning.

"Then maybe you should just shower first, then I'll go after," I teased.

"No, no. That's not environmentally friendly. We'll just have to make it work." In seconds he had his clothes completely off, with a total lack of modesty that I wished I could achieve.

"I've never done this before," I said, fiddling with the waistband of my sweatpants.

"I know." Tyler kissed me softly. "And honestly, that's the hottest thing ever. You don't have to do this."

"I want to." I did.

Nervously, I shucked my own clothes and stood awkwardly, fighting the urge to cover my various bits with my hands. But Tyler pulled me into the shower and straight into his embrace, the hot water sluicing over us.

"God, you feel so good," he murmured.

He was right. It felt intimate and warm, our hands trailing over each other's bodies, exploring, learning each other. I was curious about his piercing, and I splayed my hand over the length of him, then toyed with the metal ring, glancing down through the streaming water at it, enjoying the immediate reaction my touch brought.

His body was so different from mine, so much hard to my soft, that he was fascinating. I could touch him all day and never be tired of all that firmness.

"Rory." His hands tensed on my shoulders. "What are you doing? Damn, you're killing me."

"Why did you get this?" It seemed incredibly painful to have a rod jammed through your privates.

He shrugged. "I don't know. Seemed like it might be cool. And maybe I just wanted to see if I could handle the pain."

"So it hurt?"

"Like a motherfucker. But also it's my understanding it increases pleasure for my, uh, partner, and I figured that could only be a good thing, right?"

"I suppose."

"Does it feel good to you?"

I thought about that, moving my hands to his chest so I could look up at him, into his dark eyes. "I don't know," I told him honestly. "I have no comparison. So yes, it feels good, really good, but does it feel 'more good' than it would without the piercing? Well, I can't exactly say, can I?"

He grinned. "Spoken like a true scientist. Maybe one of these days I'll take it out but I won't tell you, and I'll see if you notice. It'll be like a blind taste test."

I laughed. "That doesn't sound right."

"You know what sounds right?"

"What?"

"I love you."

I would never get tired of hearing that. Ever. "I love you, too."

Steam rose around us as we kissed, and I forgot all about my nervousness. I forgot about everything but him.

* * *

WHEN JESSICA GOT BACK FROM THE WEDDING WEEKEND, SHE looked exhausted, dumping her suitcase down on the floor and crawling into bed, clothes and coat still on. "God, my family wears me out."

"I'm sorry," I said, but my voice sounded more perky than sympathetic.

She noticed immediately. "What's up with you?" she asked, rolling onto her side and studying me. "You look hopped up on caffeine."

"No. I'm just, you know, happy. Tyler and I are officially boyfriend-girlfriend."

"Really?" Her eyebrows went up. "Wow. Cool. Good for you."

"Thanks, Jess." I grinned, hugging myself.

Kylie came into the room, grinning. "Hey!" She flopped down on Jessica's bed next to her. "Sigh. What an awesomely, fantastic, magical, wonderland, super-amazing weekend. God, I love Nathan."

Jessica rolled her eyes. "Can you go on Rory's bed and gush with her, please? I'm tired. You two can be in love with love together."

Kylie jumped up and ran over to me. "Are you in love?"

I nodded, feeling ridiculous and thrilled and so far out of my element, yet sharply aware of being alive. "Tyler and I are dating for real. Like you and Nathan."

She let out a shriek and grabbed my hands, spinning me around until I was dizzy. "That's awesome!"

We laughed and twirled and I felt carefree in a way I wasn't sure I had ever experienced before, but that I definitely did not want to let go.

* * *

ON TUESDAY WE WERE AT TYLER'S, AND I WAS ATTEMPTING TO bake a pie from instructions pulled up on my phone. I was leaving the next day to go home for Thanksgiving, and I had wanted to make something that smacked of Turkey Day for Tyler and his brothers before I left, knowing full well they would not be having a traditional meal like the majority of America. I did cheat and buy a ready-made crust, but as I studiously measured ingredients, I marveled at how disgusting canned pumpkin smelled.

"That looks like cat barf," Jayden told me, leaning over my shoulder to look into the bowl.

"I know. But trust me, it's going to taste good."

"If you say so," he said doubtfully.

Tyler was sitting at the kitchen table helping Easton with his homework, and their mom was nowhere to be found. She hadn't told anyone where she was going. The boys had come home from school and she wasn't there, so there was no telling when she might show up. It made me nervous, I wasn't going to lie. Somehow I didn't think she would be thrilled to see me in her kitchen baking a pie. But I was determined to at least try, and if she came home and freaked, I would just leave.

"My dad's girlfriend is a really good cook," I told Jayden. "She makes six different pies for Thanksgiving."

"We had pie at the shelter last year," he said. "It was apple."

"The shelter?" I asked, though I knew what he meant. I just didn't want to believe it.

"Yeah, they give you free food on Thanksgiving."

"You're not doing that this year," Tyler said from the table, his jaw set. "You know I'm pissed Mom took you there. We can afford our own food. She's just fucking lazy. It's not right when there are people who really need it."

Knowing full well that Tyler's mother spent most of her disability checks on drugs, I figured they probably did need it, but Tyler had his pride.

"She made me go," Jayden protested, looking confused and miserable. He pushed his glasses up.

"I know, bro. I'm not mad at you. I'm mad at her."

The back door opened and a guy walked in who looked enough like Tyler to make it clear this was his older brother, Riley. He was a little shorter, a little broader, but they had the same nose, the same eyes.

"You're mad at Mom? So what the fuck else is new?" He reached out and fist bumped Jayden. "Hey, dude, what's up?" He reached over and ruffled Easton's hair. "Hey, little man."

Tyler got a cuff on the back of the head. Hard. Tyler stood up, clearly prepared to challenge him, both of them grinning, like this was normal.

But Riley had turned his attention to me and the bowl. "Hey, what's this? There's a chick in the kitchen and she's cooking? Someone call the cops, she's clearly an escapee from a mental institute."

"Hi," I said, disarmed by Riley. He was more jittery than Tyler, his smile more superficial.

"This is Rory, my girlfriend," Tyler told him. "So don't be a dick."

"Me?" Riley put his hands on his chest in mock protest. When he peeled off his flannel jacket, I saw he had a tattoo identical to Tyler's on his bicep. He put his hand out. "Nice to meet you, Rory. I'm Riley."

"Nice to meet you, too." We shook and it was a hard grip, one that didn't seem to notice or care that I was a girl. I wasn't sure if I liked that or not.

"What are you making?"

"Pumpkin pie." I added the pumpkin spice and cinnamon to the mixture.

His jaw dropped. "No shit?" He shot a grin in Tyler's direction. "Damn, brother, you done good."

Tyler looked torn between being pleased and annoyed.

"You got any friends you could fix me up with?" Riley asked me. "That cook? Preferably blond?"

"Don't answer that," Tyler said. "None of your friends deserve to be subjected to this asshole."

Riley opened his mouth to make an undoubtedly smart-ass response to Tyler when Easton spoke at the table. "Knock knock," he said.

Everyone looked at him, clearly surprised. "What?" Riley asked.

"Knock knock."

"Who's there?" Tyler asked, looking amused.

"Screw."

"Screw who?"

"Screw you," Easton said with a grin, the first one I'd ever seen him sport. When he smiled like that, he looked like he belonged with his brothers, and it made me laugh.

It had the same effect on everyone else, too. They all laughed, Jayden yelling, "Oh my God, so stupid!" as he snorted in amusement.

Easton looked pleased with himself. I didn't think it was often that he got to be center stage, and I empathized with him. He was more like me at that age than I imagined his brothers were.

"So what is the occasion?" Riley asked, watching me pour the liquid filling into the piecrust.

"Thanksgiving is Thursday," Tyler told him.

"I know that, idiot. I'm working a side job since I have the day off."

"Yeah? Good money?"

"Yep. Getting a couple hundred to do a garage roof. So this is a Thanksgiving pie?" He looked like he was having a hard time processing the concept.

"Yeah, since I won't be here," I told him. "I wanted to make something and leave it for the boys."

"You won't be here, Rory?" Jayden asked, looking disappointed.

I knew I had already mentioned that, but he must have forgotten or chosen to ignore it. "No. I'm going to my dad's for the weekend." I felt guilty even saying it. I knew that my day was going to be completely different from theirs, and it broke my heart. So before I realized what I was doing, I said, "You should all come with me. For the day, for dinner. It's only an hour away."

Jayden's and Easton's faces lit up. "Can we?" Jayden asked Tyler. But Tyler was already shaking his head. "No."

"Why not?" Jayden gave him a pleading look. "Rory asked us."

"Yeah, but Rory didn't ask her dad, and I doubt he wants three strays he's never met showing up on his doorstep for handouts."

"It's not a handout," I protested, feeling hurt that my gesture was being thrown back in my face. "You're my boyfriend. When people date, they spend holidays with each other's families and no one thinks of it as charity. It's what you do."

The argument had struck a chord with him. He knew he was being proud and stubborn. So he tried another angle. "You can't spring this on him at the last minute. They'll run short on dinner rolls."

"Susan always cooks twice as much as anyone can eat. Her parents will be there, too, and my aunt Molly." I slid the pie into the oven and set the timer. "It's pretty boring being the only one under forty. I could use the company."

"Please?" Jayden asked. "Rory says there's six pies there."

Tyler gave his brother a rueful look. "You're such a food whore. And no. I don't have the gas money."

"I'll give you fifty bucks," Riley says. "Take the boys and go have a decent dinner for a change."

I glanced over at Riley, both surprised and pleased. "You're welcome, too, you know."

He gave me a smile. "Thanks, I appreciate the offer, but I'm good. I don't want to pass this job up."

"Mom will freak out," Tyler said to Riley.

But his brother shrugged. "Mom will always freak out, bro. Can't do anything about that. Might as well get yourself some pie and deal with her bitching. Better than missing out on it and still having her at you."

Tyler nodded. "Yeah, you have a point." He looked at me, still frowning. "Are you sure? You should call your dad first."

"I will later. It's fine," I assured him, though I didn't really know that for a fact. This was uncharted territory for me. I had never invited anyone, male or female, to any family function. Dad would probably be so stunned he wouldn't know how to say no. Either that, or curiosity over Tyler would compel him to agree.

Slowly, he looked at his brothers, then at me. "Alright. Thanks, babe. That's really sweet of you."

Jayden whooped in triumph.

Tyler pulled me down onto his lap and kissed me. "I hope you don't regret this," he murmured in my ear. "The Mann boys don't have the best manners."

"It'll be fine," I repeated, because I wanted it to be. I kissed him.

"Does this mean we can eat pie today?" Easton asked.

Riley let out a snorting laugh. "I know someone who will be."

Nice. I fought the urge to squirm.

Tyler threw a lighter at him. "Shut up."

Riley caught it. "Yeah, that's going to hurt me." He used it to light a cigarette he pulled out of his pocket. "Welcome to the jungle, Rory. We take it day by day."

THE LOGICAL STRATEGY WAS NOT TO CALL MY DAD BUT TO call Susan, which was precisely what I did. I figured she was the cook, so technically she was hostess. She was the one who would have to make adjustments to her meal plan and shopping, not my dad, so it made complete and total sense to ask her instead of having him spring it on her last minute or something.

I was also terrified my dad would say no.

He had asked a bunch of probing questions about Tyler on the phone on Monday, and had commented in a faux-jovial tone that he supposed all the kids were into tattoos these days, making it obvious he in no way approved.

So I was calling Susan.

"Hey, Rory, how are you?" she asked when she answered her cell phone.

One of the things I liked best about her was that she was good at being neutral. If she was surprised I had called her, which I never did, she didn't show it. She also always managed to express interest without it sounding like concern. If I had been forced to deal with someone who was trying too hard, continually asking me if I was okay, I would have had a much harder time accepting a third person inserted into our Macintosh household.

"I'm great, thanks. How are you guys? Is Dad having a mental breakdown about Tyler?" I asked, because I was fairly sure he was.

Susan laughed. "He's . . . adjusting. He's not used to the idea of you dating."

"But he was always asking me if I was seeing anyone," I protested, as I cut across the quad, the remaining soggy leaves on campus clinging damply to my boots.

"Yeah, well, that's a man for you. Wanting it and the reality of it are two totally different things. Besides, I think your dad expected you to date someone more like him. A button-up-shirt kind of guy."

"Well, that's really egotistical of him," I said, amused. "Though I suppose I always figured I would end up with a nerd. But you can't really plan these things." I felt wise and philosophical about the whole thing.

"No, you can't. The irony is that your dad and I don't look like we belong together either, but of course he doesn't see the parallels. I'm sure once he recovers from the muscle tone and the tattoos, he'll be fine."

Good thing he didn't know about the penis piercing. That would give him a heart attack. Or the fact that I had seen the penis piercing. I grinned, glad Susan couldn't see me. "I hope so. Tyler is a great guy."

"By the way, I'm going to suggest that you and I have a quick obligatory birth control conversation right now, so that I can tell your dad we did. Then he won't attempt to have that conversation with you himself, thus resulting in mortifying all of us on Thursday and him popping seventeen antacids. I want him to enjoy dinner, and I don't want you humiliated in front of the whole family."

"Oh, God," I said, horrified. "He wants to talk to me about birth control?"

"Unfortunately, yes. So let's nip this in the bud. Are you using it?"

I didn't see any reason to deny what we were doing, and we were being safe. So I told her truthfully, "Yes."

"Okay, perfect. We're good, then. I'll tell your dad we had a lengthy heart-to-heart and we bonded and that you're not sleeping with Tyler at this point."

I laughed. "Great idea."

"Because really, is it any of his business? Not particularly."

"Um, it's not." There were some things you just didn't need to share with your father. Like how late Tyler had kept me up the night before, doing quiet and delicious things to me under my comforter while my roommates slept.

Redirecting my thoughts, I reminded myself there was a point to this conversation. "So, do you mind if Tyler comes for dinner on Thursday?"

"No, of course not. I think that's a great idea, actually. What about his family? Does he live too far away to go home?"

"No. He actually lives right here in Cincinnati. But he doesn't exactly have a standard home life. His mom is a bit of a mess," I said, trying to downplay the truth. "And he basically takes care of his younger brothers. Soooo . . . can they both come, too?"

In true Susan fashion, she didn't change tone at all. "Sure. How old are they? The older they are, the more meat they eat, in my experience. Little guys just like corn and bread."

"Seventeen and ten."

"Perfect. Are you still coming tomorrow?"

"No. I'll just come Thursday morning with Tyler. That way Dad doesn't have to drive down here tomorrow and pick me up. He can just take me home on Sunday." I adjusted my backpack and squinted against the sun. "Should I call him and tell him?"

"I can pass it on. See you Thursday."

"Thanks, Susan."

When I hung up the phone, I changed my mind and decided to call my dad. He shouldn't have to hear secondhand from Susan. That wasn't fair. It had just been me and him for a decade, and I didn't want our closeness to shift and fade away.

But it was his voice mail, so I left a message.

Thursday morning I realized that he had never actually called me back.

CHAPTER FIFTEEN

"WHOA, RORY, THIS IS WHERE YOU LIVE?" JAYDEN ASKED FROM the backseat as we pulled into my neighborhood. "Holy crap, you must be rich."

"No. Just middle class," I said, feeling awkward at his awe. I tried to see the subdivision through his eyes, not mine. To me, it was just a regular suburban neighborhood of houses built in the mid-nineties, fake colonials with brick fronts, vinyl siding wrapping around the rest. The houses weren't on top of one another, but they were close, though the builder had snaked the streets to give the illusion of privacy. There were five floor plans, and only on rare occasion did some wacky homeowner deviate from the holy trinity of shutter colors—black, burgundy, or hunter green.

It was all very ordinary. Basketball hoops and cul-de-sacs and perfectly edged front lawns. At any given moment from March to October, there was a middle-aged man taming his minimal plot of land into a perfect emerald postage stamp, with conical bushes and staggered foliage, so something was always in bloom. Women planted flowers. Kids traveled up and down drives on scooters.

At ten, I had assumed everyone except poor people in Africa lived that way.

By twelve or thirteen, I had a slightly expanded view of the world, and by eighteen, had considered myself knowledgeable of the plight of America's working poor.

But until I rode through my own childhood neighborhood in Tyler's dilapidated car and saw those streets through Jayden's eyes, I hadn't really understood. This felt alien to them, I could sense it in the tension that rose in the car. This felt unattainable. This felt like it was mocking them.

"Maybe I should have worn a tie," Tyler said wryly.

"You don't have a tie," Easton told him from the backseat. "Do you?" The idea seemed to intrigue him.

"No." Tyler lit a cigarette as he turned down the street I pointed to. "And I don't want to."

I recognized that tone. His jaw was set and he was dragging hard on his filter, blasting the smoke back out. He was uncomfortable. It made me uncomfortable. I wanted this to be fun for them, for me, not something everyone was dreading.

"This street is called Chamomile Court? Is that for real? What's one block over, Lavender?"

I didn't say anything, because he'd put me in a position where nothing I could say would be right. If I mocked it along with him, I was mocking my upbringing, which I didn't think I needed to apologize for. If I tried to put a positive spin on it, it would just irritate him.

There was no question that Chamomile Court was a stupid

name for a street. But there were a lot of stupid street names. There were whole blogs dedicated to Butt Hole Lanes and Divorce Ct. signs, right alongside intersections like Love Lane and Disaster Drive.

Whatever.

Maybe Tyler realized his mood had altered mine because for most of the drive up from Cincinnati, we had all been laughing and talking, and now I was silent. His hand snaked over and linked through mine. Sometimes I still stared in awe at our hands entwined, amazed that we were together. Our relationship felt like a Christmas gift that you hadn't asked for and weren't expecting to receive, but the minute you saw it, you knew it was perfect for you.

"Don't worry," I told him finally, brushing his skin with my thumb. "They'll like you." I pointed to the beige house with the red brick facing. "This one."

I expected him to protest, say that he wasn't worried, but instead he just gave me a half smile and pulled into the driveway.

"Is this it?" Jayden asked, sounding excited. He was wearing an extremely beat-up army jacket, a faded red Coca-Cola T-shirt, multiple braided and cloth bracelets, and a beanie. He looked like a Portland hipster, while Easton looked like he was color-blind. He was wearing an orange shirt and turquoise blue jeans. I had a feeling they had been a thrift-store purchase from the girl's department. I kind of enjoyed seeing that the younger brothers had clearly defined themselves separate from Riley and Tyler, who looked like they would fit in at a party with a crowd of Ultimate Fighters on their day off. Lots of black and chains.

Then there was me, dressed in another one of my supershort floral dresses, with thick tights and boots, a knit beret on my head.

We would make a fantastic flash mob, because no one would ever suspect the four of us were together.

I led them into the house through the garage, calling out, "I'm home," moving through the laundry room and into the kitchen.

The house smelled like Thanksgiving should, of roasting turkey, cinnamon, and wine. Susan was at the island, vigorously chopping something. "Hey! Happy Thanksgiving."

"Happy Thanksgiving. Susan, this is Tyler, Jayden, and Easton. Guys, this is Susan, my dad's girlfriend."

She wiped her hands on a towel and lamented, "Oh, Lord, I'm thirty-eight, do you know how ridiculous I feel being called someone's girlfriend?" She came around and shook each of their hands with a smile. "Nice to meet you all. We're so glad you could join us."

"Well, I'm forty-eight, how do you think being called your boyfriend makes me feel?" my dad said from the family room, standing up. "And no, I did not like it when you spent a month testing out the phrase 'manpanion' to everyone. It made me feel like your health aide."

"You could get married!" Susan's mother called from the couch. "That would solve the whole damn problem."

"I'm sorry I brought it up," Susan said ruefully.

My dad came over and hugged me. "Hey, sweetheart."

He then eyed Tyler with unguarded curiosity. When he shook Tyler's hand, I noticed his nose wrinkle up. He could smell the cigarette smoke on Tyler's clothes, and he looked none too pleased about it. Tyler was smiling, but it was forced, defensive.

"Thanks for bringing Rory home," my dad said.

"Thanks for letting us crash your family dinner," Tyler said. "That's really cool of you."

Leaving them to eyeball each other, I went over and said hi to

Susan's parents and my aunt Molly, who emerged from the dining room with another bottle of wine, glancing at me like she'd never seen me before in her life. I saw that she and Susan each already had a glass of red wine. My aunt was what I'm positive my father always feared I would morph into. She was superintelligent, with a PhD in physics, extremely quiet, interjecting random comments usually totally unrelated to the current topic. She wore sweaters that would fit a 300-pound man, and when she dyed her hair, she forgot to wipe the color off her forehead and ears after shampooing. She seemed locked in an internal Boltzmann constant equation, trying to bridge the gap between the outside macro world and the micro world of her brain.

Becoming Aunt Molly was my greatest fear as well. The truth was, my dad might have become as eccentric as his sister if he hadn't met my mother. He had been a TA for a chem professor when she was an undergrad, and by all accounts, including my own memories, she had been very social. They had been a couple of unpaired electrons until they had met, my father had always joked. Which never made any particular sense to me since electrons were composed of multiple atoms, which made them sound like a foursome, at bare minimum. Or was he saying that together they were reactive? It would have been funnier if he had made a reference to the excited state of atoms, but maybe that was just me.

When I stepped back into the kitchen, I slipped my hand into Tyler's and squeezed it. "Do you guys want something to drink?" Jayden and Easton were standing there looking around with big eyes. Tyler was chewing on his fingernail.

"I'm fine," he told me. "Thanks. Susan, do you need some help?"

This made her smile. "Actually, I could use some help. I need a strong man to pull this turkey out of the oven, and from the looks of it, you fit the bill."

He certainly did.

Though my dad looked put out about the fact.

"Sure, no problem." Tyler went over to the kitchen sink and washed his hands, and I secretly applauded. He had probably earned five points with my OCD father for that.

While Tyler helped Susan with bird retrieval, I took Jayden and Easton into the garage and showed them the little refrigerator stocked full of soft drinks and beer. "Pick whichever one you want from the soft drinks."

"How much are they?" Jayden asked.

I bit my lip so I wouldn't say anything. Sometimes I got really pissed off on their behalf. They shouldn't have to be so suspicious of people giving them something as simple as a drink. "Oh, they're free. My dad bought them all already."

"Cool." Jayden picked an orange drink and Easton picked a straight-up Pepsi.

I took a Diet for myself and grabbed a beer for Tyler. When we got in the house, Jayden wandered over to the TV to watch football. Easton stayed next to me as I held the beer out to Tyler, who had already set the giant roasting pan on the stove top. "Since I was out there," I told him.

He gave me a smile. "Thanks." He looked more relaxed.

"Should I card you?" my dad joked.

Ugh. Way to be obvious. "Dad, he's twenty-two. Don't be weird."

For some reason, this exchange made Tyler grin. "It's okay, babe. The man has a right to question whatever he wants in his own house."

My father looked mollified and shot me a "See?" look.

Maybe Tyler was just glad my dad was being honest. Or maybe he had just needed a minute to adjust to the situation. "So how did you two meet?" he actually asked my father and Susan.

"They met online. Right?" I asked, realizing a second after I said it that I didn't actually know.

"What? Why would you think that?" my dad said to me, looking surprised. "We met at the grocery store. I was the hapless nerd wandering around with a puzzled look on my face in front of the deli counter. Susan insisted I try the prosciutto."

"I seriously did not know that." But I could picture it. I wondered why in three years I had never bothered to ask what it had taken Tyler ten minutes to discover.

"I thought he was so cute," Susan said, pulling an electric carving knife out from under the counter, her blond hair falling in her face. "And he was actually interested in learning something new when I was offering him suggestions. So many people bristle, like you're calling them stupid for trying to help them make a choice. I was just trying to help, and he understood that."

"How did you two meet?" Dad asked, trying to sound casual, but not quite pulling it off.

Technically we had met when Kylie had started sleeping with Nathan. But I told him, "Tyler is my tutor." It was true.

"What?" My dad laughed. "Since when do you need a tutor?" He clearly didn't believe it.

"American Lit might as well be ancient Hebrew to me, so he helps me interpret the books I have to read."

"Really?" Now I had my father's attention. He looked at Tyler with a new respect.

"Yeah, you know how literal I am."

"You come by that honestly."

"Tyler's been really helpful."

"You had a B in the class before we started studying together," Tyler reminded me. "You weren't exactly a failure."

"For these two, a B is a failure," Susan told him.

"Well, I think tutor is too strong a word. We really met through mutual friends and started studying together. She helps me with science and math."

"Are you an English major?" Dad asked.

"No. I wish. I'm in the EMT program. I needed to do something that wouldn't take four years and would guarantee me a job afterward. I do think I'll like it if I can survive all the bio classes."

"He's graduating next semester," I said, hearing the pride in my voice.

"Wow. That's great." Mental gymnastics were going on in my dad's head, clearly.

"What about this guy?" Susan asked, touching Easton on his back as he leaned over the island, staring intently into a terrarium that my dad frequently fussed over. "What grade are you in, Easton?"

"Fifth," he said, his words muffled from his fists shoved into his cheeks as he rested on his elbows.

"Do you like school?"

"No."

"Well, at least he's honest," Dad said, amused.

Tyler wasn't. He didn't say anything, but I could see the thoughtful concern that crossed his face. He worried about his brothers, especially Easton, that was obvious to me. Frankly, he probably had a reason to. Jayden was easy to read, and he seemed like a happy enough teenager, especially under the circumstances. Easton might have a million thoughts running in his head, good or bad, and no one would ever know what they were. Or he might be thinking about a whole lot of nothing. It was impossible to say.

"Are you hungry, Easton?"

He shrugged.

"We are!" Susan's dad, Bob, called from the family room. Jayden had sat down next to him and they seemed to be discussing something about the game. There was lots of pointing on Jayden's part and head nodding from Bob.

Susan's mother, Nancy, was knitting something. I was kind of hoping it was a scarf for me for Christmas. She made those fuzzy circle scarves that were like an acrylic barrier between your skin and the wind.

"Don't be a grumpy old man," Susan told her father. "We're ready to eat. Everyone to the dining room."

As they all shuffled in the direction of the dining room, I picked up a casserole dish of au gratin potatoes. "How are you, Aunt Molly?" I asked. She was staring at the front of my father's refrigerator, water glass ready to fill, but I noticed she wasn't pushing the button.

"Hmm?" She snapped out of it and focused on me. "Oh, fine. Just battling the dragons in the physics department, as usual. How are you?"

"I'm great." I was. With the exception of Jess and Kylie, all my favorite people were in my house. I leaned closer to her. "Isn't my boyfriend cute?" I whispered, curious about whether my aunt even thought in those terms anymore.

Her eyes widened and her gaze shifted across the room to Tyler, who was directing Easton where to sit at the dinner table. "Oh! I suppose so. He certainly is the epitome of masculinity, and females are hardwired to find the strongest males as attractive in order to guarantee their future offspring will have the greatest chance at survival."

Huh. Now there was a completely nonsexy way to think about dating.

"Exactly," I told her, giving up. Hey, for all I knew, there was complete truth to it. I was overly fascinated by Tyler's muscles. I just didn't want to think in those clinical evolutionary terms. I wanted to be a girl and feel giddy and romantic.

There was no danger of me becoming Aunt Molly after all.

I sat between Jayden and Tyler at the table, Easton on Tyler's left, nervously playing with his cloth napkin.

"Why are there so many forks?" Jayden asked me.

"One is for salad, one is for your dinner, and one is for your dessert." I pointed to each one as I spoke.

"Whoa." He looked stressed out.

"Don't worry about it, U," Tyler told him. "Just pick one and stick with it if that's easier."

"No, no. I can do it right." He resolutely took the salad fork and started eating his mixed greens from the bowl Susan had placed on his plate.

The meal went a whole lot smoother than I would have expected. Bob and Nancy were chatty people, and they seemed to enjoy peppering the boys with questions. It gave them more options for conversation, because normally they tried to pry a sentence or two from Aunt Molly then gave up. My father looked triumphant as usual when he carved the turkey, having his big-man moment for the year.

Jayden ate every scrap of food on his plate for two courses, earning appreciative comments from Susan and Nancy. "Would you like more mashed potatoes?" Susan asked him as his finger came out and slid across his plate to clean up the gravy.

I knew Tyler hadn't seen or he would have reprimanded him, but I figured this was probably the best meal of his life, so why ruin it with rules? We had all licked our fingers at one point or another.

Jayden nodded. "Thanks, Mrs. Susan."

I wasn't sure where the title had come from, but Susan seemed to take it as a compliment.

Where Jayden was a bottomless pit, Easton wasn't eating much of anything. Tyler was spending half his time coaxing him to try a bite or two of everything on his plate. Easton slowly licked and chewed the smallest bits it was possible to stab with a fork. They were really glorified crumbs. What he primarily ate was bread and butter, and when the pies appeared, he definitely did not hold back on those. He ate a slice of pumpkin and apple.

He was stuffing a big piece in his mouth when he spoke for the first time since we'd sat down. "Rory made a pie. It was the best ever."

Aww. How sweet was that? "Thanks."

"You baked?" Dad asked me. "Where did you find a place to do that at school?"

"At our house," Jayden said. "Rory cooks for us."

"Just a couple of times," I protested because I didn't want to take more credit than I deserved.

"She's a great cook," Tyler said, giving me a smile. It was the kind of smile that said more than words would. It was a smile that reminded me of all that we had shared with each other, both emotionally and physically.

My heart swelled in the warm dining room, happy that I had found someone who understood me. Who appreciated me.

Though Dad and Susan exchanged a look I didn't like. They looked nervous, both of them.

Probably worried I was going to get pregnant, despite my chat with Susan. Or that my grades were going to slip or something because I was cooking dinner once every ten days. Which was ludicrous. Nothing was going to affect my schoolwork. If I had to sleep less, I would. Because I had always lived on the Dean's List and I had no intention of falling off it.

Trying not to let their looks ruin anything for me, I suddenly realized that Tyler's leg was bouncing up and down wildly. His thumb and fingers were drumming on the table, and he kept reaching for his beer before stopping himself. His face looked pinched.

I suddenly realized he wanted to smoke but knew he couldn't in the house. Or leave the table until someone else did first. He was fighting his nicotine craving in an effort to be polite and make a good impression on my family.

"Are you finished?" I asked, gesturing to his empty dessert plate, only a few crumbs left on it. Jayden was working his way through a second slice of chocolate silk, so I left him alone.

Tyler nodded, so I picked up both my plate and his and stood up. "Tyler and I are going to go for a walk," I announced. "I need some fresh air."

He gave me a grateful look as he stood up.

My father looked at me, surprised, but he just nodded. No one else even seemed to notice.

When we stepped outside after depositing the plates in the dishwasher, my fingers buttoning up my coat, Tyler leaned over and kissed me. "You're the best, you know that?"

"Nope. I had no idea." I smiled up at him as we started down the driveway in the crisp night air, carrying an empty soft drink can for him to drop the butt in when he was done smoking. Littering was frowned upon in the burbs.

Lighting his cigarette, he took a deep breath and sighed. "Damn, that feels good. I don't think I realized how much of an addict I am until I had to sit there for two hours. It was distracting and that pissed me off. Maybe I should think about quitting."

"Obviously if you can do it, you know it would be a good idea for health reasons."

He took my free hand and made a noncommittal sound. "Your dad is trying. I can see this is hard for him, but he's trying."

"Yeah, he's not used to me having a boyfriend."

"I don't think he would care if I was a polo-shirt-wearing guy from an upper-middle-class family. He thinks you can do better."

"No," I protested, even though I suspected it was true. But my father didn't know what a good person Tyler was. "He just needs to adjust to the idea."

Tyler stopped in front of our neighbor's house and stared down at me, cupping my cheek. "You can do better. But I'm too selfish to let you go."

"I don't want you to let me go. Ever."

It was as perfect a day as I could have hoped for, and when Tyler left that night with the boys after watching more football, the backseat filled with leftovers packed by Susan, I sat on the couch with Bob and Nancy and cuddled under a throw blanket, perfectly content.

The feeling lasted almost twenty-four hours, until I got the message that Tyler was in jail.

CHAPTER SIXTEEN

"WAS IT WORTH IT?" DAD ASKED AS SUSAN AND I CAME IN through the garage.

We had decided to brave the Black Friday crowds and go out in pursuit of bargains. Mostly things Susan wanted, with me along for the ride. I pulled off my boots and told him, "It was interesting, that's for sure. Though I fear for humanity."

"Oh, I already feared for humanity. I don't need a bunch of shoving shoppers to tell me that."

"But I got a breadmaker for twenty bucks," Susan said, looking smug. "And a whole stack of dollar DVDs."

"Who uses DVDs anymore?" Dad asked her.

She made a face at him. "This from the man who hasn't bought new towels in twenty years."

I went to the coffeemaker, cold from walking seventeen miles across various parking lots. My phone buzzed in my pocket. It was a text from Nathan.

Why would he be texting me? Worried, I tapped my screen to

unlock it. I hoped that he and Kylie hadn't had some long-distance blowout fight and now he wanted advice.

It was worse.

Can you call me? Tyler in jail, need bail $.

Holy shit. My pulse jumped. What stupid thing had they done? Probably got into a fight at a bar or something. Or maybe he had unpaid parking tickets. Horrified at the image of Tyler going through the booking process, I hit the Call button.

"Hey," Nathan said, answering immediately and sounding breathless. "Can I borrow a hundred bucks to post his bail? It's one-fifty and all I have is fifty bucks."

"Yes." It would put a dent in my bank account, but I had it and that was all that mattered. "What happened? Where are you?"

"I'm at my apartment. How soon can you get here?"

Crap. I turned to see Dad and Susan watching me. I wasn't going to ask them for a ride back to Cincinnati tonight. That was not going to go over well. At all. Especially given the reason.

"Couple of hours. What's the charge?" I asked quietly, trying to decide how much I was going to tell the adults in the room.

"Possession of a controlled substance."

"Possession?" I blurted out in shock, immediately blowing the plan to be vague in front of Dad. "You mean drugs? Holy crap."

"They were his mom's, obviously. I'm not sure what exactly happened because I could only talk to him for about sixty seconds, but he said they were out, and he got approached by a cop in a parking lot. He tried to call Riley, but he's not picking up. I've been trying him for the last half hour and I can't get ahold of him either. I'm going over to the house."

"Where's his mom?"

"Who knows? She didn't get picked up with Tyler so she took off."

Now that was bizarre. How had he managed to get arrested and not her, when at any given moment she was high? "Well, this was clearly a mistake. We'll just have to straighten it out."

Nathan, who had grown up in the same neighborhood as Tyler, sounded dubious. "I don't know about that. Possession is possession, Rory. You can't really get out of it."

"Won't they run a drug test and see he doesn't use any?" It seemed to me there had to be a way to prove that the drugs weren't his.

"I don't know. Look, just get here as soon as you can. Text me."

"Okay, sure. Bye." I took a deep breath and looked at my dad and Susan. I didn't really have a choice. I was going to have to ask for a ride. "Can I have a ride back to school tonight?"

"What? Why? And why were you talking about drugs?" The vein in my dad's temple was pulsing.

"You know how I told you Tyler's mom is a mess? Well, she had a back injury ten years ago and she got hooked on pain pills. It's gotten worse, and while I'm not sure what exactly happened because Nathan didn't know, it sounds like she was with Tyler and the cops pulled them over, and I guess there were drugs in the car. So he was arrested even though he has never used any of that stuff, and I have to get down there and bail him out."

I figured if I didn't stop for breath, I could get my whole explanation out before he freaked out. It didn't seem to matter.

"Your boyfriend was arrested for drug possession?" he roared. "Are you kidding me?"

"No. It's not his fault. He's totally clean. You saw him. He and his older brother are keeping that house together despite his mom."

"So you've been cooking dinner and hanging out in a house where there is a drug addict? Where there are drugs?" His voice was getting louder.

"She's never there when I am. And it's not like there are meth pipes lying around. It's pills. They're in her pockets or whatever."

"Oh my God." My dad ran his hands through his hair and pushed up his glasses. "I can't believe you are being so blasé about this. Do you know the risk you're putting yourself in? I can't believe this. I'm sick to my stomach."

He did look ill. But I felt sick myself. Tyler was in jail. Did my dad not get the significance of that? "Can we talk about this on the drive? I don't want Tyler there longer than he has to be."

Dad shook his head, scoffing in disbelief. "Do you honestly expect me to drive you an hour back down there on your holiday weekend home so you can bail out your druggie boyfriend?"

"Don't be insulting!" I protested. "I just explained the situation to you. It is not Tyler's fault that his mother has problems. He's doing the best he can to take care of his brothers."

"Look, I liked Tyler when we met him yesterday. He seems like a nice kid, and yes, it is admirable that he wants to take care of his brothers. But have you thought about any of this, Rory? What kind of future does he have? Jayden has Down's and he's probably going to need to live with Tyler forever. Easton clearly has a different father, and while he seems sweet enough, he could probably benefit from some therapy. All of that is burden enough, none of which I want you taking on, but now you're telling me that his mother is a complete drug addict? There is no way I want you involved in any of this. Let someone else bail him out."

"His friend Nathan doesn't have enough money," I said through gritted teeth. "His brother isn't picking up. He's probably at work. I can't just leave him there!"

"I'll drive you," Susan said.

My father whipped his head around to face her. "No, you won't! Rory is *my* daughter."

"Who happens to be twenty years old and wants to do the right thing and help a friend. There is plenty of time to offer your opinion about her safety later."

"Susan," Dad said, his voice tight and tense.

Uh-oh. Now they were going to argue over me. Just what I didn't need.

"Don't fight, seriously you guys, I don't want that," I pleaded. "Can I just borrow the car and go down there? I'll bring it back tomorrow, I swear."

My dad clearly grappled with this, but finally he said, "No, I'll drive you. I don't want you driving when you're upset."

"Thanks, Daddy." I went to get my purse and coat.

"Rory?"

"Yeah?" I turned to see him still standing in the kitchen, the skin of his forehead creasing with worry. "Have you thought about the fact that if you were with them, you could be in jail right now, too? It could ruin your life."

I shivered. I hadn't thought about that, no. But then again, I hadn't spent any time around Tyler's mother. Though I had been with him when he was carrying drugs.

"This isn't like getting caught with a beer at a college party. Drug possession is serious."

That's what Nathan had said. I guess I knew it, but I didn't want to consider it at the moment. So I just nodded.

*   *   *

IT WAS A TENSE RIDE BACK TO CINCINNATI. WE WOULD DRIVE
in silence for ten, fifteen minutes, then my dad would suddenly
start lecturing.

"Where does she get her drugs?" he asked at one point. "Are
there drug dealers popping in and out of that house?"

"No." Not that I was aware of. "I think she has a friend who
gets them for her."

"Where does she get the money? Is she stealing or prostituting?"

"She spends most of her disability check on the pills." I actually
suspected that the house was in the process of being foreclosed on,
because I had seen some papers left on the kitchen table last time
I was there, though Tyler hadn't said anything about it.

He snorted in derision. "Of course she does."

"I thought you also said we shouldn't be judgmental of other
people's problems." Not that I intended to defend her, not really. I
hated what she had done to her children because of her addiction.

"Sure. Except that she has jeopardized her sons and now she
has potentially jeopardized my daughter. My sympathy for her is
dried out. There is a little something called rehab if you want to
get help."

I couldn't argue with that. I didn't even want to argue with that.
These were all thoughts I had had myself about Tyler's mother.
While it was easy to understand how her addiction could have
gotten out of control, it wasn't so easy to understand how she
treated her children. Whether or not she was ever physically violent
with Jayden and Easton.

The silence lasted again almost twenty minutes, until it was
punctured with, "You know no EMT department is going to hire

a guy with a prescription-drug conviction. They'll be afraid he'll steal half the drugs off the ambulance."

I looked over at him in the dark, horrified. That had never even occurred to me, but it certainly sounded like a very real possibility. "Oh my God." My lip started to tremble. I started to cry. "Everything he's worked so hard for . . ."

Dad seemed to realize his speculation had gone too far. He suddenly hastened to reassure me. "That's if he's convicted, that is."

We pulled into the circle in front of my dorm. "Can you get your bag yourself, or do you need help?" he asked, the air between us awkward.

"I can get it. It's just a backpack." I had been planning to spend the weekend in pj's or the same pair of jeans. I had packed light, not expecting to come back on Friday. My room was going to be lonely, the dorm eerily quiet with everyone gone for the holiday.

"Let me know what's going on."

"I will. Thanks, Dad. For everything."

Then because I was me, and he was him, we didn't say anything else. That was as emotive as we seemed to be capable of, and as I got out of the car, I was already texting Nathan to let him know I was back. When I glanced back to wave, I saw Dad was on his phone, too, probably calling Susan to do damage repair.

Nathan said he would be there in ten minutes to pick me up, so I went into my room and unpacked my bag, wishing I had a way to contact Tyler's brothers myself. I was worried about them.

Mostly, though, I was worried about Tyler. My main knowledge of prison was gathered from TV and movies, but I didn't think they were unrealistic in portraying it as depressing and violent. I didn't want to picture Tyler there, some hulking guy with an attitude shoving him just for the hell of it. Or worse.

After a few minutes of pacing, I went back downstairs to wait in the lobby. When I saw Nathan pull up in Tyler's car, somehow that only made me feel worse. "We need to go to the money machine," I told him when I got in. "I didn't want to ask my dad to stop."

"What did you tell your dad?" he asked, looking as worried as I felt. His hair wasn't combed, and he was wearing his sweatshirt backward, the tag sticking out under his chin. He looked like he'd been ripped right out of sleep.

"I told him the truth, as much as I know it. He freaked out, of course, but he'll get over it." I hoped. "I'm just glad you answered the phone when Tyler called." Now that I thought of it, I wondered why he hadn't called me. Probably because he'd known I was an hour away without a car.

"I was actually sleeping."

That confirmed my suspicions.

"But for some reason I answered it. Not even sure why I did, but it was a good thing."

"Do you know where we're going?"

"Yeah. I've bailed a person or two out in my time."

"Do you know what the possible sentence is for something like this if he gets convicted?" I asked. I couldn't fathom that he would get prison time, but what did I know about it?

"It's a first-time offense," he said, pulling in to the bank. "So that's good."

That wasn't exactly answering the question, but now wasn't the time to worry about it. He took my card and inserted it into the machine, and I gave him my pin. Twenty minutes later we were walking into the lobby of the police station. I stayed close to Nathan, uncomfortable with the sounds and smell and appearance of the place. It was stark and dingy, with apathetic guards and rude desk clerks. Everyone looked miserable, and it smelled like body odor.

I let Nathan handle all the talking and the paperwork and the payment process. Then we waited on a wooden bench for forty-five minutes while Nathan tried to entertain me with jokes from his favorite comedians. I smiled and tried to give him appreciation for his efforts, but the truth was, I felt like throwing up. This was even more alien to me than the suburbs had been to Tyler's brothers. There was random yelling and psychotic muttering, and the heat didn't seem to be on. I was huddled in my coat, hands jammed in my pockets, wishing I was anywhere but there. Of course, I knew that meant it had to be ten thousand times worse for Tyler, stuck on the other side.

But finally he was let out through an electronic door and he started toward us.

"Rory!" Immediately he glared at Nathan. "What the fuck is she doing here?"

"I only had fifty bucks, man," Nathan protested. "She paid the rest of the bail."

"You didn't have to bring her here though, you idiot."

"You're welcome," Nathan retorted, clearly irritated.

"Why am I not allowed to be here?" I asked, standing up. "And hello to you, too, by the way."

"Because you don't need to be in this shithole." He took my hand and pulled me close to him, glancing around like he thought someone was going to snatch me and toss me in a cell.

When he hit the front door to open it, he was aggressive and angry, the door bouncing off the wall loudly enough that I glanced back, fearful that someone might yell at him or drag him back to jail. Nathan was walking quickly ahead of us, and we all seemed to have the same desire to get the hell out of there. Tyler was practically dragging me, and I stumbled to keep up.

"What happened?" I asked. "What happens now?"

"I may or may not go to jail, that's what happens now."

Fear crawled up my throat. "Are you kidding me? For a few pills on a first offense?"

"I don't use, so my drug test was clean. So that makes me a dealer in the eyes of the law. Why else would I have eight Oxy pills?" He gave a laugh of pure exasperated fury, yanking his car door open so hard it sprang forward and closed again. "God! Fucking God!"

After he kicked the door three times with me standing there, scared for him, maybe even slightly scared *of* him, he took a deep breath and forced himself to calm down. I could see the struggle, feel his tension as he reined himself back in and reopened the door for me. I climbed in and looked up at him, a silent question on my face.

"You know what? It will be fine. Don't worry, babe. It's not enough for a mandatory conviction. Everything is going to be okay." He bent down and gave me a soft kiss on the lips. "Thanks for bailing me out. I'll pay you back."

He didn't smell like Tyler. He had a foreign odor clinging to his hair, his shirt, one of antiseptic and sweaty palms, and I didn't like it. "Don't worry about the money. I don't care. I'm scared for you," I told him truthfully. Being called a dealer sounded really bad. Worse than bad. The end of the world awful.

I thought about what my father had said—how no one would hire a guy with a drug conviction to be an EMT. That was bad enough, that was life altering and plan ruining. But prison time? I couldn't even imagine.

"It'll be okay," he repeated, and he went around the back of the car.

I glanced at Nathan in the backseat and he studiously avoided looking at me, like he knew this was a lie.

"Can we stay at your place tonight?" Tyler asked Nathan. "I refuse to go home until I've calmed down, and the dorms are so empty this weekend they'll notice if I stay in Rory's room."

At least he had included me in the *we*. The last thing I wanted was for him to pull away from me. I had no experience with the legalities of the situation, but I was rational, logical. I could offer advice, comfort. I could feed him, lay down with him. Be there for him.

"Sure."

Tyler pulled out and we drove half a block before Nathan asked, "So how did you end up with the pills on you?"

"My mom went into the store, so she left them with me. Cop comes up to my window and starts giving me shit. Next thing I know he's patting me down and searching my car. Mom conveniently never came back out of the store."

"Your mother let you get arrested for her drugs?" I asked, disgusted. "How could she do that?"

Tyler shot me a look. "Because she knew if she got busted, they'd make her go to rehab, and we all know she doesn't want to do that. Besides, it wouldn't be her first offense. Not by a long shot."

"Why were the cops messing with you anyway?" Nathan asked.

"I don't know." Tyler grabbed his pack of cigarettes off the dash. "And truthfully, I don't feel like talking about it anymore. I just want a shower to wash the smell of loser off me and to go to bed."

"I don't blame you," Nathan said. "When I got picked up for drunk and disorderly, I got stuck in that cell for twelve hours with twenty guys. It smelled like shit and greasy hair."

Gross. Without realizing I was going to, I promptly burst into tears. I didn't want to think about Tyler in a jail cell with low-life criminals.

"Hey, hey," Tyler said, sounding alarmed. "It's okay, baby." He shot a glare at Nathan. "This is why you shouldn't have taken her there, jackass."

Nathan threw his hands up in protest.

"Don't blame him," I said tearfully, wiping at my eyes and trying to get myself under control. "I wanted to be there. I wouldn't have given him the bail money if he had said no."

"You didn't need to see any of that."

"Well, I did." As we pulled onto Straight Street, I stared at his profile. "And I can handle it." Okay, so maybe I had started crying, but it was traumatic. It didn't mean I wasn't capable of hearing or seeing the truth.

The look he gave me was dubious enough to be insulting, but I wasn't going to pursue it. This wasn't the time.

When we went into the apartment, he went straight to the bathroom, immediately turning on the shower. I had half expected that he would suggest I join him, but maybe he didn't want to in front of Nathan. Which was stupid. He wouldn't care what Nathan thought about us being naked together. More likely, he wanted to be alone. Which kind of hurt my feelings. Which made me irritated with myself. I could not be needy about any of this. I was just going to have to pull it together and be strong for Tyler.

Nathan went into the kitchen and opened the fridge. "Want a beer?"

"Yes." Without question. "What time is it?"

"After one."

No wonder I felt so drag-ass tired. I took the beer and popped it open, taking a nice, long sip. My throat felt scratchy, my eyes swollen.

Five minutes later, when Tyler came out of the shower in just his jeans, hair damp, I was nursing the beer and watching TV with Nathan, though I couldn't have told you what I was actually looking at.

"Ready for bed?" he asked me, looking exhausted and angry and sexy all at once.

"Sure." I followed him to Bill's room, too strung out to worry that we were crashing in someone else's bed. We went into the extremely neat room, and I pulled my shoes off. I wouldn't have minded a shower myself, but more important, I wanted to climb into bed with Tyler and rest my head on his chest. I needed that contact, that reassurance.

He stripped off his jeans, pulled back the bedspread, and climbed into bed. When his head hit the pillow, he sighed. I took my pants off, too, and my sweater, leaving my tank top on. I still felt a twinge of shyness walking around naked in front of Tyler, and I preferred for him to peel off my clothes if we were going there.

But he didn't seem interested in more than pulling me close against him. "How did you get back to school?"

"My dad brought me."

"You told him?"

"Yeah, I had to if I wanted to get back here."

Tyler was silent for a second. "Wow, I'm sure he's thrilled to know his daughter is dating a drug dealer and that he let me in his house yesterday."

"You're not a drug dealer."

"Tell that to the judge. And your father. I'm sure he hates me."

Hate was a strong word, but Dad definitely wasn't in a happy place about the whole thing. "He trusts my ability to judge character." I hoped. "If I say you're a good man, he'll believe me."

Tyler sighed, but he didn't say anything. He just kissed the top of my head. "Good night."

"Good night." I tried to close my eyes, but they kept popping back open, thoughts swirling through my head with the velocity of a tornado. Who was staying with Jayden and Easton? I knew that Jayden was almost eighteen, but was he really capable of looking after his little brother? Where was their mother? And how could she let Tyler take the hit for her drug use? It was just incomprehensible.

Tyler's breath slowed and evened out, and he was asleep within five minutes. Sometime much later, my fingers still splayed across his chest, I fell asleep. Only to be yanked out of a dark and dreary dream about locked boxes by Tyler's phone ringing next to me.

He leaned across me and fumbled for it, glancing to see who the caller was. "Hello? Yeah, I'm out, man, thanks." Sitting up, he held the phone away from his mouth and murmured to me, "It's Riley. Go back to sleep, baby." Then he slid out of the bed and readjusted the blankets back over me. He moved across the room, opened the door, and headed toward the living room, speaking quietly. "Rory and Nathan posted bail. Yeah, eight Oxys, charged with possession, and my drug test was clean, so you know what that means. Could be twelve months."

Twelve months? Was he serious? He had reassured me that it

was going to be fine, yet he had known that it was possible he could get sent to prison for a whole year? Tyler moved into the living room and I couldn't hear him speaking anymore, so I sat up and crept over to the door he had almost completely closed. I wanted to hear what else he knew but wasn't inclined to share with me, his suburban girlfriend who cried after seeing the police station lobby.

"Oh, she did it on fucking purpose," Tyler was saying. "I wouldn't be surprised if she called the cops herself."

I sucked in a breath. He thought his mother had set him up.

"He starts giving me some shit about how I didn't use a turn signal and why was I loitering in the parking lot. I told him my mom was in the store and I was waiting for her, and he says I have attitude and to get out of the car. It was bullshit, all of it. I was just parked there, doing nothing."

There was a pause when obviously Riley was speaking. "Well, you know she totally went off when we got home on Thanksgiving. She was fucking pissed that I took the boys to dinner at Rory's. She starts going on about how I think I'm too good to eat in her house and how my rich girlfriend is trying to steal her babies from her. Her usual shit, but now she has a new person to blame, you know?"

Me. She was blaming me.

"She threw the leftovers across the room. It was like a Tupperware grenade, man. Stuffing exploded everywhere." Here he actually laughed, ending it in a cough. "So damn stupid, and actually kind of funny except that she wasted good food. I haven't eaten like that, ever. I'm sorry you missed it."

"When does she ever have that many pills at once, anyway? She usually snorts 'em as fast as she can buy them. Or she buys heroin because it's cheaper. That was five hundred bucks in that bag, so where the hell did she get that money?"

That was a very good question.

"Not that it matters, I guess. All I know is that I'm pretty much fucked. If I'm lucky I'll get off with parole and a fine, but there's no way to know how the judge will go. Not that I have the money for a fine, anyway."

That I could help him with. I wasn't sure how, but I would figure something out. My dad could loan me the money. Which I'm sure would go over big with him.

"Yeah, I'll talk to you later."

I dashed back to bed and slipped in, closing my eyes. My heart was pounding so loudly I was sure he would hear it, but he didn't seem to notice anything out of the ordinary. He just slid back into bed beside me, his thigh warm as it brushed mine. But he didn't go back to sleep. I could tell he was looking at something on his phone because the blue screen was squintworthy with its glaring false light when I cracked my eyes.

"What are you doing?" I whispered.

He glanced over at me. "Sorry. I didn't mean to wake you up. Just playing a game." He slapped his phone back down on the nightstand.

Except he hadn't been playing a game. He had been doing a search on mandatory sentencing for drug convictions in Ohio. It may have been three in the morning, but I had 20/20 eyesight.

That he was worried, worried me.

I couldn't think about it or my head would explode.

"I'm wide awake." My hand snaked down his chest to below his waist. "And I want you."

It was probably the boldest thing I'd ever said to him, and he reacted exactly as I had hoped he would. He gave a low moan and rolled over on top of me, already tugging my tank top up as he kissed me.

I wanted to hold him close to me, to feel that deep intimate connection, to be alone with him, without our fear and thoughts crowding in.

He clearly felt the same way because he was rougher, more demanding than he had been so far, as if he could release his frustration with sexual desire. "Get on top," he demanded after a few minutes inside me. "Ride me."

Keeping us entwined, he flipped over, dragging me with him so I ended up on his chest, hair falling into my eyes. He brushed it back, tucking it behind my ears.

"Sit up," he urged, his eyes shining with something I didn't understand.

I did as he asked, pushing off his chest, finding my footing with the unfamiliar position, feeling powerful in how I was pleasing him. Tyler put his large hands over top of mine, holding me tightly in place.

Our movement, our emotions were frantic, urgent, deep and passionate.

I knew that no matter what, I had turned a corner and I couldn't go back.

I was deeply, madly, truly in love, so much so that it almost hurt.

CHAPTER SEVENTEEN

THOUGH I TEXTED MY DAD TO TELL HIM EVERYTHING WAS OKAY, I didn't call him until I got back to my room on Sunday. It was not exactly a fun conversation. I tried to downplay everything.

"So, he has to have a hearing, but it's a first offense. I'm sure it will be no big deal."

My dad wasn't buying it. "I did some research. If he isn't a drug user, then he gets charged as a dealer and the penalties are more severe."

Damn it. Why did everyone seem determined to cram that depressing bit of information down my throat?

"There's no point in speculating," I told him, which was a ridiculous thing for me to say. I was the absolute queen of speculation. It was my nature to assess something from all angles and categorize all possibilities. Being methodical was normally my path to sanity. If you imagine all the potential outcomes, then you have hypothetically faced the worst-case scenario and you are more mentally prepared if it occurs, which is usually unlikely—like thinking the knock at the back door is a serial killer instead of your next-door neighbor asking if you've seen her missing dog.

In this case, however, it was statistically likely that the worst-case scenario would become reality, and the idea of Tyler sitting in prison for twelve months was something I couldn't even allow to enter my brain for more than a half second or I would go insane.

"I just want you to be realistic," he said. "There will be a punishment of some kind—there is no question about that."

Dad of Doom. Geez.

"What do you want for Christmas?" I asked him, in arguably the most obvious attempt to change the subject in recorded history.

"For my daughter to not be dating a drug dealer."

Subtle. Dad brought it full circle. Foiled at my own game.

Irritated that he insisted on referring to Tyler as a drug dealer, I told him I had to go, and he didn't even attempt to draw out the conversation.

Team Macintosh was experiencing in-house fighting.

MY ROOMMATES WERE SUITABLY HORRIFIED AND SYMPATHETIC in a way that was much more satisfying. They took Tyler's side and called his mother nasty names, which I appreciated because then I didn't have to be the one who said them. It seemed morally cleaner that way.

"What was jail like?" Kylie asked Tyler as we sat around playing beer pong on Sunday night, though I was fake playing because I had an early class.

It was a tactless question, but she was that girl—she never realized she had said something rude until after the fact.

Tyler was drunk. I'd never really seen him loaded, and wow, was he wasted. Like slurring words, stumbling, glassy-eyed, shit-faced drunk. Before the beer, I had seen him take four shots of Jack Daniels in a very short amount of time.

"It was like watching two unicorns fucking," he told her. "All glitter and jizz."

"What?" she asked, frowning in confusion. She looked to me for guidance, but I had no idea what he was talking about.

Tyler and Nathan seemed to think this was very funny and tried to fist bump, only missed. This made it even funnier.

"You guys are weird," Jessica said, attempting to put her hair into a topknot, but only succeeding in creating a sloppy bun.

Nathan's roommate Bill was back in the apartment and he was almost as drunk as Tyler, mentioning that he and his girlfriend had broken up the day before. "I don't ever drink," he told me for the fourth time. "I'm so fucked up."

When people say it isn't all that fun to be sober when everyone around you is drunk? They are one hundred percent correct. I was tired and I felt impatient with the conversation, or really lack thereof. It made sense to me that Tyler needed to blow it out, given what had happened on Friday, but I felt the opposite. I just wanted to crawl into bed and sleep for about three days to avoid the reality of the situation, not drink myself into a fuzzy stupor.

I was clearly in the minority.

After another hour, I realized there was no way we were getting back to the dorm unless I drove Tyler's car, and even that seemed unlikely since I wasn't sure I could shoehorn a drunk Jessica into the car without help. And no one in the room was in any position to assist me in anything other than making me feel good about my ability to pronounce my *T*s and *S*s.

It was decided that Jessica could share Bill's bed, and Tyler and I would sleep on the couch. Which meant that I was crammed against the back cushions in approximately twelve inches of space, while Tyler snored loudly, out cold. Every time he moved, he pulled the blanket off me, and I was in and out of a restless sleep, cold and stiff.

Which was why I was actually awake when he rolled toward the coffee table and vomit shot out of his mouth.

Holy crap. I leaped over him and ran for the kitchen wastebasket. Angling it under him, I held it, stroking his head while he heaved over and over. "It's okay," I told him, adopting a soothing voice I used on agitated stray animals that needed grooming. "You're okay."

"Fuck," he said finally, wiping his mouth and falling back onto the couch, his eyes watering. He gave a weak cough.

I tied off the trash bag to minimize the smell and got him a damp paper towel. I swiped it across his face. He grabbed it from me, annoyed. "I got it."

He turned his back on me, and I was forced to take the edge of the couch, which was worse than the interior I soon discovered. I woke up on the floor twice before rousing Tyler at seven in the morning.

"Tyler, I need to get to class. Can I borrow your car?" I whispered.

He jerked awake and looked at me like he'd never seen me in his life. He groaned and rubbed the top of his head. "God, I feel like ass."

"I put water and aspirin on the coffee table. Where are your keys?"

"My pocket."

He made no move to retrieve them for me, so I went under the blanket and dug into the pocket of his jeans. The only acknowledgement I got was a brief opening of his eyes, then nothing. I knew he was hurting if he didn't use the opportunity to point out how close my hand was to his penis and how much closer still it could be.

I checked on Kylie and Jessica, but Kylie waved me off and Jessica never even woke up, despite my shaking her gently. She was snoring loud enough to wake the devil, but it didn't seem to be disturbing Bill, who inexplicably was sleeping with his glasses still on his face.

For some stupid reason, instead of feeling grateful that I wasn't hungover like the rest of them, I felt lonely. Like I had missed out on a mutual experience.

Or maybe I was just acutely aware that Tyler was stuffing his emotions down his throat alongside the beer and not leaning on me the way I would like him to. It bothered me that he hadn't shared with me that he and his mother had fought over his Thanksgiving trip to my house. I had waited for him to explain what had happened, but he hadn't, and that hurt my feelings.

Ironic, considering I had never been one to share the majority my thoughts with other people.

IT SNOWED AGAIN ON TUESDAY, AND KYLIE AND NATHAN HAD the brilliant idea to go sledding. We only had two sleds, but it seemed like a great way to continue to ignore Tyler's hearing, which had been set for mid-December at the tail end of exams week. There was a substantial hill behind Nathan's apartment, so Tyler and I went to his mom's house to collect the two sleds he was sure were in the garage. I wasn't thrilled to be going to his house, because I was kind of scared of his mother after hearing she had thrown such a fit about Jayden and Easton coming to my house, but she was sleeping on the couch.

Jayden and Easton were in their bedroom, playing video games that Tyler had rented from the library for their ancient gaming system.

"Come on, guys, get some warm clothes on," Tyler told them. "We're going sledding."

"Really?" Jayden asked eagerly. Then he frowned. "Sledding is for little kids."

"No, it's not. I'm doing it."

That was all the permission Jayden needed. In five minutes, he and Easton were wearing sweatshirts and coats, their hands crammed into gloves. Tyler and I had retrieved two sad-looking sleds out of the garage, and when we went into the kitchen, Riley appeared.

"Why does everyone look like they're about to cross the Bering Strait on foot?" he asked, leaning against the kitchen counter with a disposable gas station cup of coffee in his hand.

"We're going sledding. Want to come with us?" I asked. It didn't seem like a Riley kind of activity, but I was being polite. Besides, I wanted the chance to get to know Tyler's older brother a little better.

He stared at me, then at his brothers. Finally he shrugged. "Why the hell not?"

"Woot!" Jayden said.

Riley plucked his flannel shirt off the kitchen chair, and we filed out. I rode in the backseat between Jayden and Easton and listened to Tyler and Riley banter in the front. It felt good, warm, cozy. The best I'd felt since I had gotten that text from Nathan on Friday.

When we got back to the apartment, our friends were waiting for us on the hill, tossing snowballs at each other. Kylie looked like the pink abominable snowwoman, dressed from head to toe in fuchsia fur. I wasn't even sure where each piece stopped and started. It was just one giant fluffy assault on the senses.

"Is that a Care Bear?" Riley asked.

He and Tyler laughed.

"Ladies and children first!" Kylie declared as we all hiked up the hill.

"That's Rory and Easton, then," Tyler told her with a smirk. He handed me the sled he was carrying and kissed me.

Kylie smacked him.

Jessica was busy amassing a snowball stockpile, so she didn't look like she cared about getting first dibs on sledding. So Easton and I lined up next to each other, my feet awkwardly jutting out in front of me, gloves curled around the handles. That hill looked steeper from the top than it did from below. The lamplight of the parking lot cast a harsh glow over the sparkling snow, fresh flakes falling gently on us.

"Race ya," he told me with a smile.

"You're smaller than me," I told him. "My weight will slow down the pull of gravity."

To which his response was "Go!" as he pushed off.

"Hey!" I wiggled back and forth until I finally shot down the hill after him.

Holy crap, immediately I was going faster than I would have thought possible. Yet instead of being scary, it was exhilarating. The wind swept past my cheeks, my hair whipping back behind me, cold air filling my lungs. I could hear the guys up on the hill, cheering us on, and the whoosh of my plastic sled over the crystal snow. It was cold, only in the twenties, so it was perfect snow for sledding, crisp and icy, not wet and heavy. Enjoying the freedom, I only panicked briefly when I got to the bottom and realized I was careening straight toward the parking lot. Easton was already standing up, having beat the snot out of me in our race. I hurled myself sideways off the sled into the snow with a clumsy but effective dismount. The sled kept going and hit the concrete speed bump at the edge of the parking lot and flipped up into the air.

Standing up and smacking the snow off my butt, I high-fived Easton.

"That was awesome!" was his opinion.

"Totally!" I grinned at him as we collected the sled and trudged back up the hill. My butt was wet, but it was worth it.

"My turn!" Kylie said, and this time, she took the sled directly from me, not waiting to hear anyone else's opinions.

She and Jayden squared off, and Riley gave them both a shove to get them going. Both shrieked the entire way down the hill, Kylie's pink hood flying off her head and flopping on her back.

Tyler gave me a grin. "Damn. I'm not sure who screams more like a girl." He pulled me into his arms. "By the way, sorry again for puking on you."

I snuggled into the warmth of his chest. "I told you, it wasn't on me. It was the floor. And it's no big deal, for the third time. You took care of me when I was hungover. I'm just sorry I had to go to class. I felt guilty for leaving you." I did. I'd gone back at lunch with some soup from the food court, but Tyler had still been sleeping, so I had headed back to campus for my afternoon classes.

"There wasn't anything you could do but let me sleep off that whiskey, which is what I did. I did eat the soup eventually, at seven."

He shook his head. "So stupid. I can't believe I had to call off work. Lost fifty bucks for no reason."

I was about to tell him he was entitled to get drunk after the weekend he'd had, when I heard Jessica's voice rise.

"Your opinion is meaningless to me since I don't even know who you are," she said, voice haughty as she glared at Riley.

He seemed to be offering her a suggestion on snowball packing, given that he was squatting down on his haunches and had a handful of snow. "Fine, have shitty snowballs," he told her, standing back up and letting the half-formed ball fall out of his hands. "And I'm Riley, Tyler's brother. Who are you?"

"Jessica. Rory's roommate."

Neither one said it was nice to meet the other, as it apparently wasn't. Tyler shot me an amused look when Riley rolled his eyes and moved away to take his turn, which he did by running and diving onto the sled on his stomach with a whoop. I laughed.

"Please," was Jessica's opinion, her eye roll matching Riley's earlier one.

Kylie started shrieking when Easton hit her with a snowball. It was a bold move for him, but I guessed the fuzzy pink target was too tempting. She looked like the snack food Sno Balls, and I would imagine that at ten years old, sugar factored into the majority of his fantasies. He probably couldn't help but be fascinated. Nathan took a turn down the hill, and Tyler and I went together, me tucked between his legs.

But we were too heavy as a two-man team and stalled halfway down the hill..

"That was a rip-off," he said as we trudged back up to the top. "The only good thing about it was your ass rubbing on my junk."

Now it was my turn to roll my eyes. It was like guys came with a manual titled *Gross: The Least Romantic Things Ever to Say to Women*. All of which seemed to crack them up.

"Don't be a tool," I told him, which also seemed to crack him up.

Jessica had climbed onto the free sled but was having second thoughts. "I don't want to crash."

"You'll be fine," Kylie reassured her. "It's fun."

"But what if I hit the cement thing? I could break my ankle."

It surprised me, but she really did sound anxious. I didn't tend to think of Jess as being afraid of anything, but she was clutching the handles tightly and her shoulders were tense.

"You're not going to break anything," Kylie assured her.

"Either go or get off and let someone else have a turn" was Riley's suggestion.

That clearly pissed Jessica off because she hunched forward, like she was steeling herself to go. "I'm going. Just give me a second."

But Riley's boot came out and he gave the sled a mighty shove, sending her flying down the hill, her screams of terror ripping through the quiet night. Clearly pleased with himself, he chuckled.

"Dude," Tyler said in a vague reprimand, but it was clear he was struggling not to laugh himself.

"That was mean," Kylie told Riley.

"What? She was hogging the sled."

We all watched as Jessica tumbled off into the snow, clearly concerned enough about her ankle to arrange for an early exit from the plastic sled. She rolled about four times before coming to a stop with her arms and legs spread out like a snow angel. She was completely still for a second, long enough for me to take two steps, intent on running down the hill to see what she'd broken. But then she sprang up, yanking her hat off and throwing it on the ground.

"You're an asshole!" she screamed up at Riley. "I could have been killed."

This made him give up the fight and start laughing out loud. "You're not that fragile," he told her. "You look like you have a decent amount of padding."

Uh-oh. Given that it was the furthest thing from the truth, he clearly was just yanking Jessica's chain, but she wasn't someone I would necessarily want to mess with.

"Ouch, bro, that was a little harsh," Tyler told him. Yet he was chuckling under his breath.

"Screw. You." Jessica stomped up the hill and threw the sled at Riley.

It bounced off Riley's arm, his feeble attempt to block it marred by his laughter. He was practically doubled over, he was so entertained by himself. "Don't. I could be killed." Then he burst out laughing again after mimicking her words.

"Dick," she said, walking right past him. Then with a speed that a ninja would envy, she scooped up one of her snowballs, turned, and smashed it right into Riley's face.

His laughter cut out, and he swiped at his face. "Hey!"

Jessica smiled in pure satisfaction.

Tyler eyed me. "You're not going to smash a snowball in my face, are you?"

"No. I'm more subtle than that." I shivered. "Am I the only one who thinks its freezing out here?"

"You can go in if you want," he told me, hugging me close. "I'll stay out here with the boys."

Easton and Jayden took another turn down the hill while Kylie and Nathan made out. Yeah, I wouldn't mind going in and escaping the snow piling up on my eyelashes. I kissed Tyler and called to Jess, "I'm going in. Want to come with me?"

"God, yes."

I glanced back at all the guys and Kylie, watching them laugh and urge Easton to go down the hill on his stomach. The night was almost perfect, filled with the people I cared about the most, minus my family. The air was crisp and clean, and the snow blanketed the dirty parking lot in pure white.

For one moment the world seemed beautiful, and I was happy.

But tomorrow the snow would most likely melt, leaving behind a slushy brown muck that we had to sludge through whether we liked it or not.

CHAPTER EIGHTEEN

IT IS AMAZING WHAT WE CAN IGNORE. WHAT WE CAN COM-partmentalize and put in a box labeled Later. How we can let the motions of ordinary, everyday life distract us from real, looming problems. For two weeks Tyler and I ignored his upcoming hearing. We went to the coffee shop and I ordered lattes and he ordered black coffee, like we always did. We watched movies and studied and took turns sleeping in my dorm room or at his house if his mom was gone. I cooked. I went to my work-study job. Tyler went to the convenience store. Each day clipped along as it always had, and we laughed and talked and made love.

It was like if we just ignored the future and lived in the now, it would magically sort itself out.

Twice I tried to ask Tyler about the hearing, possible outcomes, and what his court-appointed lawyer had told him. Both times he brushed it off, saying, "It is what it is, no point in worrying about it."

We took our finals and made plans for him to come up for a

few hours on Christmas Eve when I was at home for break. I didn't exactly have permission from my dad for that, but I figured once the hearing was over, we could work on damage control. He had said himself he liked Tyler.

The morning of the hearing, I was still arguing with Tyler about going to the courthouse with him. "I can talk to my professor."

"Absolutely not," he said as he put on a dress shirt he had borrowed from Bill. It was a little small, but it was preferable to wearing a Metallica T-shirt to court. "You have your lit final today, and we don't know if we'll be done in time for you to get back for it."

We were in my room, and Kylie and Jessica had already left for their respective exams. I did have the lit final at one thirty, and thanks to Tyler I actually felt somewhat prepared. Riley and Nathan were going to court with Tyler, but I still felt a pit of anxiety in my stomach. I wanted to be there. I couldn't change the outcome in any way, but the control freak in me thought somehow I could. That I could ask the right questions. That I could support Tyler. That by the sheer force of my will I could make the outcome a positive one.

"I'm sure I can reschedule it."

"No." He gave me a firm look as he tucked the blue shirt into his black jeans. "That's the last thing in the world I want is for you to be rearranging your exams because of me. You have your scholarship to think about, you can't be risking your grades. Your dad will hate me more than he already does."

He was right, about all of it. But I still wanted to be there. "Text me the minute you're done. I'm going to be freaking out."

Tyler smiled and brushed his hand across my cheek. "No freaking out. It's all going to be cool. What's the worst that can happen?"

We both knew the worst that could happen. He could get a year in prison.

"My lawyer says I won't get the maximum sentence. Now I need to go before I'm late."

Tyler kissed me, a long, lingering kiss that made my tension loosen and my bare toes curl into the carpet. "Mm," he said. "Love you."

"Love you, too."

I HADN'T HEARD ANYTHING BY ONE, SO I TURNED OFF MY phone when it was time for my exam and took my seat. I floated my way through Hemingway, Fitzgerald, and Williams. It amazed me that two parts of my brain could coexist so easily—one methodically plodding through symbolism, the other in a courtroom downtown with Tyler.

As I answered essay questions on *A Streetcar Named Desire*, I remembered my first conversation with Tyler about Stella's reaction to Stanley throwing a shoe. Tyler had been right. I hadn't understood then that love and passion weren't logical, that you could stand outside and observe and say that someone was behaving ridiculously, but that when you were the one in the room, nothing made sense but the volcano of emotion that erupted when you were with your lover.

I still wasn't convinced that tossing a shoe didn't mean you harbored an anger-management problem, but I did understand love now. How it wrapped around you and made you more aware of the prickles on your skin, the roots of your hair, the intensity of every touch and every inch of you. It was like life in hi-def. Everything was sharper.

After I turned in the exam and left the room, the first thing I did was turn on my phone. I walked down the hallway, impatiently waiting for it to make its various tech noises as it fired up, then as I received texts and e-mails.

There was no text from Tyler.

But there was one from Nathan.

Got 30 days and 1500 fine. Starts serving now.

Relief that he had not gotten a year was immediately replaced by panic. Wait a minute. Did Nathan mean he had been taken straight to prison? For thirty days? That meant I wouldn't be able to see him. He would be behind bars for Christmas, too.

I dialed Nathan's number and he answered. "Hey."

"Hey. What does that mean? Tyler's in jail already?"

"Yeah. They took him into custody to immediately start serving his sentence. His lawyer said he could do weekend jail for the next four months but that he was more likely to not serve the full time if he just went right in. He decided to just get it over with."

I stopped walking, sinking onto a bench by the water fountain. Students moved up and down the hallway and I tried to think, tried to process what I was hearing. "So they clearly didn't believe he was innocent?"

"He pleaded guilty. His lawyer took a plea for him that they worked out with the prosecutor last week. He knew he'd be going to jail today unless the judge decided to suspend the sentence, which wasn't very likely."

"He took a plea? He didn't tell me that."

There was an awkward silence as we both realized Tyler had kept fairly important information from me, which he had shared with Nathan. "He probably didn't want you to worry. Taking a plea is pretty standard, I guess."

"He kept telling me it was going to be okay." My throat tight-ened. "He told me not to come today."

"Tyler is a protector, Rory. That's his personality. He didn't want you to blow your exams."

"I didn't get to say good-bye or anything." I was crying now.

Nathan swore, probably pissed that he was forced to deal with Tyler's hysterical girlfriend. "He didn't die, for fuck's sake. It's okay. You probably said good-bye to him this morning, right? It's like if someone goes out of town for a few weeks. It's no different. He'll be back before classes restart in January."

"Do you promise?" I asked, which was absolutely a ridiculous thing to ask of Nathan. He had no control over any of this.

But he laughed. "Yes, I promise. Thirty days is thirty days. They don't tack on more to your sentence. The truth is, he was lucky to get off so easy. And he was lucky he didn't have any more pills on him than he did. If that had been a whole bottle, he'd be gone for a year, no question about it."

Somehow I wasn't feeling that any of this was particularly lucky, given they weren't even his drugs. But there was no point in being bitter.

"Can I go see him?" Though the thought of entering a prison made my palms sweat, I wanted to show Tyler I supported him.

"No. He won't be in long enough. Besides, he would rip my balls off and stuff them down my throat if I let you go."

That made me laugh a little through my tears. Nathan was probably right. "Maybe Tyler should trust I'm not going to flip out."

"You're crying, aren't you?" Nathan teased. Then he said, se-riously, "Look, Rory, don't take it personally. Some things a guy just has to deal with himself, and this is one of those times. Tyler is ashamed, you know, and you seeing him behind bars would only make it worse. He needs to keep his pride, that's all."

I knew Nathan was right. I stared down at the cracked tile of the floor. "You're right. Thanks, Nathan. Hey, can I have Riley's number? I was planning to talk to Tyler about getting Jayden a present for his birthday on Sunday. I still want to get Jayden something, even if Tyler isn't here."

"Sure. And don't worry. It's all a lot better than it could have been."

"Thanks."

I ended the call and stared at the screen, not sure what the next logical step was. After sitting there for ten minutes, trying to calm down, trying to fit the pieces of the legal puzzle into place, I concluded that the only thing I could do was go back to my room and study for my final exam, a nine a.m. bio test the next day.

Because I couldn't make Tyler's mother go to rehab, and I couldn't turn back the clock and have her take her pills into the store with her, or have the cop drive down a different street. I couldn't wipe Tyler's record clean and have him stay in the EMT program. Nor could I drive down to the county jail and see him.

It felt like once again I was the girl behind the glass wall, walking alongside and watching everyone around me, but unable to interact with them. The other students all moved down the hallway, some talking and laughing in groups, others studying their phones, some hurrying, some lingering. For me, it felt like I had stopped moving and the world was spinning around me, a noisy whirlpool of confusion, and I couldn't make any sense of it.

But I decided that if Tyler could sit in prison for a month, I could hold my shit together for the same amount of time in my relatively easy existence. I only had three days before my dad was picking me up for winter break, and after my bio final, I felt myself seized by motivation to get everything done before I left. I packed a few weeks' worth of clothes and toiletries into a jumbo suitcase and propped it up by my closet. I cleaned all the food out of our mini-fridge. I bought a Christmas gift for Tyler, a hand-stamped metal disc on a chain. The letters spelled *TRUE* across the worn metal, and I thought it was cool and personal and his style. I got excited every time I glanced at it, tucked in a resealable plastic bag in my purse.

I also called Riley and made arrangements to go to the house to give Jayden a birthday gift and to bake them Christmas cookies. I had always been planning to do that, but now it felt more urgent.

It was odd to spend time with Riley, who offered to drive me to the grocery store to get the ingredients, though he did shake his head and say, "I don't think U needs cookies. He's getting a little thick in the middle."

"Who cares?" I asked. "He likes sugar, and it's not like he's going to be dating a whole bunch of hotties and he needs six-pack abs. Let him have a Christmas cookie."

Riley still looked skeptical. "Alright. But I'm not buying him new pants when his jeans don't fit."

"It's his birthday. Give the guy a break." I clutched my purse tightly to my chest in the cold car and hoped I had enough money for everything I was planning to do. It was going to be an expensive day. "Did you make the appointment?"

"Yes, for the third time. It's at eight. You're one of those organized people, aren't you? I would have just shown up as a walk-in."

"I like to be prepared."

He glanced over at me. "Tyler's lucky to have found you."

The compliment caused my cheeks to burn. Riley wasn't one to blow smoke up anyone's ass. "Thanks."

I bought cookie cutters in the shape of Santa and a snowman, and sprinkles and decorative icing in a squirt bottle. Riley scoffed, but an hour and a half later, I was quick to note that he spent a huge amount of time decorating the crap out of a Santa cookie.

"My Santa is pimped out," he declared, holding up his handiwork for everyone to admire. He had filled in the beard and the hat with icing and shaken sprinkles on top of the iced cap. It was impressive.

"Whoa," was Jayden's opinion. He was biting his lip as he tossed sprinkles on a snowman until it looked like it had repeatedly rolled in a field of red and green grass clippings.

Easton was wearing more icing than his cookie, and I noticed that he kept slipping his finger into the mixing bowl to scrape up the remaining bits of dough and pop them in his mouth.

The kitchen smelled delicious, and the boys were happy. The only thing missing was Tyler, but I took pictures on my phone to show him.

Riley glanced at his phone. "We should get going here soon. We have a birthday surprise for U."

"Really?" Jayden abandoned his cookie. "What is it?"

"It's not a freaking surprise if I tell you, now is it? Let's put these cookies away in your room so Mom doesn't toss them, then we'll go." Riley helped me collect all the masterpiece creations and put them in a plastic storage container. I gingerly made layers so I didn't mess them up.

"Okay, Easton, you take them in your room and lock the door behind you. I'll be waiting to catch you."

"What?" I asked, bewildered as Easton ran down the hall, the cookie container tucked under his arm. He went into his room, and I distinctly heard the lock click in place.

"If he locks the door from the inside, our mom can't get in. Easton jumps out the window and I catch him. Then when we get home, I toss him back up. It's foolproof."

"Ingenious," I agreed, giving him a grin. I could learn a thing or two from their survival techniques. They repeatedly just made the best of their situation.

"It's how we hide food and money from her. Once she tried to kick the door down, but she broke her big toe so she never did that again."

Jayden and I followed Riley out the back door and into the yard. Easton was sitting on the window ledge, legs dangling. When he saw Riley, he turned around so his backside was facing us.

"Alright," Riley told him. "Jump."

He dropped down and his brother caught him. Riley reached up and pulled the window down until it was almost closed.

"She doesn't just try to go in the window?" I asked.

Riley scoffed. "That would require a ladder and coordination. Strength and ambition, none of which she has."

"These guys are lucky they have you," I told Riley quietly. "I can't imagine what would happen to them without you and Tyler."

"I can't even think about it," Riley said, his jaw set as we walked down the drive to his car. "Or I'll punch a wall."

Jayden immediately realized what was happening when we pulled up to the tattoo parlor. "Am I getting a tattoo?" he asked, bouncing in the backseat with excitement.

"Yep. You're eighteen today so you don't need permission. Rory and Tyler and I all chipped in to get your tat started. We can have them do the *TRUE* today, and we'll have to add the *Family* part later when we have more money."

"Oh, my God, this is awesome!" Jayden looked like he might die from pure bliss.

Seeing his joy made me grin. I was happy to be a part of this with him.

As we got out of the car, Riley reminded him, "You know this is going to hurt. Bad. You can't be jerking around or it will get messed up. And if it hurts too much we can stop."

"I can handle it!" Jayden sounded offended.

Riley rolled his eyes at me. "I hope this isn't a disaster," he said under his breath. "If he ends up smacking the tattoo artist, I will never live it down."

After a round of greetings and wassups and Riley showing the guy his own tattoo and how he wanted it replicated on Jayden, they were ready to get started. Jayden sat on his hands to keep himself from jerking around. Easton had wandered away to look at pictures of the shop's work hanging on the walls. Riley kept his hands on Jayden's shoulders, and I stood next to him, trying to distract him by offering suggestions on what he could do on Christmas break from school.

As the artist worked on Jayden, he made a lot of noise, wincing and yelling out and looking like he wanted to die, but he toughed it out. Riley had suggested the outline of all the letters be done first, so if we needed to bail, at least it would read as something more than a half-done tattoo. Jayden did explain the meaning of the letters to the heavily pierced and tattooed guy working on him, and I think the guy was genuinely touched.

"That's cool, man. Every tattoo should have personal meaning."

"Hey, Rory, how do you spell your name?" Jayden asked me.

"R-o-r-y."

"Hm. So it starts with *R*?"

"Yes." I watched the letters of their own names appear on Jayden's arm and I suddenly realized that if you added an *R* to the end, *TRUE* became *TRUER*.

Tears filled my eyes. It was like I belonged there. That I had always been meant to be added to their family.

"Are you crying?" Easton asked, coming over to us.

Busted. "No, I just have something in my eye." But I pulled him in to my side and forced him to hug me, even though he squirmed. There was something to be said for touching the people you cared about. I was sorry I had spent the majority of my life avoiding it.

When Jayden had had enough, and the letters were outlined and shaded, we decided to call it quits. I took pictures of him before they bandaged his arm, and we let him go into the store next to the tattoo parlor and pick out some candy for his birthday.

"This is the best birthday *ever*," Jayden declared. Then he looked stricken, like he had said something inappropriate. "Except Tyler's in jail."

That was definitely hitting the nail on the head. I was missing Tyler more than ever. He should have been able to share this with us.

So the next day, on my own, I went back to the tattoo shop and had him ink *Truer* on the inside of my wrist in small, feminine, scrolling letters. I wanted to be able to look down at any time and see those letters linked together, a visible reminder of Tyler and my commitment to him and to his brothers.

Permanent.

Like love.

CHAPTER NINETEEN

"EXCUSE ME?" I ASKED MY FATHER, BLINKING ACROSS THE dinner table at him. He could not have just said what he did.

"You're forbidden to see Tyler," he said, stabbing a spear of broccoli with his fork and avoiding my eye. "I'm sorry, Rory, I know you care about him, but I can't have you putting yourself at risk."

Very, very carefully I put my own fork down as I tried to calm myself down enough to be rational. Arguing wasn't going to accomplish anything. "You can't forbid me to see him. I'm twenty years old and I don't even live here the majority of the time."

"I'm still your father and given the circumstances, I have every right to limit your involvement with him."

I suppose I shouldn't have been so surprised, but I was given that I had been home an entire week and nothing had been said to me about Tyler at all. My father had been ignoring that he even existed and for the time being, that had been fine with me. Dad knew Tyler was serving his sentence in jail because I had told Susan, who had told him. There had been no response from my father, until now, two days before Christmas.

"Well, I'm not going to stop seeing him," I said flatly. "So you can just forget about it." I tugged at my sleeve, making sure my new tattoo was covered. I didn't need to give him anything else to freak out about.

"Yes, you are." Dad stared at me, as if the force of his will could convince me.

Except I was just as stubborn. "No. This is a *serious* relationship, Dad, do you understand that? This isn't just some guy I kind of like. I would *marry* Tyler if he asked me." Not tomorrow, but in a few years. But I wanted Dad to get it. This was no casual first crush.

He blanched. "You wouldn't dare."

"No, I won't, because I'm not ready for that," I admitted, punching holes in my argument. But I was hardwired for honesty, I couldn't help it. "But I'm telling you, I won't stop seeing him."

"Then I'll stop paying your tuition."

My jaw dropped. "Are you serious?" I whispered.

He nodded. "He's in prison, Rory! He's a convicted felon. His future is ruined. I don't want him dragging you down with him. I'm sorry for the circumstances of his life, but that doesn't change the fact that if you stay with him, he'll ruin your potential. I am not going to just stand here and let that happen, and you can be as angry at me as you want, but I'm not going to back down."

"Susan," I said, my voice strangled, looking to her for help. "Tell him this is ridiculous."

But she just shook her head, lips pinched. "I'm not getting involved in this. You've already been using me as a shield, and I can't be a part of this. It's between the two of you."

She was right. I had been. "I'm sorry," I told her. "But listen to him. He's being ridiculous!"

"Maybe I should have encouraged you to date more in high school. Maybe Susan shouldn't have moved in here. I don't want you to feel like you need some sort of replacement family because you've been displaced here."

I stared at him in disbelief. "Are you kidding me? Do you honestly think my relationship with Tyler has anything to do with you at all? Because it doesn't! I don't give a crap if Susan lives here or not . . . that's between you two. And you could have encouraged me to date in high school as much as you wanted to, and it wouldn't have mattered because no guys wanted to date me! This isn't some weird plea for attention or a lashing out because I don't want you to date. God, Mom has been gone for twelve years. I think I'm okay with you having a love life." Why did parents always think it was about them? So, so annoying. "I met Tyler and we clicked. He's a wonderful guy. That's it. End of story."

"I'm not going to back down on this."

"I'll just lie and tell you I'm not seeing him. How are you going to know?" I asked, defiantly.

"I can check your cell-phone records and watch your social-networking posts and check-ins."

That was playing dirty. But he meant it. I could see it on his face. "Then I'll get student loans and pay the tuition back myself."

I could see he was considering whether he would have a legal leg to stand on to block my getting a loan, but I knew that loans could be taken in my name. And since I was over eighteen, he had no say in it. So we just stared at each other, both strategizing.

"Don't push me out of your life," I told him. "Is that what you want?"

"I'm looking out for your best interests. You'll thank me in ten years when you're a coroner and you have a respectable husband."

"Tyler is respectable," I said, tears suddenly in my eyes. "He has an incredible sense of honor and loyalty and right and wrong. Whether you choose to look past the tattoos and the metal T-shirts or not. Respectable doesn't always come wrapped in a sweater vest." I shoved my chair back. "Never judge a book by its cover, you always said. You're being a hypocrite."

I took my plate over to the kitchen sink.

"I didn't make up the fact that he's sitting in prison right now."

I paused, water running straight down the drain as I slackly held my dirty plate. "Yes. He's in prison. And I'm going to still be his girlfriend when he gets out."

"So you're going to leave college with a hundred thousand dollars worth of debt? You're making the biggest mistake of your life."

I shook my head. "No. The biggest mistake of my life was spending most of it not letting people get close to me."

IT WAS NOT A FUN CHRISTMAS AT OUR HOUSE. AFTER A TENSE gift-opening session that morning, I sat on the couch and watched movies in my pajamas all day. Susan was trying to be cheerful. Dad and I were sullen and polite.

The highlight of my day was a text from Riley. It just said "Merry Christmas," but for him, I felt like that was a pretty grand gesture. Riley didn't seem like a guy who discussed his feelings. At all.

Kylie sent me a text asking what I was doing. What did she

think I was doing? I wondered with a rueful shake of my head. I texted her back.

Nothing. Trying not to strangle my dad.

Are you going out tonight?

Did she think I went clubbing on Christmas night?

Nope. Hot date with the couch and a horror movie marathon.

K. Have fun.

I stared at the TV, listening to my dad and Susan in the kitchen, making coffee and talking. Probably about me, given their low tones. Whatever. I didn't for one minute believe my dad would really force me to pay for all of my tuition on my own. But if he did, fine. I had a scholarship that took care of everything but my room and board and books, so if I moved into an apartment, I could get a loan to pay for that and my living expenses. I would manage. He wasn't going to blackmail me.

Two hours and one slasher film later, the doorbell rang. I heard my dad go to answer it, figuring it was the neighbors bringing over a bottle of wine or something as a gift.

Instead, I heard Tyler's voice. Holy shit. I jumped up, tossing the blanket back, ecstatic that he was out of jail almost two weeks early. On Christmas.

But then I heard my dad say, "I'm sorry, you can't see her."

Oh, no, he didn't.

I shoved my feet in boots.

"I'm sorry for interrupting on Christmas, but please, Mr. Macintosh, just give me ten minutes with her."

I didn't wait to hear my dad's response to that. I grabbed the gift bag with the necklace for Tyler in it from under the Christmas tree, and I ran out the back door, across the deck, down into the yard, and around to the driveway.

"Tyler!" I called, breathless from running in the cold. He turned.

My father spotted me, and I saw the anger on his face in the porch light. "Rory! You get back in this house, right now!"

Instead, I jumped in the passenger seat of Tyler's car and locked the door. Tyler got in and stared at me. "What's going on?"

"Just drive."

But instead he leaned over and cupped my cheek and kissed me, breathing in deeply. "God, I missed you."

"I missed you, too. Are you out for real? They cut your sentence short?"

"Yeah." Tyler stared at me for a second, his expression serious, before he suddenly seemed to remember where he was. "Is your dad going to come out here if we just sit in the driveway?"

"I don't know," I told him truthfully. "But probably not. We could go somewhere."

"It's Christmas, everything is closed. I just wanted to see you, let you know that I'm okay. I'm not going to stay long. I need to go home and see the boys. Riley hasn't told them I'm out yet."

"Oh, okay." He had come to see me first. My heart swelled and I clutched the gift bag in my lap. "Are you okay? Was it horrible?"

But he just shrugged. "It wasn't the best time I've ever had. But it wasn't anything I couldn't handle." He bit his fingernails and stared at his steering wheel, clearly thinking again.

I felt like I was waiting for something, for him to share what he was thinking. My euphoria started to deflate. I had the sense something was wrong. This wasn't the blissful reunion I had been imagining, us sitting in his car silent.

"You should have told me you took a plea," I said, because I was still upset by that. "You don't need to protect me."

He lit a cigarette and glanced at me. "Actually, I do need to protect you. What's going on with your dad? I take it he's pissed about me going to prison?"

It was my turn to shrug. "He said I can't see you. But he's just upset. He's not really going to cut me off and stop paying my tuition. He'll get over it when he sees I'm serious."

Tyler took a long drag off his cigarette, his gaze still focused on the dashboard of his car, his knees apart and up as he leaned against the door. "Rory, I had a lot of time to think when I was sitting in there. Nothing to do but think."

"Yeah?" I asked, suddenly nervous. Why was he acting so weird? My heart started to thud unnaturally.

"I don't think we should see each other anymore."

Oh, God. He did not just say that. My heart started to splinter, my words tumbling out, desperate and anxious. "What? Don't be ridiculous. My dad will get over himself."

But Tyler's jaw was clenched, and he shook his head. "Your dad is right. I've got nothing to offer you, Rory. Nothing. The money I had saved for tuition went to pay my fine. I have to drop out of school, and truthfully, the university would probably kick me out anyway for having a felony conviction. I'll never be an EMT now. That's done. No one is going to let me be around prescription drugs. Everything has changed, and I don't want you to have to deal with the fallout from my problems. It's not fair to you."

"We're not doing this again," I told him firmly, quietly. "We've already had this talk and I told you that you can't make my choices for me. Not you, not my father. *I* make my decisions."

"That was before!" he said, finally looking at me, the ember of his cigarette glowing in the dark. "I'm a criminal now, don't you understand that? If I'm lucky, Riley can get me some construction work, but that's it. My only option. I lost my job, shitty job that it was. We're nine months behind on paying the mortgage on the house, and as soon as the bank weeds through their red tape, they're going to kick us out on the street. That is the reality of the situation."

I blinked back tears. I could feel his worry, the tension emanating from him. "Which is why I want to stick by you. Relationships aren't for good times only."

But he scoffed and shook his head. "You don't get it. I'm a loser, a capital L loser." He formed the letter with his fingers on his forehead, just in case I didn't get it, apparently. "And that's all I am ever fucking going to be. You have so much more potential and I won't be able to stand myself if I ruin all of that for you."

"Stop being so fucking noble!" I told him, furious. I never swore, and he looked startled that I did. "So you're broke! I am too, you know. If I'm telling you I don't give a shit, then I don't give a shit."

"Don't make this harder on me than it is."

I laughed, tears in my eyes. "Hard on you? You're the one dumping me on Christmas."

"I had to see you. I couldn't let it go on longer than this so that we both wound up even more hurt. It's better to just get it over with."

My eyes narrowed at him. "Just get it over with? Like it was nothing. What happened to us being the real deal? Forever? I love you?"

His fist tightened on the steering wheel and he pitched the cigarette butt out the window. "I meant those things. But I need to do what's right."

"What's right is what we have. You and me."

"Rory, go in the house. Please. I can't do this." He sounded agonized, but I had no sympathy.

So that was supposed to be it? He was going to leave because he couldn't deal with it?

Screw that. "No. I'm not getting out of this car until you stop acting like an idiot." I folded my arms to prove my point.

"Your father is watching out the window. You need to go in." Then he opened up his door and retrieved the butt he'd thrown, like he had suddenly remembered where he was. He stuffed it into his ashtray, slamming the door shut. "Please. Just go."

I shivered in the cold, tears streaking down my cheeks. "I trusted you, Tyler. I gave you my virginity."

"Don't put that on me. That was your choice," he said, his voice distant, and a little impatient. "I tried to stop you. I told you that you would regret it."

That made me furious. I smacked his shoulder with the gift bag. "Don't dismiss me like that! If your goal was to be an asshole, you've achieved it."

His response was to lean across me and shove my door open.

That shattered me. I had no fight left. He really was dumping me on Christmas. He had driven an hour right out of prison to tell me he never wanted to see me again.

For a second, I couldn't actually breathe. I thought I was going to faint. But I swallowed the bile that was rising in my throat and turned to get out. With shaking fingers, I dumped the colorful gift bag on his gearshift. "Merry Christmas."

He stared down at the green bag, red tissue popping out of it, then tried to shove it back at me, looking stricken. "I can't accept this. I don't deserve this."

"No, you don't," I told him, flatly. "But it's meaningless to me. I have no use for it."

I climbed out of the car and slammed the door shut, my lip trembling, teeth chattering.

Without looking back, I ran into the house. My dad was standing there, waiting, clearly having been watching.

"I hope you're happy!" I screamed at him. "Tyler just broke up with me, and it's partly your fault!" Maybe that wasn't fair. Tyler had come to the conclusion we couldn't be together before he'd pulled in the driveway, but I don't think my father's threat to cut me off had helped the situation.

Running up the stairs, still in my muddy boots, I slammed my door shut as hard as I could, locking it. With a scream, I slapped a pillow off my bed and onto the floor. Then I screamed again and threw another pillow. I did it again and again until there was nothing on the bed but the fitted sheet, while my dad pounded on my door. When my throat was raw from screaming, I fell on the torn-apart bed and sobbed.

I cried until my eyes were swollen and tears ran down my cheeks, soaking my sleeve. I cried until I was choking on my own mucus and my head was throbbing and there was no liquid coming from my eyes anyway, and I was just a snuffling, painful, congested sobbing mess.

I cried until I heard my father and Susan talking in the hallway.

"I should take the door off. I need to talk to her," Dad said to Susan, his voice anxious.

"Leave her be. She's had her heart broken. Don't you remember having your first love break your heart?"

"No. I married my first love."

Which only made me start crying all over again.

Then I tortured myself by looking at all the pictures on my

phone of Tyler. There weren't many, because he hated having his picture taken, but there was one of him in bed, asleep, his face relaxed, his chest bare. I loved that picture. It showed him as tough, yet vulnerable. I clutched the phone to my chest and stared out my bedroom window into the black night, the hurt so overwhelming it took effort to breathe.

When my mother died, when I saw my father crying as he came out of that hospital room for the last time, and I realized what had happened, I bawled into my grandmother's arms in the waiting area, as nurses stopped to whisper words of comfort and other people around the hospital shot sympathetic glances our way. I remember thinking that this was wrong, this couldn't be right, that we couldn't live in a world that was so mean, that moms shouldn't just die. As my grandmother picked me up and rocked me on the hard chair in that waiting area, tears on her cheeks, her scent of rosewater surrounding me, she had murmured to me that the world had stopped for a moment and gone dark, but tomorrow, the sun would rise all over again. It would do that every day, until one day we were okay.

And it did.

So I picked up the phone and called my grandmother.

The next day, I boarded a bus to Florida to spend the week before classes with her and my grandfather.

CHAPTER TWENTY

JANUARY WAS COLD AND DARK. ALL THE WAY AROUND. IT WAS icy winds, slippery sidewalks, five o'clock sunsets, and a hole in my chest that couldn't be filled no matter how many Fritos I stuffed down my throat.

I got up every day and I went to class and I studied and I hung out with my roommates. Sometimes I even laughed. I was determined not to let Tyler ruin my life. I was determined to recover, be normal.

But sometimes I also found myself doing strange things. I took the bus to Tyler's neighborhood and I walked down his street, knowing I could get caught, but not caring. I stood at the corner and I looked in, seeing his mother passed out on the couch and catching a glimpse of Jayden in the kitchen.

I walked away, dissatisfied with my voyeurism.

I started to send texts, then deleted them.

I walked alone, a lot, in the dark, prompting Kylie to express concern. But I liked the cold, the angry, howling wind. I liked how my cheeks stung and my lips cracked and my eyes teared up from the cold. I blew my breath out and watched it and listened to it, the quick huff, that illusion of steam. I liked the way my nose went numb and my toes went numb and my fingers went numb in my pockets. I felt alive, I felt like my body was slicing through the night, through the darkness, warm, blood pumping.

I refused to listen when Kylie and Jess tried to tell me what was going on with Tyler. I refused to go to Nathan's.

Yet I found myself online searching databases, finding Tyler's mug shot from his arrest, and printing it out. I carried it in my notebook, his tight sullen face staring out at me when I flipped through my calculus notes.

Once on campus I thought I saw him, and I ducked behind a tree, feeling like I was going to throw up.

I scratched out the *R* on my tattoo with a black marker, then washed it off three seconds later.

And every day the sun rose, and every day I healed a little more.

I started tutoring at the local elementary school, working with at-risk kids. I quit my work-study job, deciding that the bookstore didn't need yet one more middle-class kid making eight bucks an hour. My time could be better spent at the grade school and the shelter.

One time in late January, I saw Easton in the hallway. I hadn't even realized I was at his school, but it wasn't that far from the house, so it made sense. I called out to him, ridiculously relieved and excited to see him. His head turned and his eyes widened. Then he bolted away from me, shoving another kid to get down the hall, his lip trembling.

I stopped, crushed.

* * *

ON VALENTINE'S DAY I CALLED MY DAD. WE HADN'T SPOKEN
since I had left for Florida. Six weeks was a long time to go without
contact. I had sent him texts so he would know I was okay, but I
hadn't been able to bring myself to call him. He hadn't called me.
It was a pattern we needed to break, immediately, or we were going
to do it forever.

"Rory?" he answered, sounding anxious.

"Hi."

"How are you, sweetheart?"

"I'm okay." I was in the study lounge, the only person there, as
usual. Kylie was out with Nathan, and Jessica had gone out to the
bars with Robin. I had declined an invite, preferring to distract
myself with studying.

"I've been worried about you."

I put my feet on the coffee table and inspected my slippers,
sighing. "Look, Dad, we need to quit doing this. Ever since Mom
died, you and I have avoided talking about the hard stuff. We just
ignore our feelings and it's not good. I really am having a hard time
right now and I need to know that you're there for me."

"Of course I'm there for you. I just wanted to give you space."

"If you could be in my face about me not seeing Tyler, you can
be a little more in my face about making sure I'm okay. That's all."

"You're right. You're absolutely right. It's hard for me to . . .
share how I'm feeling."

"I know. I am pretty much a carbon copy of you. But I don't
want us to be strangers to each other. We're all we've got. I mean,
well, you have Susan, but you're my father. My family."

"You're the most important person in the world to me, and I want you to know that."

It was good to hear. It was what I needed to hear.

"How were your grandparents? I should call them more often."

"They're good." My mother's parents were more like her, talkative and full of energy and life. Even in their seventies, they were in about seven different clubs and activities down in Naples. "It was nice to see them. And I think I gained five pounds the week I was there."

"You could use the meat on your bones. You got my scrawny build."

"Thanks a lot. I thought thin was in." I crossed my ankles, feeling a sense of peace settle over me. "So what are your Valentine's plans? It's nine o'clock. I hope I'm not interrupting foreplay."

"Rory!"

I laughed. It was almost like I could hear my dad blushing.

"I have to accept you're not a little girl anymore, don't I?"

"It looks that way," I told him. "I grew up when you weren't looking."

"Damn. And I can still remember when you would bring home Valentine's Day cards from school. One was a clock that said 'Just in Time, to be Mine.'"

I grinned. The man was getting sappy. Clearly we should not go six weeks without talking ever again.

"Rory. I'm sorry about Tyler. I really am."

My chest tightened. "Thanks."

Thirty minutes later, I said good-bye and went down to my room, ready for a studying change of scenery. I opened the door and flicked on the light. It took me a second to realize the room wasn't empty. Jessica was on her bed, head thrown back in pleasure, a guy between her thighs. When he lifted his head to see what was happening, I realized it was Bill, Nathan's roommate.

"Oh, geez, sorry! I didn't know you were in here. I'll go back upstairs." Embarrassed at what I'd seen, I went straight back to the lounge. I crammed a bunch of quarters in the vending machine and bought myself a bag of chips, trying not to feel envious that I wasn't spending my Valentine's Day that way.

I'd been fine, all day. Really okay.

Now I had a pit in my gut and a desperate desire to check my phone every three seconds for a text I knew was not coming.

Twenty minutes later, the door opened and Jessica came in, wearing her pajama pants and a giant sweatshirt. Her hair was tousled. "Hey."

"Hey. Where's Bill?"

"I made him go home. I don't want him to get the wrong idea about what this was."

"What was this?" I asked, curious, as she flopped down next to me and drew her knees up to her chest.

"Just bored, and he has been flirting with me for weeks. I wanted to have an orgasm and so I did. I told him straight out I wasn't going to screw him." She made a face. "Don't judge me. I get enough of that as it is."

I shrugged. "I'm not judging you. I figure as long as you're honest with the guy, you have a right to do whatever you want." That kind of casual sex wasn't for me, but if she could handle it, more power to her.

"Good. Because I get so sick of slut shaming, you know? It's like a guy can fuck anyone he wants and no one says a word. But we're not supposed to have physical urges at all. We're supposed to want to have sex only because we're in love, and the truth is, my body doesn't seem to know the difference. It just knows it likes touchy." She grinned at me. "Lots of touchy."

"I envy you the touchy right now," I told her honestly. It had been far too long since I had been touched.

But I also knew that I would never go backward. I wouldn't undo what I had done with Tyler. I was never going to be able to emotionally distance myself from the people around me the way I had most of my life, and I didn't want to. Being a loner was ultimately selfish, and if you never gave of yourself, you never got in return. The risk of being hurt was higher when you put yourself out there, but it was worth it.

My phone beeped to indicate a text.

My heart jumped and I grabbed it, a small seed of optimism planted.

It was from Kylie saying she wuv'd me.

Sweet, but not what I wanted.

I tossed my phone back down, disgusted with myself.

"He's miserable," Jessica said, quietly. "He looks like hell, you know. And he asks about you."

"It doesn't matter." It didn't. He had shattered my faith, my trust, my heart.

And yet the sun rose again the next day.

And I still loved him.

IN MARCH, TYLER'S MOTHER OVERDOSED AND DIED. JESSICA called to tell me and I sat there on my bed, in shock. "What? Oh my God. How?"

"Heroin. That black heroin they buy because it's cheaper, only it's way more dangerous."

"Oh, no." I closed my eyes. "Was she at home? Who found her?"

"Tyler. His brothers were still at school."

I was grateful Jayden and Easton weren't home, but I couldn't imagine how Tyler had felt. How helpless and sad, and maybe in a small part of him, relieved. His mother's suffering was over.

"She died last night. They're burying her tomorrow."

"That fast?"

"Yeah, they can't afford to do a wake or anything."

What a sad ending to a sad life. "I'm going to go. I have to," I said.

"I think you should." Jessica gave me the details, the time and the cemetery.

That night I went on another of my nocturnal walks, the weather still grim, still firmly in the grip of winter, the paths around campus filled with slushy, muddy snow that melted each day and iced over each night.

And for the first time in over two months, I gave in to the urge to text Tyler. I simply wrote

I'm sorry.

It said many things to me. I was sorry for his mother's death, sorry for the reality of his life, sorry that I had been given so many more opportunities than he had. Sorry that I had screamed at him, sorry that for whatever reason, he couldn't trust in my feelings for him. Sorry that my future no longer held him in it.

I didn't know if he would answer me. But he did, immediately.

Thx. Me 2.

So he hadn't deleted my number.

And I was entitled to read all the subtexts I wanted into that brief text. That "me 2" meant he was sorry not just for his mother, but for us.

Maybe that wasn't logical. But I had learned that sometimes logical didn't feel as good.

CHAPTER TWENTY-ONE

I SAW TYLER FOR THE FIRST TIME IN TWO MONTHS, BENT OVER his mother's grave, his arm around Easton's shoulders.

Jessica and I had borrowed Robin's car. Kylie had gone with Nathan earlier. It was raining, a steady, drizzling cold mist. The snow had all melted, except for what clung to the curbs and the giant piles in parking lots. The ground was soft, wet, as we crossed the grass to reach the grave site. The attendance was low. There were Tyler and his brothers, Kylie and Nathan, Tyler's aunt Jackie, and a woman who I thought might be their next-door neighbor. That was it. Ten people, including Jess and me.

Without saying anything, we just slid into place beside Kylie, listening to the priest, who was softly speaking a prayer. When I looked down at the simple casket, I saw there was a picture on it of Tyler's mom when she was much younger, when she had still been Dawn, a girl with dreams and a future. I was amazed to see her wide smile, to see the joy and life on her face, to see the care she'd taken with her hair, teasing it to enormous heights, her eyeliner a dramatic teal color. I thought maybe it was her senior portrait.

Jessica squeezed my hand, and I knew she was thinking the same thing. "I'm never touching that shit ever again," she murmured to me. "Never."

"Good." I glanced over at Tyler, unable to resist, wondering if he had seen me.

He was looking right at me, and he gave me a nod of acknowledgement. He was dry-eyed, his expression closed. Easton was silent, too, but Riley was wiping at his eyes, and Jayden was openly crying. My heart broke for them.

When the priest was done, giving the sign of the cross over the casket, he turned to Tyler and Riley and spoke quietly to them for a minute. Then he moved off, giving the family their last moments alone with their mom.

But none of them lingered. Jess and I drifted back a little to give them privacy, but Riley immediately came over to us. He hugged me. "Thanks for coming. I appreciate it." He nodded to Jessica. "Thanks."

"I'm so sorry," I told him. "I lost my mom, too. I know how hard it is."

"Well, this wasn't exactly unexpected. She was on borrowed time. But it's still a kick in the gut." Riley glanced over at his brothers. "Going to be hard, all the way around."

"I'm sure. If I can help, just me know."

"Thanks." Riley patted my shoulder, then walked back.

I could hear Tyler and his aunt arguing. "Just let it go, Jackie. I swear to God, don't do this right now or I will lose it."

"I'm just saying, we should be able to press charges. Dealers shouldn't be able to sell you bad shit." Jackie was smoking a cigarette, wearing jeans and a nylon jacket, her hair up in a pony-tail. She pointed at Tyler, her voice raising. "You know your mom could handle her shit, so for her to OD, it had to be bad stuff. Someone should pay for this."

"Someone did pay for this. Jayden and Easton paid for this. They paid for every day of her addiction, and I don't want to hear it. There is no one to blame here but her and her love of the little white pills."

"Don't talk bad about your mom when she's barely cold."

But Tyler just shook his head. "Jackie, I'm not doing this. I love you, but I'm not doing this."

I felt like I was hearing something private I shouldn't be hearing, so I went over to Jayden and gave him a hug. He had stopped crying, but his eyes were red and he was wiping his nose with the sleeve of his coat. I dug a tissue out of my purse and handed it to him.

"I miss you," he told me, sounding every kind of miserable you could be.

"I miss you, too." I did. He was a lesson in being grateful. He was funny and clever and one of the most genuine people I'd ever met. "If it's okay with Tyler, you and I can hang out sometime. Just because Tyler and I aren't together, doesn't mean you and I can't be friends."

"Really?"

"Really. As long as it's okay with Tyler." I didn't want him to think I was trying to infiltrate his family or win him back by using his brothers. I would die if he thought that.

Of course, I should have realized Jayden would ask Tyler immediately. "Tyler, is it okay?"

"Is what okay?" Tyler came over to us, giving me a brief smile, his hands in the front pockets of his jeans.

"Can I hang out with Rory sometime? She said we're still friends even if you and her aren't."

"Of course you can." Tyler looked at me, his eyes searching, earnest. "I would like to still be friends with Rory, too."

Only if I had a heart of steel, which I didn't. Maybe in six months or a year, but right now, I knew I wasn't capable of just being his friend and not wishing every second that I was something more to him.

"We can be the kind of friends who care about each other, but never see each other or talk," I told him, trying to be honest. Of course, that sounded much ruder than I intended.

But the corner of Tyler's mouth turned up. "Only you, Rory."

Only me.

"U, can you and Easton go wait in the car with Riley? I want to talk to Rory for a second."

"Don't be mean to her," Jayden said, clearly figuring that must be the reason we were no longer together.

"I won't," Tyler said, annoyed. "Now go."

"Well, I'm relieved you're not going to be mean to me," I said, fighting the urge to smile. It was good to see him, even under the awful circumstances. Even with the rain dampening my hair and seeping into my shirt from the gap of my coat collar. Even with him looking so solemn and damaged, the dark circles under his eyes prominent, angry slashes of bruised purple skin.

"I think I've been mean enough to you already. But I want to thank you for coming. That was really sweet of you."

"I'm just sorry about your mom. I really am." I hoped my voice conveyed my sincerity, that he could hear that I still cared about him. "What are you guys going to do?" I meant about the house, the future.

But he just shrugged. "We'll manage. We'll be fine."

"If there's anything I can do . . ." I started to say, but I trailed off. It sounded trite saying that to Tyler.

After a moment of silence, he spoke. "You look good," he said, and his voice cracked. He cleared his throat, glancing over to the left, to the open grave. "Just as beautiful as I remember. I thought, you know, that maybe I had exaggerated in my mind what you looked like, but I didn't. You're beautiful, and I was a complete dick to break up with you on Christmas." He swung back to stare intently at me. "I hope someday you can forgive me. It wasn't that I didn't love you. I did. I do. I love you. But . . ."

"I know." I stopped him. I didn't need to hear all this again. "I do forgive you. It doesn't mean I don't wish it was different though, because I do."

"Are you . . . dating anyone or anything?"

Was he stupid? I made a face. "No. And I don't want to."

"Why not?"

"Because they're not you." Idiot. "What about you? Seeing anyone?" I jammed my hands into my coat pockets, immediately sorry I had asked that. Why did I need to torture myself?

But he shook his head. "No." He rubbed the stubble on his chin and I waited, recognizing the sign that he was trying to force words out. "Rory?"

"Yes?" Whatever he was going to say, it didn't matter, because I already felt a hundred pounds lighter. Just seeing his face, reading in his eyes that he loved me, hearing him say it, was enough to fill that last hole in my heart with spackle. It was patched up, not perfect, but intact.

But then I saw what was dangling from his neck. It was the necklace I had given him for Christmas. I recognized the black rope chain and the dented metal with the typography letters stamped on to it. Except it didn't read *TRUE* like it had when I'd placed it in that gift bag, wrapped in tissue paper. It read *TRUER*.

"What is that?" I asked, voice trembling, afraid I might suddenly cry. "Why is there an *R* on your necklace?"

"What?" Then he glanced down to where I was pointing, and he smiled softly. "Oh. *R* is for *Rory*."

Oh, God.

"Jayden pointed out to me that your name starts with an *R*, and I realized that you belong on this necklace, right here, in this gift that you gave me. The best gift I've ever gotten." He ran his callused thumb over the metal. "Next to my heart, where you belong."

I did start crying. I couldn't stop myself. I pulled my coat sleeve up with trembling fingers and turned my arm so he could see the tattoo on the back of my wrist. "So you're always with me."

Tyler stared at it, his jaw clenched. Then he said, "Oh, God, Rory, I love you. I shouldn't tell you that, but I can't . . ."

He lifted my wrist and he kissed the tattoo, staring deep into my eyes while his lips brushed across my flesh. Mist droplets were scattered all over his hair, and he caressed the inside of my arm. Then he murmured, "It wouldn't be fair to ask you to be with me."

That's what I had been waiting to hear. I would have let it rain on me all day if those words were at the end of twelve hours. "Why don't you give it a shot?"

"But your dad . . ."

"Will get over it. We've come to a new understanding."

He laced his fingers through mine. "What do I have to offer you?" he asked, pleading.

"You're my best friend. My English tutor. The guy who keeps

me from becoming a lab recluse." I shook my head at him. "But I'm not going to talk you into it. This one is up to you. We've proven that we can survive apart."

I gave him just a second or two, watching the struggle on his face, then I whispered, "Good-bye, Tyler," and started to walk away. I wouldn't, couldn't, be with a man, no matter how much I loved him, who wasn't sure it was what he wanted. In some ways, the breakup had been good for me. It had given me a new appreciation for myself and the people in my life.

Even the ones who might not be able to be in it.

Ignoring my tears, I was all the way across the grass and to the street when I heard him yell, "Rory, wait!"

I turned and there he was, right behind me, reaching for me, pulling me into his embrace as he stared down intently at me. "Don't go, please, God, don't go."

My heart swelled, but I shook my head. "You don't mean that."

"Yes, I do," he said tenderly. "I don't want to be without you. Not for another day. Not for another minute. I've been miserable without you. Opening that car door was the stupidest thing I've ever done in my life, even if I thought it was the right thing to do."

I kissed him. Hard. Wanting him to understand that none of that mattered. That what mattered was here, now, me and him and a promise to be the best we could, for ourselves, for each other.

"I love you," he whispered in my ear. "And I'm never going to let you go."

Then the horn blaring made me jump. We were still standing in the street by the cemetery and Riley had hit the car horn.

"Seriously?" Tyler said shooting an annoyed look at his brother. "What a jack-off."

I smiled, giving a watery laugh. "Maybe we should discuss this somewhere else."

"I don't think there is really anything else to discuss." Tyler cupped both of my cheeks with his hands and kissed me again, softer this time. "Except how happy I'm going to make you."

"You already have." I sighed, so relieved to feel him close to me, to smell his scent, to have his fingers caressing me. I had missed him so much. "But you do owe me a Christmas present."

He laughed, leading me over to the car, holding my hand firmly in his. "Good point. I'll work on that. How about a matching necklace?"

"That's kind of a cop-out, but effective," I told him, because frankly he needed to work a little harder than that.

"Rory Macintosh, what am I going to do with you?"

"I can think of a thing or two."

"So can I."

Keep reading for a special treat:
original bonus scenes from

TRUE

Never before published!

TYLER

THE FIRST TIME I SAW RORY WAS AT A PARTY AND I WAS BORED.
Same people, same apartment, same cheap-ass beer, same stupid
conversations about who was hooking up with who, and stupidly
arrogant and generic politic assertions that no one knew how to
discuss or back up with facts. I was sitting on a kitchen stool, a
beer in my hand, trying to avoid a girl who was hitting on me. She
was attractive enough in a typical sort of way but she opened her
eyes really wide when she giggled, which was all the time, and she
misused words constantly. Someone was always luxuriating or
eradificating when she talked and I was torn between wanting to
laugh and wanting to be a total prick and correct her. When she
told me she admired my muscularity I knew I wasn't a good enough
actor to hide my amusement. Or horror, really. I mean, was this
higher education? Weren't we all in college here? I am no brainiac,
but, dude, pick up a book and read.

So I excused myself to go get another beer on the other side of
the kitchen and when I turned, I saw Rory.

She stood out immediately in the crowd, the only chick there not sporting a summer tan or wearing as little clothing as was possible outside of a strip club. Her hair was in a braid draped over her left shoulder and it was an intriguing auburn shade, her skin creamy and fair. She was wearing a little dress that showed no cleavage and had hints of granny to it. That all was enough to make me pause and stare for a minute, but it was what she was saying that really caught my attention.

"That movie is medically improbable," she told the guy next to her. "If you attempted to interconnect living humans in that way, they would die of asphyxiation, dehydration, or a bacterial infection. But most likely asphyxiation would occur first. You can't swallow with your jaw distended like that."

"How do you know? And who cares? It's just so gross it's awesome."

I saw that she wanted to grimace at his response, but she tried to hide it. "I'm curious, then, what constitutes disturbing to you."

I found myself fighting a grin.

But the guy seemed insulted. "Lighten up. God. It's a movie."

"You're right," she agreed, and she looked contrite. But then after a slight pause, she spoke again, like she couldn't stop herself. "A scientifically inaccurate movie."

And right then, she lit a spark of interest in me that grew each time I saw her over the next few months. She was quiet, always letting Kylie and Jessica upstage her, but I watched her the way she watched everything else, the silent observer, and I couldn't get her out of my head. She fascinated me, the way her hair moved, the way her hands were so small and feminine, the fact that I learned she was a premed student. I studied her, I fantasized about her, I dreamed about her. I tried to think of a way to talk to her, but she always looked through me, like I wasn't worthy of her attention. Which I wasn't. I knew that.

It didn't mean I didn't want to be.

But once she and I started hanging out, after Grant scared her, once she started to look at me like I was something, I tried to hold back. I tried to do the right thing. I tried to resist touching her, kissing her, but when you're presented with the perfect package of temptation that seems like it was designed just for you, to trip you up, it's too hard to pass it up.

So I didn't, and even though she blew me off for a week after we made out, I kept at her until she caved.

And then I just felt like I couldn't get enough of her. It was like Edgar Allan Poe said: "I became insane, with long intervals of horrible sanity."

That guy was messed up and I finally understood him. Falling in love felt crazy, like I had a fever, but I couldn't stay away, couldn't stop myself, and we hadn't even had sex yet. I figured it would probably kill me if we didn't soon. But then again, it might kill me when we actually did.

We were walking across campus after classes and I snaked my hand over to take hers. "How much studying do you have tonight?"

"A ton," she said, glancing up at me and smiling. "I have a molecular biology exam on Friday."

So going to the movies or something was out. But I wasn't going to go home and not see her for the rest of the day. I'd only seen her for an hour. "I have to go home and work out but then do you want to go to the coffee shop? I can pick you up around seven."

She nodded. "So, how often do you work out?"

"Five days a week." She'd seen me without a shirt, touched me, but she never said anything about it other than to comment on my tattoos. Though I'm not sure what I thought she was supposed to say. But hey, I wanted her to think I was hot. I wanted all that time spent doing pull-ups and crunches with a weighted ball to have her in a girl puddle of appreciation. I wasn't doing this shit just for my health, let's be honest.

"That's dedication."

"There's a fitness test you have to pass to be an EMT, so I want to make sure I can."

"I'm sure you will." Her hand was soft in mine, cold from the November air. "You seem very . . . fit."

She was so cute when she was being shy. Even her pale cheeks turned a slight pink.

"So you like my muscularity?" I joked. "That's masculinity paired with muscular. It's a hybrid—like vajazzle."

Part of me wondered if she even knew vagina bedazzling existed, but then again, she roomed with Jessica and Kylie. If I had twenty bucks to bet, I would lay it down on Kylie's south side looking like it did when they turned on the lights at Great American Ball Park for a Reds game.

"Did someone call the plumber?" she asked.

"What?" That totally threw me off. Her expression was serious, like it usually was. "What do you mean?"

She pulled her hand from mine and reached up to squeeze my biceps through my leather jacket. "Because the pipes are here."

I started laughing so hard it turned into a cough. She grinned at me.

"Oh, my God." I tried to breathe. "Did you hear that from a seventy-year-old guy with a pinup girl tattoo?"

"Sure. Because that's who I hang out with when I'm not with you."

She was killing me. And every time she spoke, I fell further and further into love with her, one deadpan joke, one scientific observation, one kind word to my brothers at a time. It was like the adrenaline rush of working out paired with a whiskey buzz, and I couldn't stop smiling.

But that was when I was able to shove aside reality and just exist, with her.

When the truth of who I was and where I came from became something I couldn't ignore, I fucked up and ruined things.

Then I fucked up and ruined them again.

And I didn't know how to ask for a third chance.

RILEY GOT ME A JOB PLOWING PARKING LOTS WHEN IT SNOWED, and it was better than working at the convenience store. At least on the scale from "sucks a little" to "sucks hard and long." I could listen to my metal music while I drove the truck, and there was something methodical and organized about going down row after row, pushing the snow, the scrape of the plow on the asphalt loud in the still morning hours, sparks flying.

But it gave me too much time to think, and when I had time to think, every thought centered around Rory. I wondered what she was doing. If she hated me. If she was dating some engineering student with a high IQ and a big-ass bank account. If she realized how much I loved her and how every single goddamn day I questioned if breaking up with her had been the right thing to do. It didn't feel like the right thing, not for me. I missed her so much it hurt worse than the time Riley had accidentally missed the punching bag I was holding for him and nailed me in the face, busting my nose. My face had throbbed for days, and that's what this was like—a burst of pain followed by a pulsing agony, all my own fucking fault because I had been stupid enough to let myself go there with her. To fall for someone I could never really have.

Every time I stepped into my house, I remembered all over again why I had bailed. After finishing up by eight a.m. and kicking the snow off the side of my boots, I walked in the back door and found the usual scene—my mother screaming at Riley, who had come over on his way to work to drive Easton and Jayden to school since the weather sucked.

"Get out of my house!" she shrieked, wearing jeans that might have fit her at one time, but now hung loosely on her thin body. Her hair hadn't been washed in days and it stuck to one side of her head, limp and matted.

"I'm going," Riley told her, shaking his head. "Jesus Christ."

"Don't you be sacrilegious in front of me," was her response, her hand reaching up to slap at Riley.

He ducked and missed the blow, though it wouldn't have had much impact. The heroin was doing a number on her and she was emaciated, weak, a constant tremor in her hands.

"Let's go, little man," he told Easton, who was eating dry cereal. "Mom's riding the crazy train today."

That was every day. She had a lifetime ticket to ride.

The house was freezing, since we kept the thermostat at sixty-two to save money, and it smelled like stale cigarettes and something more pervasive and indefinable. But it was like a sour stench of neglect, dust, old food, and my mother's own peculiar odor. She smelled like she was rotting from the inside out, and it scared the shit out of me.

As much as I hated what she had done to our family, I didn't want her to die. But she would. Whether she died tomorrow or ten years from now, she was killing herself one needle, one pill, one fifth of Jack at a time.

This was why I had broken up with Rory.

She didn't deserve to be stuck with this. I'd been born into it, and if I'd had a choice, I would have walked away years ago, but I had Jayden and Easton to worry about. And my mother. I couldn't leave her alone, because somewhere buried beneath the desperate drive for drugs, there was a woman who had loved us.

Rory was better than this. Better than a guy with a record, no real future to speak of, and a lousy five bucks in his pocket.

So why had I started to text her about a dozen times, only to stop myself?

Why did I torture myself over and over with the memory of her staring up into my eyes, confessing she loved me, her voice earnest, her expression sincere. Why did I wonder if some other dude was touching her body, kissing her in places that only I had kissed before?

And why had I spent money I didn't have on a box of chocolates for her, very much aware that Valentine's Day was in two days?

The box of truffle samples was burning a hole in my coat pocket and I pulled it out and tossed it on the table next to the overflowing ashtray. "Here," I told Jayden, who was trying to throw his cereal into his mouth one puff at a time, with little success. "You can have these, U."

His eyes lit up. "Really?"

Riley, who had been stepping into his boots, gave me a curious look. "You want to talk about it?" he asked.

"No." What the hell was there to say? I was a dumb-ass, end of story. Even if I got over the fact that I would be dragging her down, why the hell would Rory take me back? I broke up with her on Christmas Day in the mother of all dickhead moves, and a drugstore box of chocolates wasn't going to earn me forgiveness for that.

"Mom, you want one?" Jayden asked, tearing the exterior wrapper off like I might change my mind. He had the lid off in three seconds and a truffle in his mouth.

"What?" she asked, eyes vacant as she looked around, like she wasn't sure where she was. Hell, maybe she wasn't.

"Leave one for Mom, and take the rest with you," I told Jayden. "You and Easton can share them. Now shove off before you get a detention for being late."

The minute they left I decided I couldn't stay in that house either. The walls were closing in on me. My mother only looked at the chocolate I tried to hand to her, without taking it. I put it up to her mouth and she took a small bite. For a brief second her eyes focused on me. "You look like your father," she said.

"I know."

"He's an asshole."

"I know."

"But you're a good boy, Tyler, you always have been."

"Thanks, Mom. I try." I pushed her down into a chair and put a blanket around her shoulders.

Taking the truck I used to plow, I went out into the morning, knowing that I wasn't in a good place. Every day stretched before me, the same, void of any true pleasure. I was just existing, in a

Groundhog Day life, wake up and do it all over again. Fingering the necklace Rory had given me for Christmas, I drove toward campus, trying not to let the bitterness I felt at having to drop out crawl too far up my throat.

My phone rang and I saw it was Riley. "Yeah?" The truck skidded around a corner in the snow and I turned the wheel to accommodate for the loss of traction, craving a cigarette. Not enough hands. Not enough of a lot of things.

"Hey. Phoenix just got arrested. He came home and found Aunt Jackie's dealer boyfriend cutting her up with a knife."

"What?" Now I wanted that cigarette even more. My aunt was notorious for dating drug dealers who treated her like ass. "Jesus. I take it Phoenix stopped him? So why the hell is he in jail?"

"You know him. He didn't let it go at just stopping him. He beat the shit out of him. The dude is in the hospital."

That didn't surprise me. My cousin was two years younger than me and he had a temper that exploded without control. But in this case, I couldn't say I blamed him. What would if I do if I saw someone treating my mother like that? "I knew this day was going to be shit. What do you need me to do?"

"Pick up Jackie at the ER. She's at University, getting stitched up, and the cops are interviewing her. Make sure she doesn't say anything stupid that might get Phoenix in even more trouble."

I sighed. My head was starting to throb with a headache. "Alright, I'm on my way," I told my brother.

After I skulked in the back of Rory's dorm parking lot, like the loser that I was. She had a nine a.m. class, and every day she came out that front door at exactly 8:40. I might have done this once or twice before.

"Do I need to scrape together some bail money?" Though I

wasn't sure where it was going to come from. Paycheck advance off Riley's job, most likely.

"Bail is set at five grand. He's going to have to sit in jail."

"Holy shit." Then I guess my only other option was to go and visit him and give him some words of encouragement. Jail fucking sucked and I felt for him. "Alright, I'll call you later."

The door had opened and Rory came out, wearing a navy blue coat and an emerald green cap on her head, her hair in a braid on the side of her face. She had her bag over her shoulder like she always did, and she looked at the ground as she walked, kicking up the fresh snow with her boots.

My chest felt tight and I hated myself for the self-inflicted torture. Why the hell did I do this? Just seeing her, even from this distance and through a row of cars, made it worse. I wanted to touch her in the worst way. I wanted to close my eyes and breathe in her scent, my mouth on hers, arms holding her against my chest.

God, I missed her.

She glanced toward the parking lot and I wanted her to see me. I wanted to be busted so I could beg her to forgive me, to take me back. So I could tell her that, like my mother, I was rotting from the inside out without her.

Rory paused.

I opened the door, one foot out, ready to go after her.

But she was only adjusting her bag, and she strode forward again without another glance.

Pulling my leg back into the truck, I shut the door. "Happy Valentine's Day, Rory," I murmured to her, staring after her receding figure.

Then I cranked up Metallica, lit a cigarette, and headed toward the ER.

* * *

THAT DAY IN MARCH WHEN I CAME HOME, I KNEW IT THE MINUTE
I kicked my boots off in the kitchen and closed the door behind
me. I could smell death, and my first reaction was to glance at my
phone to see how much time I had before the boys got home from
school. I didn't want them to see our mother dead, because I knew
that she was. I'd left her that morning on the couch, staring up at
the ceiling, scratching herself aggressively in that way that addicts
do, digging nails into arms until the skin broke and bled.

And now there was a stillness to the house that made my gut
sink. Not the kind of unmoving air that tells you no one is home,
but an absence of life or something. I just knew that I knew, and
when I went into the living room, there she was, exactly where I
had left her. Eyes still open, still staring at the dingy ceiling. But
now she had a needle dangling from the vein in her thigh, her jeans
pushed down to her knees for access. The veins in her arms must
have collapsed.

Maybe I swore. Maybe I cried. I'm not really sure, because the
moment is both a confused blur and a sharp distinct vision. She
feels so sharp and focused in hindsight, that is all I can see, but
me . . . I'm hazy. I can't remember what I did exactly.

But I was aware that no one but me should ever see her like that,
so I used my sleeve and I pulled the needle out of her arm and tossed
it on the coffee table. I pulled up her jeans, just enough to cover
her. And I called 911.

What happened then was the worst part of all—because somewhere, deep inside my soul, I felt relief. Sure, that her suffering was
over. But relief that *our* suffering was over. It was a terrible, black,
shameful, and selfish feeling, and I decided right then and there

that if we were going to survive, my brothers and me, we had to take everything good that was offered to us and be damn grateful.

So when Rory came to my mother's funeral, and offered me forgiveness, and a third chance I didn't deserve, I took it.

That night she came home with me and she cooked dinner for the boys. I didn't have any appetite, but I was just so grateful to have her there, to see her smile at me, to hear her whisper in my ear that she loved me. Her presence helped lift the heavy sadness, and the scent of her cooking permeated the house, covering the smell of stale air and that peculiar odor of death I was sure I could still detect.

When she climbed in bed beside me after eleven, I was exhausted, and embarrassingly, tears pricked at the back of my eyes. "I'm so glad you're here," I said, as she rested her head on my chest. I buried my nose in her hair, wanting to smell her sweetness.

"Me, too. I missed you so much, Tyler."

"I missed you, too." Getting control over my emotions, I hugged her tight. "Thanks for being there today and for letting the boys know you care about them. They missed you, too, and I feel like shit for that." Then, because I had to be honest, I added, "I feel like shit about a lot of things."

"It's going to be okay, you know," she said. "Just promise me you won't try to think for me. I have a fairly impressive brain. I can manage to make my own choices about my life."

She was right. "I know that. I always knew that. I knew you wanted to be with me. That was never it . . . It's that I didn't trust that I wouldn't just be one huge regret some day in the future. I didn't trust that I wasn't being totally selfish and ruining your life. I hurt you so I wouldn't hurt you." I gave a laugh. "Damn, that sounds stupid."

"It is stupid." Rory wasn't one for not saying what she was thinking. "But I do understand and that's why I forgive you. But if you do it again, I'll be the one to end it this time, and I'll do a tattoo cover-up of a surgical scalpel."

There was a terrifying future. "You'd cover *Truer* with a picture of a scalpel? Would you make it bloody, too, while you're at it?"

"Maybe." Half sitting up, she kissed me softly. "But that's not going to be necessary, is it?"

"No." It felt like a vow, a promise I would do everything in my power to keep. "I love you."

Then she surprised me by staring to cry. "I love you, too."

Trying to pull her closer, alarmed, I wiped at the tears. "Hey, hey, it's okay." A surge of protectiveness rose in me and I captured her mouth with mine. "I'm not going anywhere."

Her kiss turned passionate and she moved her tongue against mine and I slipped my hands down her back. I wanted to feel her tight body with mine, all of it. Her leg moved to the side so that she could grind against me. I was only wearing boxer briefs but she was in jeans and a T-shirt. We clawed at clothes, me yanking her shirt off so hard her head popped through and sent her hair up in all directions from the static created. But neither one of us paused or commented, just tore at fabric until we were naked together, her slim body aligned over mine, the hot center of her thighs teasing over my cock.

"Rory," I murmured, a horrible, aching thought occurring to me. "I don't have any condoms."

"I went on the pill," she whispered, her fingers and eyes raking over my chest. "It made my father feel reassured."

My vision actually went black for a split second as I realized what that meant. "I don't have to use one?" We had never done that. I had never done that. Not with anyone.

"You don't have to use one."

I flipped her on her back and hauled her knee up. For a second I just stared down at her, memorizing the perfect tilt of her nose, taking in the rise and fall of her chest, the goose bumps on her flesh from arousal, the love that shone so clearly in her eyes.

"I need you," I told her.

"You have me."

Then I sank inside her open body and gave a groan at the unbelievable sensation of her without a condom.

"Oh, God," she said, her eyes going wide. "That's . . . it."

Exactly.

Sometimes there are no words.

Sometimes there is just emotion.

Keep reading for an excerpt from the second
book in the True Believers series
from Erin McCarthy

SWEET

Available now from InterMix!

JESSICA

I COULDN'T GO HOME FOR THE SUMMER. I JUST COULDN'T.

Going home would mean endless worried looks from my mother, and reminders about following curfew and the dangers of alcohol and premarital sex. My father would force me to volunteer—which was *such* an oxymoron—to teach Sunday school at his church and threaten to throw out all of my revealing clothes. Like shorts. Because wearing shorts in summer was so scandalous.

I couldn't deal with it, a whole summer ruined with their good intentions and their high moral standards that only a saint could live up to. And I'm no saint.

So I lied and told them I was spending the summer in Appalachia building homes for the poor with a Christian mission group when I was actually staying in Cincinnati and working at a steakhouse. I know. That was kind of a shitty lie.

But it was the only one that would have worked, so I had gone with it and there was no turning back now. Maintaining my freedom was worth a little guilt that I wasn't actually helping people in need, though I suppose I could argue I was at least fueling the economy by serving beef. So the only thing still unresolved was where I was going to stay for a week in the gap between when I had to leave my dorm and when I could take over a sublet on an apartment June first.

I had a plan. Turning the doorknob, I stepped inside and assessed the situation. My roommate Kylie, snuggled with her boyfriend, Nathan, who lived in the apartment. Tyler and my other roommate, Rory, also cuddling. The sap factor in the living room was huge, with Kylie on Nathan's lap, their fingers entwined, while Tyler did that weird thing he was constantly doing where he played with Rory's hair and made me want to smack his hand away on her behalf. She always seemed okay with it though, go figure.

"Hey, Jessica!" Kylie said brightly. "Cute top."

"Thanks." I had put on the tight red tank absently, then had wondered if more cleavage would be better for what I had in mind, then had been disgusted with myself for even thinking such a thought. So then I had decided no cleavage was necessary to my self-respect and pulled a Union Jack shirt on over the tank. Appearance was such a process. "What are you guys up to?"

"I'm watching *Inglourious Basterds*," came a voice from the kitchen. "Everyone else is engaged in foreplay."

Ugh. Trying not to sigh, I turned and saw Riley Mann, Tyler's older brother, popping the top of a beer can. He was not who I wanted to see.

"Jealous?" I asked him lightly, forcing a sardonic smile. Everything about Riley annoyed me, from his sarcasm to his inability to ever be serious, to the fact that he was hot as hell and so clearly knew it. I didn't see him very often since he worked full-time in construction, which was perfectly fine with me. It was easier to breathe without his testosterone choking the room.

He shook his head. "No. Sex is not worth the headache of a relationship. And my hand doesn't expect me to text it twenty times the next day."

There was mental imagery I did not need, though I couldn't argue with his opinion that relationships were a crapload of work. I made a face. "You're always so charming. Is Bill here?"

"He's studying in his room," Nathan told me. "He has a physics final tomorrow. God, I'm so glad I'm done with my exams."

I was done, too, which was why housing was becoming something of an issue. I only had two days until I had to vacate the dorms. "Okay, thanks." I started down the hall to Bill's room.

"You're going in there?" Nathan called after me. "I'm warning you, he's in a mood."

"I'm sure it's fine. I just want to say hi." Bill had been crushing on me for six months, ever since his girlfriend from high school had dumped him for a basketball player at Ohio State. We had hooked up a few times, but I had been totally clear about not wanting to date. I was not in the market for a relationship at all.

Without knocking I went into Bill's room. He was at his desk, and with the exception of the books and papers spread out in front of him, his room was neat as usual, bed made, no sign of finals stress. Until you got to his hair. Then the tension was evident in the floppy curls sticking out in various directions, looking like he hadn't made nice with a hairbrush in days. His glasses were sliding down his nose when he looked up, and he was a very cute, modern interpretation of the absentminded genius.

"Hey," he said, looking vacantly at me.

"Hey. How's studying going?" I propped a hip on the corner of his desk and smiled.

"Not bad, but I still have a lot to go through. Did you need something, or did you just want to hang out? Because I can't until tomorrow."

"I wanted to know if I can stay here with you, in your room, for a few days." Okay, so it was more like eight days, but who was counting?

"What?" He frowned. "What do you mean?" He tapped his pen on his lips and blinked up at me.

"I need a place to crash until I can get in the apartment I sublet. There's no way I'm sleeping on that couch in the living room. It's like chain mail. But I can sleep in your bed with you, right?" I smiled and used the tip of my finger to push his glasses up. "I promise I won't kick you in my sleep like I did last time."

For a second he didn't say anything. Then he shook his head. "No."

That was definitely not the answer I was expecting. "What? Why not? Okay, so I know I can't promise to have control over my limbs when I'm sleeping, but you can always kick me back. I don't mind." He couldn't be seriously telling me no. My heart rate started to increase, anxiety creeping up over the back of my neck.

"I don't care if you kick me, it's not that." Bill sighed. "Look, Jess, we both know it's no secret I like you, and you've been totally straight up with me about not returning the sentiment, and I appreciate that. Maybe it's insane of me to say no, because sometimes I do manage to talk you into hooking up when you take pity on me, but I can't share a bed with you every night for a week and not feel like shit about it. I just can't."

My jaw dropped, and I felt a hot flood of shame in my mouth, which made me angry. I hadn't done anything to feel bad about, despite what my dad's opinion about it would have been. "You make it sound so sketch. We're friends. We've hooked up when we both felt like it, not because I was desperate and you were my only option or because I felt sorry for you. I'm not that nice of a person that I'll blow you out of pity. I just like you as a friend and I think you're cute. We have fun. Apparently, I was totally wrong in thinking you felt the same way."

"I do feel the same way," he insisted. "The problem is, I feel more than that, and I'm just not into torturing myself. I want you to be my 'girlfriend.'" He made air quotes. "Pathetic, I know."

The thought of being anyone's girlfriend made me want to throw up in my mouth a little. There was no way I wanted to give a guy that much control over my emotions and my time. I had finally gotten away from that for the first time in my life.

"I'm sorry. It's not pathetic, it's just . . ."

"It's you, not me." He rolled his eyes. "I know. You can save the let-him-down-gently speech for another dude. I get it."

I had to admit, that was kind of a relief. "This is awkward," I told him.

"Probably more for me than for you," he said with a nervous laugh. "Look, you can stay on the couch in here."

"Except now it will be weird." It already was.

"No, it won't. I won't be needy or anything. I just need to have some self-preservation."

"Okay, I understand." I did. But it made it different. I couldn't casually touch him anymore. I couldn't flirt without feeling like I was leading him on, and I would have to be careful around him. I fought the urge to sigh. Why did everything have to be so complicated between guys and girls? Curse hormones. "Good luck on your final."

"Thanks." He gave me a smile, then he returned his attention to his book.

I left, feeling deflated and oddly sad knowing Bill and I couldn't quite be friends in the same way we had been. But then again, maybe we'd never really been just friends, because I had always known he liked me. And why did that suddenly make me feel so guilty?

"That was fast," Riley said the second I came into the living room, his feet up on the coffee table, expression bored. "I guess that's why they call it a quickie."

"Shut up," I said, with more vehemence than I intended. I was feeling bad, and I couldn't precisely figure out why Bill's rejection had bothered me so much. I didn't need Riley judging me.

"What's wrong?" Rory asked, peeling herself off Tyler's chest, where she was splayed like plastic wrap.

"I just don't have anywhere to stay for the next week, that's all." I didn't want to say in front of Riley that Bill had turned me down. It would be like handing him the material for a ten-minute stand-up routine at my expense. No, thanks.

"You can stay here," Nathan said.

"Thanks, but I don't think that's going to work."

"Why not?" Kylie asked.

I shot her a look, hoping she'd get the hint.

"Did you and the nerd have a fight?" Riley asked. "Is he not putting out enough for you?"

It really wasn't fair that such a beautiful face was on such an asshole of a guy. Riley was a little shorter than Tyler, just as muscular, but whereas Tyler had a certain hardness to his face, Riley had been gifted with adorable dimples and large eyes. It was almost tragic he was such a jerk-off. I ignored him, but it wasn't easy, because he seemed to take great pleasure in pissing me off. I really wanted to throw something at him. Like my fist. Right into his cocky face.

"You can stay at my house," Tyler offered. "The boys and I are going to Rory's dad's for a week, remember, so you'd have a bed to sleep on."

There was a thought, though it was an intimidating one. "Is it safe?" I asked, before I thought about how rude that actually sounded. Tyler and Riley lived with their two younger brothers in a lower income neighborhood in a house the bank was in the process of foreclosing on since their mother had died. Riley had lived in a basement before that, but once his mom overdosed, he had moved back in. I'd never been there, but I was picturing a drug infested neighborhood with drive-by shootings and prostitutes on every corner. My parents lived in a minimansion in a small town, so I didn't exactly have street cred. My experience with poverty was limited to movies and episodes of *Cops* on my laptop. It was like a bear walking through the desert. I had no previous exposure.

"I mean, won't the neighbors think I'm breaking and entering?" I added, as a very lame cover to my initial question.

"Princess, I don't think anyone is going to think you've broken into our shithole and are squatting," Riley said, rolling his eyes. "If anything, they'll just think you've come over to score drugs."

"Rory stays with me all the time," Tyler added. "No one will even notice. People keep to themselves in our neighborhood."

"I never feel unsafe there," Rory said. "But then again, I'm never sleeping there alone. Tyler is always with me."

"I've never lived alone," I said. Even for a week, the thought had a certain appeal. No one's opinion but my own. No rules. No guilt. No feeling bad that I could never live up to anyone's expectations. It sounded awesome and scary. I wanted to try it, just to see what it would be like. "That sounds great, Ty. Thanks for offering."

"Have both of you forgotten something?" Riley asked, picking up his beer.

"What?" I said, wary. I just knew I wasn't going to like whatever he was going to say.

"I'm not going to Rory's dad's to swim for a week like a kid at summer camp. I'll be here, working. Living in my house."

Oh, God. I couldn't help it. I made a face.

The corner of Riley's mouth turned up. "That's exactly how I feel about it, princess."

"I think it will be good for you guys," Kylie said, an eternal optimist. Or suffering from massive delusions. "You can become better friends this way."

"Maybe we don't want to become friends," Riley told her. "Maybe we like not liking each other."

I almost laughed. There was a certain truth to that. I basically felt like I'd seen all I needed to see to know I didn't need to see more. But if I said that Kylie's head would explode. She was a very honest and kind person, and she didn't always get my point of view. Or anything involving math.

"How much will you even see each other? You both work and it has three bedrooms," Tyler said. "It seems stupid to sleep on a floor somewhere when there's plenty of room at the house."

"It's up to Riley," I said, because that only seemed fair. It was his house. "Maybe he wants some alone time with all of you gone."

I didn't mean that to sound quite as weird as it did.

He laughed. "Does that come right after Me Time and Circle

Time?" He stood up and moved further into my space than was strictly appropriate.

It was a game of chicken, and I lost by instantly backing up. Damn it. He smirked in triumph.

"I'll be fine. I can handle it if you can."

I was playing right into him and I knew it, but I couldn't stop myself. "Of course I can handle it. What's there to handle?"

He stared at me, his eyebrows raised, a challenge in his deep brown eyes. The stubble on his chin was visible, and I could smell the subtle scent of soap and a splash of cologne. He looked and smelled very, very masculine, and I was suddenly aware of my body in a way that made me seriously annoyed.

"Bring some beer."

"I'm not twenty-one." Not that it had ever stopped me from drinking, but I wasn't going to give Riley anything I didn't have to. I did not want to feel like I owed him. It was Tyler who had made the offer of a place to crash, so if anyone deserved thanks, it was him, not his arrogant brother.

For a second, Riley's eyes roamed over my chest, like he could gauge my age by my boobs. Such a tool.

But then he just said, "You can borrow my ID."

And I couldn't help it. I laughed. "Because we're practically twins."

He nodded. "Though I am *slightly* better looking."

I snorted. "I have better hair."

"I can drink more whiskey than you."

"I'm smarter."

"I'm stronger. We should mud wrestle so I can prove it."

I bit my lip so I wouldn't throw a scathing response back at him, or worse, laugh. He didn't deserve the attention, or knowing he'd gotten under my skin, which was what he wanted.

But for a split second I wondered if I should sleep on the couch after all. Because Riley seemed to be the one person who could get an emotional response out of me, even if it was just anger.

And emotions were dangerous.

They led to being trapped, like my mother, in the pretty prison of my father's house.

I was never going to let that happen.

"I call dibs on the bathroom first in the mornings," I told Riley.

Then to let him know that he did not intimidate me, and that I was always in control, I turned and walked away.

Keep reading for an excerpt from
the third book in the True Believers series
from Erin McCarthy

BELIEVE

Available now from InterMix!

ROBIN

I SPENT MY SOPHOMORE YEAR IN COLLEGE PARTYING. I WASN'T
even original about it. Just the totally typical pattern of skipping
class and going out every single night. If there was a keg party I
went, if there was a shot I drank it, if there was a guy I made out
with him. I wore short skirts, showed as much cleavage as I could,
and I felt sexy and confident while having the time of my life. I
threw up in more than one toilet, made out with a taxidermied
deer on a dare, and came home without my shoes, dorm key, or
phone on a regular basis.

Later, I tried to look back and figure out why I had slid so easily
into party girl, but all I could come up with was maybe I just
wanted a louder voice, and drinking gave me that. I wanted some
attention, I guess, or maybe just to have a good time where there
were no rules. Or maybe there was just no reason at all.

It all seemed normal. What you do in college, right? You party.
You make superficial friends. You drink. Do stupid things that you

laugh about the next day and take pictures that will prevent you from ever being a senator.

It wasn't anything I felt bad about. I mean, sure, I could have done without some of those hangovers, and I did end up dodging a few guys who wanted to date after I spent a drunken night telling them they were awesome, but nothing to make me feel ashamed.

Until I hooked up with one of my best friend's boyfriend when she was out of town.

Then I hated myself and the existence of vodka. Because I wasn't one of *those* girls. Or I hadn't been. Never, under any circumstances at all, would I have come even remotely close to doing anything with a friend's guy sober, so why would I do that?? How could alcohol make me cross a boundary so high and thick and barb-wired? I wasn't even hot for Nathan. I never had been. I mean, he was cute, whatever, but it wasn't like I nurtured a secret crush or anything.

So how did I end up waking up next to him on his plaid sheets, his arm thrown carelessly over my naked chest? I came awake with a start, head pounding, mouth dry, for a second wondering where the hell I was and who I had had sex with. When I blinked and took in the face above that arm, I thought I was going to throw up. Getting to the apartment, sex, it was completely a black, yawning hole of nothing. I didn't remember even leaving the party. No idea how Nathan and I had wound up in bed together. All I had was a few flashes that suddenly came back to me of him biting my nipple, hard, so that I had protested, my legs on his shoulders. Nothing else.

As I lay there, heart racing, wondering how the hell I could live with this, with myself, the horror slicing through me like a sharp knife, Nathan woke up.

He gave me a sleepy, cocky smile, punctuated by a yawn. "Hey, Robin."

"Hey." I tried to sink down under the sheet, not wanting him to see me naked, not wanting to be naked.

"Well, that was fun," he said, smile expanding into a grin. "We should do that again before we get up."

The thought made my stomach turn. "But Kylie," I said weakly, because I wanted to remind him that his girlfriend was back at her parents' for the summer, but she still very much existed. His girlfriend. My best friend.

"I love Kylie, but she's not here. And we're not going to tell her." He shrugged. "I didn't expect this to happen, but it did and we're still naked." He pulled my hand over his erection. "No reason we shouldn't enjoy it."

And he leaned over to kiss me. I scooted backward so fast, I fell off the mattress onto my bare ass. "I'm going to puke," I told him.

"Bummer."

Grabbing my clothes off the floor, I stumbled into the hallway, hoping his roommate, Bill, wasn't around. In the bathroom, I leaned over the sink, trembling, eyes that stared back at me in the mirror shocked, the skin under them bruised. I didn't get sick. I wished I would. I wished I could vomit out of myself the horrible realization that I had done something terrible, appalling, unforgiveable, mega disgusting.

I couldn't use vodka as an excuse. And now I knew Nathan was an asshole on top of it all.

Without asking him if I could shower, I turned on the water and stepped in, wanting to wash away the night, the dirty, nasty smell of skank sex off of my skin. I felt like a slut, like a bitch, like someone I didn't even know, and my tears mixed with the steady stream of water from the shower as I scrubbed and scrubbed.

I spent the rest of the summer sober, far away from parties, guilt nibbling at my insides, making me chronically nauseated, and I avoided everyone. I begged Nathan to stop when he kept sending me sexy texts, and I ignored my friend Jessica, who had stayed in town for the summer and who kept asking what was wrong.

By August I was consumed by anxiety and the fear that someone knew, that someone would tell, that I would be responsible for Kylie having her heart broken.

I slept whole days away and I couldn't eat. I thought about getting meds from the doctor for sleeping or for anxiety or for depression or for alcoholism or for sluttiness. But what was done was done and a pill wasn't going to fix it. Or me.

When Jessica called and said Nathan's friend Tyler was picking me up whether I liked it or not and we were going to hang out, I tried to say no. But then I decided that I liked to be with myself even less than I liked to be with other people.

Besides, once Kylie got back in a week, I wasn't going to be able to be friends with any of them anymore, and this might be my last chance to spend time with them. I couldn't be in the same room with her and pretend that I hadn't betrayed our friendship in the worst way possible. I wasn't going to be able to sit there and have her and Nathan kissing on each other, knowing that he had spent all summer trying to hook up with me again.

I was going to have to find a new place to live and disappear from our group of friends.

If only it had been that simple.

If only I had walked away right then and there.

Then I never would have met Phoenix and my life would never have changed in ways I still don't understand.

TYLER WAS A GOOD RIDE, BECAUSE HE DIDN'T NEED TO TALK. He just drove and smoked and I stared out the window, my art supplies in my lap. I had promised to paint a pop art portrait of Tyler's little brother Easton, and I had to do it tonight because I might never see him again if I had the guts to follow through with my plan to move out of the apartment. I hadn't painted all summer. I wasn't inspired. And I didn't want to now, but I had promised I would back before the morning after with Nathan.

So since I couldn't explain any of that, I stayed mostly silent. I did say, "Rory gets back tomorrow."

It was a stupid comment. Of course he knew his girlfriend was coming back to school. But I wanted to make some sort of effort. It was hot, even for August, and the windows were open, air rushing in and swirling his smoke around in front of me.

"Yep. I missed her. A lot."

I didn't doubt he had. And I didn't think for one minute he would have betrayed her the way Nathan had Kylie. Even if he wasn't living with his brother and Jessica, who were also dating. Tyler just wasn't that kind of guy. Both Riley and Tyler were loyal, and I wondered why I always seemed to attract the wrong kind of guy. The liars, the cheaters. My boyfriend freshman year had been a douche, flirting with other girls in front of me, laughing it off when I complained. My high school boyfriend had told me he wanted a girl who had her life together, who had goals. What kind of goals was I supposed to have at seventeen? At that point I already knew I was going to college to study graphic design, wasn't that good enough? So apparently his way to fix my deficiency was to hook up with his ex at a party and humiliate me.

It was hard to believe that someday there would be a guy in my life who would love me the way my friends' guys loved them.

Of course, I was never going to find that guy at a keg party. Another reason I had stopped going to the frat house all-nighters. I didn't have the stomach for so-called living in the moment fun since I had woken up next to Nathan. So maybe I didn't have my life all mapped out, but I knew that I was done with the superficial crap. I knew that I had crossed a line I never wanted to cross again and if that meant giving up alcohol forever, then that's what I was going to do because I had gone from being cheated on to the cheater, and I could barely live with myself.

And if I couldn't live with myself, what guy would want to?

When we went in Tyler's house, there was someone sleeping on the couch. I couldn't see his face since he was turned away from the room on his side, but he had black hair and a serious lack of a tan. "Who is that?" I asked Tyler.

"My cousin, Phoenix. He's crashing here for a while." Tyler kept walking past him to the kitchen. "Do you want a beer?"

"No, thanks." I hadn't had a drink in ten weeks and I didn't even miss it.

Jessica was in the kitchen, heating up food in the microwave. It was weird to me that she lived there with her boyfriend and his three younger brothers. I had never been to her parents' house but I knew she had grown up with a lot of money, and this was no spacious colonial in the suburbs. The house was small and dark and hot and was rundown, but truthfully she seemed the happiest she'd been since I'd met her. Riley came in from the patio and kissed the back of her head, looking at her like he thought she was the most beautiful creature the world had ever created.

"Want some?" she asked me, dishing up rice and vegetables onto four plates.

"I'm good."

She switched out plates in the microwave and said, "Then let's go in the other room. I want to talk to you alone." She touched Riley's elbow. "Can you put these in for the boys?"

"Got it."

I followed her back into the living room and she sat on the floor by the coffee table. "Sit. I want to talk to you about what the hell is going on."

I did want to tell her. I wanted to get the awful truth out and ask her what I was supposed to do about Nathan. But I couldn't. All I could tell her was a small portion of the truth. I looked nervously at the sleeping cousin. "He can hear us. I feel weird talking in front of him."

"He's totally out. He just got out after five months in jail and he's been sleeping for two days."

"Jail?" I whispered, a little horrified. "For what?" How could she say that so casually, like it was no big deal?

She scooped rice into her mouth. "Fuck me, that is so good." She closed her eyes and chewed. "I'm going to have to step up the workouts but I think carbs are worth it."

I didn't say anything, sitting down on the floor next to her, drawing my knees up to my chest. I was wearing a sloppy T-shirt and I dragged it over my bare knees, making a tent, cocooning myself.

"Okay, so what is going on? Seriously. You won't drink, you won't go out. You've lost weight. You don't answer my texts. You're even dressing differently. I'm totally worried about you."

I was worried about me, too. I couldn't seem to drag myself out of the anxiety that had been following me around. "I'm moving out of the house as soon as I find a new place to live."

"*What?* Why the hell would you do that?"

Tears came to my eyes before I could stop them. "I just have to. I need to stop drinking."

"But, it's not like Rory is a big drinker. And I'm sure Kylie would respect it if you said you wanted to chill with the alcohol." She looked hurt. "We would never pressure you to party. God, that's so not us."

"I know." It made me feel even worse. "It's just I feel like I need to be alone for a while. I was even thinking about moving home and being a commuter. It's not that far to my parents, only like a forty-five-minute drive to class."

"You would seriously want to move home? That just blows my mind." Jessica stared hard at me, tucking her blond hair behind her ear. "Besides, this is going to leave Rory and Kylie with a whole house to pay for since we've both bailed on them. I feel really bad about doing that."

So did I. But I felt worse about screwing Kylie's boyfriend. What would I do when Nathan came over to hang out? I couldn't play it cool, like nothing had happened. I wasn't drawn that way. "Didn't Tyler say he wouldn't mind moving in with Rory?"

"Yeah, but I don't know if he can actually afford it." Jessica frowned, picking up her fork. "I guess I can ask him. I guess maybe Nathan could move in there, too, with Kylie. Bill is moving into the engineering frat house."

I dropped my knees, alarmed. That was not what I wanted to happen. I didn't want Kylie to become even more dependent and more in love with Nathan.

"This is so weird," she said. "This is totally not what we planned. It's like complete roommate shuffle. What happened?"

Rory fell in love with Tyler. Jessica fell in love with Riley. I blacked out and had sex with Nathan.

Not exactly the same happy ending for me. I wanted to tell her so desperately I swallowed hard and clamped my mouth shut. Telling her would only mean she would have to keep a secret from Kylie. From Riley, too. Telling Kylie would only hurt her to appease my guilt.

I couldn't do it.

Shrugging, I said, "Things change."

"Robin."

"What?"

"If you got attacked or something you would tell me, right? You know you can tell me." She reached out and touched my arm, expression filled with concern.

And it went from bad to worse. Now she thought I was a victim. I nodded. "I would tell you. It's nothing like that, I swear."

"Because it seems like you started acting strange after the party at the Shit Shack. Something is obviously wrong. So if that Aaron guy did something to you, tell me."

"No, he didn't." I shook my head emphatically. Aaron had just been a guy I had danced with, flirted with, kissed. Before he ditched me and somehow I ended up going home with Nathan.

"Did something freaky happen? Did you do something you regret, like anal?"

Not that I was aware of. I couldn't prevent a shudder. "No. No anal." Though I did do something I regretted, more than anything else I'd ever done. The person who said that life was too short for regrets clearly had never done something super shitty.

"Jessica!" Jayden called her name from the kitchen. "Can you come here?"

"Yeah, I'll be right there, buddy." She set down her fork. "Be right back."

Jayden was eighteen but he had Down syndrome and I knew that Rory and Jessica both cut him a lot of slack. If he asked for attention, they gave it to him, and I was totally grateful for the interruption. I wasn't sure how much longer I could lie to direct questions.

As Jessica went into the kitchen, the guy on the couch suddenly coughed. I turned and saw dark eyes staring at me. He had rolled onto his back and was sitting up on the arm roll, his hair sticking up in front. My palms got clammy and I stared back, horrified.

Not only was he completely and totally hot, he had obviously been awake for more than thirty seconds. He looked way too alert to have just opened his eyes.

"Uh, hi. I'm Robin," I said, my hands starting to shake. What had we said? Nothing incriminating, I didn't think. I hadn't admitted anything. Though I had said anal out loud and that was awkward enough. All those nasty jokes about prison popped into my head and my cheeks burned.

His expression was inscrutable, but he nodded. "Phoenix."

"Nice to meet you," I said, because that's what you say even if there was zero truth to it. It wasn't nice to meet him. He was a criminal and I was a lying cheat and I was way too preoccupied with my own self-hatred to have anything interesting to say to him.

"Yeah. Sure." He sounded about as enthusiastic as I felt.

Agitated, I sat down on the coffee table next to the couch, wiping my hands on my denim shorts. "Sorry if we woke you up."

He shrugged. "No big deal."

I wasn't sure what to say after that. He wasn't wearing a shirt, and like his cousins, he had tattoos covering his chest and arms. The one that caught my attention was the bleeding heart. It looked severed in two, the blood draining down his flesh toward his abdomen. It was beautiful and creepy and bold. Was it a metaphor? It seemed a little poetic for the average guy, but something about his steady stare suggested he was no ordinary guy. His dark hair stuck up then fell over one eye, so it felt like he had an extra advantage, that he could watch me from behind that cascade of hair.

Jessica hadn't told me why he had been in jail and I decided I really didn't want to know. Phoenix was trouble and trouble was exactly what I was trying to avoid.

"I'm not a big fan of anal either," he said.

Giving or receiving? I couldn't tell if he was making fun of me. He didn't seem to be trying to lighten the mood with a joke for my benefit since he still looked stone-faced. It made me super uncomfortable.

"We thought you were asleep."

"What difference does it make? You didn't confess to a crime."

Thank God. "I don't like just anyone hearing my personal business. You don't even know me."

"You're right, I don't." He threw back the blanket that had been covering him below the waist and he stood up. He was in his underwear, black boxer briefs that clung to his thighs. "Robin." He added my name at the end like it was an accusation.

His body was lean and wiry, yet muscular. He looked like he worked out constantly, but had been born with a raging high metabolism, so he would never be bulky, but every muscle was obvious, the V of his hips so defined, it made my mouth thick with saliva in a totally inappropriate way for the situation. He bent over and picked up a pair of shorts off the floor, stepping into them and drawing them up. But he left them partially unzipped, and the belt clanked against his thighs as he moved out of the living room and down the hall into the bathroom without another word to me.

I watched him, unnerved. There was something hard about him, mysterious. His name suited him, unusual and intriguing. Annoyed with myself, I went into the kitchen, where Jessica was clearly laying out the situation for Tyler.

"So what are we going to do? Kylie and I were supposed to share and Rory and Robin each had their own room, but now there's an empty room completely."

"Can you guys just break the lease?" Riley asked. "I mean, what difference does it make? Everyone can move out."

"My dad and Rory's dad are the ones who signed the lease. I don't think either one of us needs to piss our dads off any more."

Riley frowned. "No. That's no good." He looked at me. "I guess you should find a replacement, since you're the one moving out."

Hovering in the doorway, I crossed my arms over my chest, miserable. "I'll just move home and I'll pay my portion of the rent. I can cover it with my paychecks from waitressing."

I was trying to be fair. To not stick them with either a bigger rent or with a roommate they didn't know and may not get along with, but Jessica's eyes narrowed in suspicion.

"Wait a minute. So you'd rather live at home with your parents who are like sixty years old, and your ancient, evil-eye-giving grandmother, while paying rent on a place you don't live in, than room with Kylie and Rory? Okay, I call bullshit. What the fuck is going on?"

When she put it like that, it did sound insane. "Nothing is going on. I just need time to . . . reevaluate."

But Jessica was tenacious. "There is something going on and you need to tell me what it is."

Phoenix strolled into the kitchen, scratching his chest, and went to the fridge. "I think if she wanted to tell you she would have already," he commented.

That about summed it up.

"And who asked you?" Jessica said, whirling to glare at him as she yanked Jayden's empty plate out from in front of him and started scrubbing it aggressively in the sink.

"Just an observation."

"Well, mind your own business."

"I think Robin would probably say the same to you."

They stared at each other and I felt the tension between them. Phoenix being in the house obviously upset the balance of Jessica being house princess. She was a strong personality, and she enjoyed being the only girl in the house. Somehow Phoenix was challenging her, and it was obvious to Riley, too. He held up his hand.

"All right, chill out. Both of you."

"Please don't fight because of me," I pleaded, feeling even more horrible with each passing second. "Just please don't." And to my horror, I started crying, tears welling up and rushing out of both eyes silently.

Everyone looked at me in shock and no one seemed to have a clue what to say. I wasn't known for being particularly emotional. Fortunately, Easton intervened. "Hey, aren't you supposed to draw me?" He tapped the canvas Tyler had propped on the floor next to the table. "When are you doing that?"

"Now," I said, taking an empty seat next to him and wiping my face, concentrating on drawing my breath in and out, slowly, evenly. "I just need some space."

That was definitely a metaphor.

Jessica went into the other room, clearly agitated, and Riley followed her, murmuring in a low voice. Tyler encouraged Jayden to go outside and shoot hoops with him. It left me at the table, methodically squeezing my oils into my paint tray, Easton across from me, bouncing up and down on his chair, and Phoenix leaning on the counter eating rice straight out of the container.

He was watching us, but I ignored him. Yellow, pink, blue. Squeeze, squeeze, squeeze. If I just focused on one thing at a time, I could function.

And it actually felt good to have my brush in my hand, the smell of the oils familiar and soothing. I felt calmer.

There was a knock at the back door and Easton jumped. "Who is that?"

"It's probably my girlfriend," Phoenix said. "Or my ex-girlfriend if this conversation doesn't go well. She's supposed to come over."

So of course the gorgeous bad boy had a girlfriend, despite his incarceration.

Phoenix opened the back door and I have to admit, I tried to pretend I was busy working, paintbrush in my hand as I used a bold magenta to do the outline of Easton's head. But I snuck a glance up at the girl who walked into the kitchen and I tried not to be judgmental. She looked hard. Older than she probably was. Bad dye job, turning naturally brown hair bleach blond, drying the texture out. Lots of eyeliner. Bad skin. Her jeans were too tight in the waist and too big in the butt. Not the prettiest girl I've ever seen but maybe she was super sweet. And who was I to judge?

"Hey," she said and tried to kiss Phoenix.

He shifted out of the way and rejected her effort. "Why didn't you come see me when I was locked up?" he demanded with no other greeting. "Not once. I didn't know what the fuck was going on, Angel."

Oh, God, seriously? Her name was Angel? I threw up a little in my mouth. I couldn't think of a name less suited to a girl who looked like she could beat the shit out of me if I looked at her wrong. Carefully, I set down my paintbrush and pushed my chair back. Clearly this was a private conversation and I had enough drama of my own. I didn't want to be involved in someone else's.

"Who are you?" she asked angrily, shooting me a glare as the noisy scraping sound of the chair made her aware of my presence.

"I'm just going in the other room," I said carefully, not wanting to go a round with her. I had no doubt I would lose, especially in my current emotional state. Easton obviously felt the same way. He bolted into the living room without a word.

"Good," Angel said, playing with the ring in her nose.

"She doesn't have to leave," Phoenix said, gesturing for me to stay. "This is only going to take a minute. So what did you want to tell me, Angel?" He crossed his arms and leaned on the kitchen counter.

I stood up anyway, despite his words.

"I'm pregnant."

I couldn't prevent a gasp from leaving my mouth. Yeah, I should have left the room. But Phoenix didn't react at all. His face never revealed any surprise, and the only movement he made was to flick his eyes over her flat stomach.

"You don't look six months pregnant to me."

"I'm not. I'm only two."

He'd been in prison more than five months. Jessica had said that. I knew that. What I didn't know was why I cared one way or the other about it being his baby, but I felt horrified for him that he'd been cheated on, and a little bit of relief that he wasn't the father.

"Then I don't need to know that." Phoenix went and opened the door. "Bye, Angel."

"Don't you even want to know what happened?" She looked disappointed. "Who the father is?"

"No. All I wanted was to know for sure that we're broken up, and we clearly are, so good luck. Lose my number."

"You're an asshole," she said.

I wasn't sure how he qualified as the jerk in this situation, but I kept my eyes on the canvas as she stomped out the back door, and he slammed it loudly behind her.

"Well, now I guess we're even," he said.

I glanced up, curious to see if he was going to rage or look upset. But he didn't. He looked . . . neutral. "Even how?" I asked.

"Now we both know each other's personal business."

I finished my brush stroke. "True. And I'm going to stay out of it, like you did with me." I just wanted to paint, to lose myself in the wet sound of sliding paint.

He came over and looked down at my canvas. "You don't need Easton here to paint? You're doing it from memory?"

"Yes."

"Cool."

He watched me for a minute, and I didn't actually mind. I didn't need quiet or solitude to paint pop art and it felt good to lose myself in the narrow focus of creating lines on canvas. But while I wanted to respect his privacy, I also knew that it had to have hurt him that his girlfriend hasn't visited him in prison, that she had cheated on him. I also felt guilty that I was a cheater, that if it ever came out, I would be the one causing pain. I hated that.

"I'm sorry," I told him, glancing up, hoping he would understand.

"For what?"

I didn't want to be specific. I didn't think he would appreciate that. "For what I heard. For what you heard."

"That you heard it? Or because it happened?"

"Both. But mostly that it happened. It hurts, I know. And I'm sorry."

Phoenix shrugged. "I'll live. I've survived worse."

I wanted to say that she wasn't good enough for him anyway, that she was a liar and a cheat and a shitty girlfriend who didn't deserve him, but did I really know that? And if I was no better than her, did I have any right to say anything?

"Sometimes we do stupid things." Very stupid things. Sometimes we needed forgiveness.

"Yeah. Some of us more than others." Phoenix pulled out a chair and sat down across from me. "I've never painted before. I sketch. It must be hard to get the subtlety of the lines and the shading in paint."

"You sketch?" I asked, amazed, then not sure why.

He nodded. "And I do tattoos. I guess the difference is with oil paint you layer on top, right? With a tattoo you do a little, but mostly it's about precision and shading."

"Do you have pictures of your work?" I asked, curious to see it. The idea of tattooing someone with a needle scared me. There was no retracting a mistake.

Sort of like life.

"Nah. But I did the original design for my cousins' arm tat, the one they all have, and I did Tyler's dragon on his leg."

"Cool. That dragon is beautiful."

"Thanks." He drummed his fingers on the table. "We're a fucked-up family, you know. We haven't always gotten along, depending on whose mom was hooking the other on what drugs."

"Why aren't you living with your mom?" I finished the outline of Easton and started shading in his strong features. Even in the brilliance of yellow and magenta, I wanted to capture the deep sensitivity of his eyes.

"I don't know where she is. She didn't leave a forwarding address."

So not only had his girlfriend cheated on him when he was in jail, his mom disappeared and neglected to tell him? I wasn't sure I could be so casual about it. In fact, I knew I couldn't. My parents were all about family. They loved me and my older brothers in a way that was almost smothering, and I was grateful for it. "Oh my God, I'm sorry."

He shrugged. "She'll turn up eventually. But Riley and Tyler are being cool and letting me stay here."

I wasn't sure what to say. "Family seems important to them."

Those fingers increased their rhythm, but the rest of him stayed completely still. The only movement seemed to come from those anxious fingers and the intensity of his stare as his eyes raked over both me and the canvas. I was never still. My mom had always commented on that. I fidgeted and shifted and couldn't stay in a chair longer than ten minutes without creating a reason to get up for a task before sitting down again. I struggled to sit through movies, and I hopped up and down off a bar stool, going out on the dance floor and outside to smoke cigarettes I didn't even like.

Even now I was bouncing my knee up and down and chewing hard on a piece of gum. His immobility fascinated me.

Which may explain why I said, "Do you want to paint? I have another canvas and brush."

Again, there was no reaction. I wondered what it would take to draw emotion out of him. "Nah, I don't want to waste your supplies."

"It's a cheap canvas. It was only five bucks."

But he just shook his head. Then a second later he asked me, "Do you have a boyfriend?"

"What?" I almost dropped my paintbrush. "No. Why?"

His phone slid across the table toward me. "Then give me your number."

"Why?" I said again, which was a totally moronic thing to say. But I didn't get any vibe he even liked me, let alone was interested in me.

For the first time, I saw the glimmer of a smile on his face. The corner of his mouth lifted slightly before he controlled it again. "Why do you think?"

For a split second, I felt like myself, and I said the first thing that popped into my head. "So you can send me honey badger videos?" I joked, because it seemed like a safer response. He was just out of prison and he had just broken up with his girlfriend ten minutes earlier. So not a good idea to get involved with him. I wasn't up for dating anyone, let alone him.

"Yes. And kitten memes."

"Well, in that case." I took his phone because I wasn't exactly sure how to say no. It seemed super rude, and I doubted he was actually going to ask me out. He would probably send me a typical guy text of "hi" or "what's up?" and I could say "hi" back or "nothing" and we'd be done with it. Guys put no effort at all into communication or pursuing a girl. If you didn't go into a huge long text of explanation of what you were doing and dug deep into their text to get an adequate response back, the conversation just died. A big old waste of time, that's what most texting with guys was.

So I typed my number into his phone with my name. It was an old smartphone, with a cracked screen, like he had dropped it on the pavement. I set it back on the table.

Tyler came back into the kitchen and looked over my shoulder at my work. "Hey, that's cool so far. You got Easton's nose just right."

Out of the corner of my eye, I saw Phoenix palm his phone and put it back into his pocket, tossing his hair back. Then he just stood up and left.

My phone buzzed in my own pocket as Tyler went to the fridge and started rummaging around. I pulled it out and saw it was a text from a number I didn't recognize. When I opened it, there was a honey badger video. "At your request" was the message.

I smiled for the first time in what felt like weeks.

Way better than writing "hi."